Praise for John Harvey

"Harvey's series about Charlie Resnick, the jazz-loving, melancholy cop in provincial Nottingham, England, has long been one of the finest police procedural series around."　　—*Publishers Weekly*

"The characters in John Harvey's urban crime novels are so defiantly alive and unruly that they put these British police procedurals on a shelf by ~~themselves~~." ~~The~~ *York Times Book Review*

"Without d ... ne beat. Harvey has set a benchma ... ieasure up to." 　　—*Literary Review*

"One of the masters of British crime fiction."
　　—*Sunday Telegraph (London)*

"Harvey reminds me of Graham Greene, a stylist who tells you everything you need to know while keeping the prose clean and simple. It's a very realistic style that draws you into the story without the writer getting in the way." 　　—Elmore Leonard

"Much like Elmore Leonard and James Lee Burke, John Harvey has far transcended his genre." 　　—Jim Harrison

"Charlie Resnick is one of the most fully realized characters in modern crime fiction ... Lifts the police procedural into the realm of the mainstream novel." 　　—Sue Grafton

"Harvey's Resnick novels are far and away the finest British police procedurals yet written." 　　—*GQ*

"Nobody writes police procedurals better than John Harvey. Nobody." 　　—*Booklist*

STILL WATER

JOHN HARVEY

BLOODY BRITS PRESS
Ann Arbor and Alnmouth
2008

Bloody Brits Press
PO Box 3671
Ann Arbor MI 48106-3671

BLOODY BRITS PRESS FIRST EDITION
First Printing September 2008

First published in Great Britain in 1991 by William Heinemann

Printed in the United States of America on acid-free paper

Cover designer: Bonnie Liss (Phoenix Graphics)

Bloody Brits Press is an imprint of Bywater Books

ISBN 978-1-932859-60-7

For Sarah: something changed

One

It was the night Milt Jackson came to town: Milt Jackson, who for more than twenty years had been a member of one of the most famous jazz groups in the world, the Modern Jazz Quartet; who had gone into the studio on Christmas Eve, 1954, and along with Miles Davis and Thelonious Monk, recorded one of Resnick's all-time favorite pieces, "Bag's Groove"; the same Milt Jackson who was standing now behind his vibraphone on the stage of the Broadway Media Centre's Cinema Two, brought there with his new quartet as part of the Centre's Film and Jazz Festival; Milt, handsome and dapper in his dark gray suit, black handkerchief poking folded from its breast pocket, floral tie, wedding ring broad on his finger and catching the light as he reaches down for the yellow mallets resting across his instrument; Milton "Bags" Jackson, born Detroit, Michigan on New Year's Day, 1923, and looking nothing like his seventy-three years, turning now to nod at the young piano player—relatively young—and the crowd that is packed into the auditorium, Resnick among them, holds its breath, and as Jackson raises a mallet shoulder high to strike the first note, the bleeper attached to the inside pocket of Resnick's jacket intrudes its own insistent sound.

And there is a moment, Resnick bulkily rising from his seat near the center of row four and fumbling inside his coat as he excuses himself, embarrassed, past people's knees, in which Jackson, expression shifting between annoyance and amusement, catches Resnick's eye and grins.

Out in the foyer, Resnick hurried to the ticket desk and asked to use the phone. Jack Skelton's voice was clipped and sharp: the body had been discovered less than twenty minutes earlier, trapped

1

beneath the lock gates of the canal, just where it flows into the Trent. Resnick's sergeant was already on his way there, along with three of the team. Resnick glanced at his watch and estimated how long it would take to drive through the city, heading west.

"Shall I send a car for you, Charlie?" the superintendent asked.

"No, it'll be all right. No need."

He had driven to the theater that night with Hannah, or rather, she had driven him, preferring to wait for him in the Café Bar. Jazz she could tolerate, but not for hours on end.

Resnick picked her out immediately, sitting at a table close to the back wall with Mollie Hansen, Broadway's head of marketing. Hannah with her hair just short of shoulder length, brown shading gently into red, a man's dress shirt, not Resnick's, worn loose over a deep blue T-shirt, blue jeans. Wearing black beside her, Mollie seemed slighter, younger, though the difference between them was no more than a few years; Mollie's hair was shorter, her face sharper, pale skinned, bright eyed.

"Not over already?" Mollie said with a grin.

Resnick shook his head. "Something's come up." He tried not to notice the concern cross Hannah's face.

"Work?" she asked and Resnick nodded. She took her car keys from her bag and dropped them into his hand.

"Shame about the concert," she said.

Resnick nodded again, distracted, anxious to be away.

The air was hazy and humid, warm for June, and even with the windows of Hannah's Beetle wound down, Resnick could feel his shirt beginning to stick beneath his arms and along his back. The streets seemed to grow narrower, the houses smaller the closer he came; there was the scent of something sweet and sickly like honeysuckle and though it was still light, the moon hung in the sky, almost full, its reflection misted in the still water of the canal.

An ambulance was parked near the intersection of Canal Side and Riverside Road; several police vehicles were pulled back alongside the recreation ground that led to the lock. Resnick left the VW behind these and walked to where Millington was standing on the narrow lock bridge, talking to a sergeant from the river police.

2

Lynn Kellogg was on the towpath, notebook in hand, questioning a youth in a baseball cap and a girl in a skimpy top and skirt who could have been no more than fourteen. He saw Naylor crouching down by the far lock gate, something stretched along the gravel beside him, covered in a plastic sheet. Carl Vincent was perhaps a dozen yards away, chatting to a pair of paramedics. There were people standing curious at windows and in open doorways, clustering in twos and threes at the pavement's edge.

As he approached the bridge, Resnick could hear clearly the roar of river water as it tumbled over the weir beyond the lock.

"Graham."

Millington nodded a response to the greeting. "You know Phil Given, river police? Charlie Resnick, my DI."

"I think I've bumped into you, County ground," Given said, "season or so back."

"Likely." Resnick was looking beyond them, down toward the water. "What do we know?"

"Couple of kids found her," Given said, "half-seven, thereabouts …"

"That's them," Millington interrupted, "talking to Lynn now."

"Must've floated down to the gate here and got wedged somehow against the support of the bridge. Trapped by her arm." Given pointed below them in the direction of the bank. "Above the water line, look, you can just see the marks."

"Any idea how long she'd been there?" Resnick asked.

Given shook his head. "Couple of hours. Maybe more."

Resnick nodded. "Doctor not here yet?"

Millington finished lighting a cigarette. "Parkinson. On his way."

"I don't suppose we've any idea who she is?"

Millington shook his head.

Resnick left them standing there and walked to where Lynn Kellogg was still talking to the kids who'd reported the body. He listened for a few moments, not interfering, moving on to where Naylor was still standing guard, the young DC's face yellow and strained. Some came to think little more of a corpse than roadkill; for others it was new every time.

"You could have a word with some of that lot standing round

gawking," Resnick said. "Get Carl to give you a hand. One of them might have seen something, you never know."

Resnick lowered himself onto one knee and folded back the sheet: the face had lost much of its definition, the skin was puckered fast in some places, loose in others as an ill-fitting glove. There were marks—what might have been tiny bite marks—around the sockets of the eyes. High on the right temple, a gash opened, raw and washed deep into the bone. After or before, Resnick wondered, straightening? After or before?

"At least it's not four in the morning, Charlie," said a voice from behind him. "You'll be grateful for that."

"Maybe," Resnick said, lowering the plastic carefully into place. "And maybe not." He imagined the impeccable flow of notes from Jackson's vibraphone, their rise and fall stretching out across the becalmed evening air.

Parkinson smiled benevolently over his half-moon spectacles and unfastened the center button of his suit. "Bridge, that's what this saved me from. Going two off in four clubs, what's more. Four clubs, idiotic call."

"I dare say," said Resnick, for whom card games were as enticing as Gilbert and Sullivan or a quick game of croquet.

"Time and cause," Parkinson said, "I'll do what I can. But don't hold your hopes. Not yet awhile."

There was enough water in the lungs for death to have been caused by drowning, though the blow to the head was severe and would have caused considerable trauma and loss of blood. A contributory factor, then, though whether the blow had been administered before or soon after the body had been introduced into the water, remained unclear. As for the exact nature of the instrument which had delivered the blow—something heavy, probably metallic, sharp but not pointed and traveling, at the moment that it met the head of the deceased, with considerable speed, propelled with considerable force.

She was a young woman, twenty-four to twenty-seven years of age, of average size and build. She had had an appendectomy in her late teens, a pregnancy terminated within the past eighteen

4

months. One of her front teeth was capped with a chrome crown, a procedure normally carried out only in Eastern Europe. Her clothing—denim shirt and cotton trousers, underwear—was of a type obtainable in chain stores in most major and medium-size cities of the world. Her feet had been bare. The silver ring on the little finger of her left hand had no idiosyncratic marks or features of design. The inexact photograph taken after basic reconstruction and forwarded to police forces throughout the United Kingdom and Europe resulted in no positive identification. Attempts to link the death to those of three others, two female, one male, whose bodies had been discovered in canals in the preceding seven years—two in the East Midlands, one in the North East—proved inconclusive.

Nothing happened.

After three months, the file was marked Pending.

Media references to the Canal Murders were spiked or stillborn. Resnick knew from occasional comments overheard in the canteen that the victim was referred to as the Phantom Floater, the Woman Who Went for an Early Bath. But for Resnick it was always the night he missed hearing Milt Jackson; the night Milt Jackson came to town.

Two

"Charlie, is it tarragon or basil you don't like? I can never remember."

Resnick was sitting in the downstairs front room of Hannah's house, dark even though it was shy of seven on this late September evening, dark across the park that faced the small terrace through shrubs and railings, and Resnick sitting close by the corner table lamp, glossing through Hannah's back copies of the *Independent*'s Sunday magazine.

"Tarragon," he called back, "but it's not that I don't like it. A bit strong sometimes, that's all."

In the kitchen, Hannah laughed quietly. From a man who regularly crammed sandwiches with everything from extra strong Gorgonzola to garlic salami, she thought that was a bit rich. "You could open the wine in a few minutes," she called back.

"What time are they coming?"

"Half-seven. Which probably means not till eight. I thought we could have a glass first."

Or two, Resnick thought. He hadn't met these particular friends of Hannah's before, but if the rest were anything to go by, they would be artsy, Labour-voting liberals with a cottage they were slowly rebuilding somewhere in southern France, a couple of kids called Ben and Sasha, a Volvo estate, and a cleaner who came twice a week; they would laugh at their own jokes and the cleverness of their cultural references, be perfectly amiable to Resnick, and at the end of the evening try not to appear too resentful that his presence was keeping them from skinning up and passing round a spliff. He suspected they had cast him as one of Hannah's passing idiosyncrasies—like taking her holidays in Scarborough or eating fish fingers mashed between two slices of white bread. "Okay," he said, "I'll be there in a minute."

One of Hannah's CDs was playing, an album he'd chanced on by Chris Smither with a version of "Statesboro Blues" that wouldn't have Willie McTell turning blind in his grave. He waited till that track had finished and then stood by the window for some moments, staring off into the dark.

Come Monday morning, Resnick was thinking, the newly formed Serious Crime Squad would be moving into its headquarters in a converted building that had once been part of the General Hospital. Twenty detective constables, four sergeants, a smattering of support staff, one inspector, and, running the show under the general super-vision of a detective superintendent, a freshly appointed detective chief inspector.

There were those—and at times Resnick surprised himself by being among them—who thought it should have been him.

Jack Skelton, heaven knows, had nagged at him long enough—get in that application, Charlie, it's maybe your last chance; even the chief constable designate had buttonholed him in the Central Police station corridor and asked him point-blank what had happened to his ambition.

Still Resnick had prevaricated. He knew there would be over a hundred applicants, fifteen of whom would be selected for inter-view, at least six of those thirtyish high-fliers from the Police Staff College at Bramshill, their cards already marked.

"Charlie, am I opening this wine or are you?"

There were those high up in the force, Resnick knew, who valued his experience, the fact that he had dedicated all his working life to the city. And there were others who saw him as small-minded and provincial, a good copper certainly, but past his sell-by date where promotion was concerned. So finally Resnick had forgone the pleasures of giving a five-minute presentation on the major problems of policing in the year 2000, and of sitting with his fellow candidates in some anonymous examination room sweating over a string of questions. He had convinced himself that doing what he was doing, running a small CID squad from a sub-station on the edge of the city center, was still challenge enough to see him through the next five years. He had a team that by and large he trusted, whose strengths and weaknesses he knew.

But one of his DCs, Mark Divine, had still not returned after almost six months' leave of absence, and another, Lynn Kellogg, having passed her sergeant's board, had surprised him by applying for a transfer to the Family Support Unit. Even Graham Millington was murmuring darkly about going back into uniform and moving himself and Madeleine out to Skegness.

Some days, Resnick felt like a captain who was busily lashing himself to the mast while everyone else was resolutely jumping ship.

"Charlie?" Hannah's voice behind him was soft and questioning. "You okay?"

"Yes, why?"

She gave a small shake of her head and smiled with her eyes. "Here," holding out a glass of wine, "I thought you might like this."

"Thanks."

"You sure you're all right?"

"Yes, sure." And looking at her then, standing close, her fingers still resting on his as they held the glass, it was true.

"The risotto will be ready in twenty minutes. If they're not here by then, we'll eat it ourselves."

Alex and Jane Peterson arrived shortly after eight, bearing apologies and flowers, a bottle of Sancerre and another, smaller, of Italian dessert wine the color of peaches.

Alex, as Hannah had explained earlier, was a dentist, one of the few still working inside the National Health Service, a balding man of around Resnick's age, some ten years or more older than his wife. Unlike Resnick and Hannah, they had both dressed with a degree of formality, Alex in a loose cream suit with burgundy waistcoat, a white tie-less shirt buttoned to the neck; Jane was wearing a black linen jacket and black flared trousers, her hair, streaked blonde, cut short and close to her head.

Throughout the meal, Alex talked vociferously, often humorously, holding strong and sardonic opinions on almost everything, and when he lapsed into silence, managing to convey the impression that he was holding back in order to give the others a chance.

8

Jane, who taught at the same school as Hannah, seemed tired but cheery, her pale face flushed as the evening wore on. Only when the subject of a day school she was helping to organize at Broadway came up, was she really animated.

"Not sure what I think about all this, Charlie," Alex said, pointing at Resnick with his fork. "What is it, Jane? Something about women and television, women and the media? Where d'you stand on that, Charlie, seminars on popular culture? Some academic from the university giving forth about stereotypes and the like."

Resnick passed.

"Personally," Alex went on, "I'd sooner slob out in front of *EastEnders* without thinking I was going to be interrogated about its gender issues the minute it was over."

Jane could scarcely wait for him to finish. "That's nonsense, Alex, and you know it. For one thing, you *never* slob in front of the TV, you've just read about other people doing it, and for another, you jump at the opportunity to intellectualize absolutely anything faster than anyone I know." She stared at him, defiant. "And just to set the record straight, it's about women and sexual violence and it's in next month's program. Hannah, you should get Charlie to come along, I think he might enjoy it."

Hannah smiled and said that she would see.

Alex leaned toward Jane and deposited a kiss on the side of her neck.

The risotto was followed by pork loin with red cabbage and sweet potatoes, *crème brûlée*, and a plethora of cheeses.

"Do you cook yourself, Charlie?" Alex asked, helping himself to more wine. "Master of the *nouvelle cuisine*?"

"Can't say as I get much of a chance."

"Lucky to find a woman then who can. Who can do it as well as this." Alex raised his glass. "Hannah, we owe you a vote of thanks."

Jane reached over and squeezed her hand and Resnick wondered why he should be feeling embarrassed on Hannah's behalf when she obviously seemed so pleased.

"And now," Alex said, "if you could pass me a smidgen more of that delicious cheese. Yes, that's it, the Vignote."

They took their coffee through into the living room and Hannah surprised Resnick by playing the Billie Holiday compilation he had given her for her birthday and which she seemed to have ignored ever since.

"This doesn't sound like you," Jane remarked with a smile, Billie stalking her way through "They Can't Take That Away from Me."

"Charlie gave it to me."

"Educating you, is he?" said Alex.

"Not exactly."

"Well, I like it anyway," Jane said. "Don't you, Alex?"

Alex jinked his cup against its saucer. "All right for selling lipstick to, I suppose, Italian cars. Modishly moody. Just a shame she can't really sing."

Resnick bit his tongue.

Hannah had lit candles, three of them in glass holders, and they burned with a thick vanilla scent. The bed was in the center of the attic room, low between rugs, two pine chests of drawers. A cloud of orange city light spun down from twin skylights, angled toward each other from either side of the sloping roof.

Resnick had washed the dinner things, Hannah had dried and put away. They had sat ten minutes longer in the front room, enjoying the silence, the virtual dark. Now Hannah was on her side, knees pulled up under the hem of the oversize T-shirt she wore in bed, and Resnick lay close in behind her, one arm running along the pillow between Hannah's shoulder and chin.

"So?"

"So what?"

"Was it as awful as you thought?"

"Who said I thought it would be awful?"

"Oh, Charlie, come on! Your face, your voice, everything about you. You were mooching around downstairs before they came like someone waiting for—I don't know—something dreadful."

"Like waiting for the dentist, you mean."

"Funny!"

Resnick edged forward a touch more and angled his arm downward so his hand could cup one of Hannah's breasts.

10

"Seriously," she said, "what did you think of them?"

"They were okay. I liked her. Quiet, but she seemed nice enough. She's fond of you. Alex, I'm not so sure. Small doses, maybe."

"And together, as a couple?"

"I don't know … they seemed to get on well enough, I suppose."

Hannah turned over to face him, dislodging his hand from her breast. "He's a bully, Charlie. He bullies her. It upsets me to see it, it really does."

Slowly, she rolled away from him and when Resnick reached out for her he felt her tense against his hand.

Three

At a quarter to six that morning, the air was raw; mist silvered across the flat expanse of the park and the Asian taxi-driver waiting for Resnick at the corner of Gloucester Avenue sat rubbing gloved hands.

"Why don't you leave some of your things here?" Hannah had suggested once. "There's plenty of room. Then you could go straight to work without having to get us both up at the crack of dawn. You could walk it in ten minutes."

But there had been the cats—there were always, for the foreseeable future, the cats. So whenever Resnick stayed over the alarm was set for five thirty and, one of his older jackets he'd forgotten aside, Hannah's wardrobe remained her own. Despite his assurances that she didn't need to get up with him, she persisted in doing so, making coffee for him and tea for herself; once Resnick left, taking a second cup back to bed and reading and dozing her way through the next hour.

Resnick's return was always greeted with preening disdain by the largest of his four cats, Dizzy presenting him with a proud backside and running ahead of him along the length of stone wall that skirted the drive, jumping down and waiting with studied impatience by the front door.

By the time Resnick had showered, changed, fed the cats, made toast and more coffee for himself, and driven the short distance across town to the Canning Circus station, it was close to half past eight. Carl Vincent had more or less finished getting the night's files ready for Resnick's inspection and was wolfing down a bacon and egg sandwich he'd fetched from the canteen. In the corner of the CID room, on the cabinets alongside Resnick's partitioned

12

office, the kettle was simmering, ready to make tea for the assembling officers.

"Much activity?" Resnick asked.

Vincent swallowed too hastily and came close to choking. "Not really," he finally managed. "Quiet. One thing, though. Those paintings we thought someone was trying to lift a few months back. One of those big houses in the Park. April, was it? May?" He opened the file and pointed. "Here. Someone broke into the place last night. Had them both away."

Resnick recalled the occasion clearly; he even remembered the paintings. Landscapes, both of them, quite small. Around the turn of the century? Somebody called ... Dalzeil? Dalzeil. He didn't think it was pronounced the way it looked.

He remembered waiting outside the house for the intruder to leave, others keeping watch over the side fire escape and the rear. Except that when Jerzy Grabianski let himself out of the house it was by the front door and the holdall he was carrying proved to contain nothing but a Polaroid camera, a torch, and a pair of gloves.

"Knew him, didn't you?" Vincent asked. "Some connection?"

Aside from the fact we're both Polish, Resnick thought, ancestry anyway? And, he might have added, that we both top six foot and are heavy with it. The first time he had seen Grabianski, it had been a little like walking into a room and coming face to face with your double. Save that he was a copper and Jerzy Grabianski was a professional criminal, a thief.

"We pulled him in a few years back," Resnick said, "along with a nasty piece of work called Grice. Stolen jewelry, other valuables, cash, half a kilo of cocaine ..."

Vincent whistled. "They weren't dealing?"

Resnick shook his head. "Came on it more or less by chance and tried to get rid."

"Still, must've drawn some heavy time."

"Grice, certainly. Still away somewhere for all I know. Lincoln. The Scrubs."

"Not Grabianski?"

"He helped us nail somebody we'd been after a long time. Big supplier. We did a deal."

13

"And he got off? Nothing?"

"A few months. By the time it came to trial …" Resnick shrugged. "Get yourself out to the house first call. If nothing else has been disturbed, clean entry, place looking more like it's had a visit from an overnight cleaner than a burglar, Grabianski might be in the frame."

"Right, boss."

From the shrill version of "This is My Song" that came whistling up the stairs, Resnick knew DS Graham Millington was about to make an appearance.

Hannah had said little more about Alex and Jane Peterson. She and Resnick had soon fallen asleep—the consequence of good food and good wine—and their morning had been too rushed and sleepy for much in the way of conversation.

Sitting in his office now, shuffling papers, Resnick thought back to the previous night's dinner, trying to recall any signs that would support Hannah's accusation. Alex had been the more dominant, it was true; domineering even. He clearly felt his opinions counted for a great deal and was not used to having them contradicted: a consequence perhaps, Resnick thought, of talking to people whose mouths were usually stretched wide and crammed with metal implements.

But while Jane had been quiet, she had scarcely seemed cowed. And when she had stood up to him about the Broadway event she was organizing, he seemed to take it well enough. Hadn't he kissed her as if to say he didn't mind, well done? While Resnick was aware that Hannah would probably regard that as patronizing, he wasn't sure he altogether agreed.

How long, Resnick wondered, had they been married, Alex and Jane? And whatever patterns their relationship had formed or fallen into, who was to say they were necessarily wrong? What best suited some, Resnick thought, sent others scurrying for solace elsewhere—his own ex-wife, Elaine, for one.

He was mulling over this and wondering if it wasn't time to wander across to the deli for a little something to see him through till lunchtime, when Millington knocked on his door.

14

"Our Carl, called in from that place in the Park you were talking about earlier. Wondered if you might spare the time to go down there. Reckons how it'd be worth your while."

The photographs showed the paintings clearly. One was a perfectly ordinary landscape, nothing especially interesting about it that Resnick could see: sheep, fields, trees, a boy of fourteen or fifteen, a shepherd with white shirt and tousled hair. The other was different. Was it the photograph or the painting that had slipped out of focus? As Resnick continued to look, he realized it was the latter. A large yellow sun hung low over a plowed field patched with stubble; undefined, purplish shadows bunched on the horizon. And everything within the painting blurred with the tremor of evening light.

"What do you think of them, Inspector?" Miriam Johnson asked. "Are they worth stealing, do you think?"

Resnick looked down at her, a small keen-faced woman with almost white hair and an arthritic stoop, voice and mind still sharp and clear in her eighty-first year.

"It seems somebody thought so."

"You don't like them, then? Not to your taste?"

When it came to art, Resnick wasn't sure what his taste was. Which probably meant he didn't have any at all. Though there were reproductions here and there in Hannah's house that he liked: a large postcard showing a scene in a busy restaurant, a man talking earnestly to a woman at a center table and leaning slightly toward her, hand raised to make a point, the woman in a fur-trimmed collar and reddish flowerpot hat; and another, smaller, which was tucked into the frame of the bathroom mirror, a woman painted again from behind, seated, but looking out across reddish-brown rooftops from one side of a large bay window—Resnick remembered the white vase at the center holding flowers, a sharp yellow rectangle of light.

"I think I like this one," Resnick said, pointing at the second photograph. "It's more interesting. Unusual."

Miriam Johnson smiled. "It's a study for *Departing Day*, you know. His most famous painting, in so far as poor Herbert was

15

famous at all. He made the mistake of being British, you see. Had he had the foresight to have been born French ..." She tilted her head into an oddly girlish laugh. "French and Impressionist, it's almost as if they were brought together from birth, don't you think? Whereas if you were to stop some person in the street and ask them what they knew of our British Impressionists all you'd get would be so many blank looks.

"Even among the knowledgeable few," she continued, "it is Sargent who is remembered, Whistler of course; but not Herbert Dalzeil." She pronounced it De-el.

"Excuse me if this is a daft question," Vincent said, "but if he's not famous, why would anyone go out of their way to steal his work? Especially if it's not like, you know, the one that's reckoned his best?"

Miriam Johnson smiled; such a nice boy, that soft dark skin, not black at all, but polished, almost metallic brown. And he wasn't brash, like some young men. Polite. "He painted so little, you see. Especially toward the end of his life. He would have been, oh, sixty I suppose when he did his best work, but then he lived on another thirty years." She laid a finger on Vincent's sleeve. "It's extraordinary, isn't it? He was born right in the middle of the last century and yet he lived to see the first years of the Second World War." Again she laughed, girlishly. "He was even older than I am now. But he lost his health, you see. His eyesight, too. Can you imagine, for a painter, what a loss that must be?"

She smiled a little sadly and Vincent smiled back.

"It's their rarity, then, that would make these worth stealing?" Resnick asked.

"And not their beauty?" Miriam Johnson countered.

"I don't know. To a collector, I dare say both. Though I doubt anyone would try to sell them on the open market; any reputable dealer would know they were stolen."

"Japan," Vincent said, "isn't that where most of them go? There or Texas."

"I should have given them to a museum," Miriam Johnson said, "I realize that. That's what was intended to happen to them, of course, when I died. It was all arranged in my will. The Castle would

16

gladly have added them to their collection, they don't have a single Dalzeil. I know it was wrong to cling onto them, especially once I couldn't afford the insurance premiums. But I was so used to having them, you see. And I would look at them every day, not simply pass them by but really sit with them and look. Of course, I had the time. And each year I thought it can wait, it can wait, there can't be long to go, just let me keep them for now." Her eyes as she looked up at Resnick were bright and clear. "I was a foolish old woman, that's what you're thinking."

"Not at all."

"Well, Inspector, you should be."

Like many in the Park, the house had been built in the latter half of the last century, testimony to the wealth which coal and lace had brought to the city. Not converted into apartments like so many of the others, it lingered on in drab high-ceilinged splendor, slowly declining into terminal disrepair. The burglar—and they were assuming it was one person acting alone—had risked the rusting fire escape and forced entry into an unoccupied second-floor bedroom. The window frame had been so rotten the catch had been easy to prize away whole. In the drawing room, pale rectangular patches on the heavy wallpaper showed clearly where the paintings had hung, one above the other. Nothing had disturbed the owner, asleep at the rear of the ground floor.

"Careful," Vincent remarked. "Professional."

"Yes."

"Professional enough for your friend Grabianski?"

Resnick remembered the smile that had settled on Jerzy Grabianski's face, the hint of smugness in his voice. "Half an hour with one of the unsung masters, worth any amount of risk. Besides, you'll not bother charging me, not worth the paperwork. Nothing taken. Not as much as a speck of dust disturbed."

All right, Resnick thought: that was then and this was now. "Maybe, Carl, maybe. But there are ways of finding out."

Four

The Sisters of Our Lady of Perpetual Help lived in an undistinguished three-story house midway between the car park for the Asda supermarket and the road alongside the Forest recreation ground, where the local prostitutes regularly plied their trade.

There but for the grace of God, as Sister Bonaventura used to remark, bustling past. Whether she was referring to whoring or working at the checkout, Sister Teresa and Sister Marguerite were never sure.

All three of them were attached to the order's outreach program, living in one of the poorer areas of the city and administering as best they could to the unfortunate and the needy, daily going about the Lord's business without the off-putting and inconvenient trappings of liturgical habits but wearing instead civilian clothes donated by members of the local parish. Plain fare for the most part, but ameliorated by small personal indulgences.

Sister Marguerite, who came out in a painful rash if she wore anything other than silk closest to her skin, purchased her underwear by mail order from a catalog. Sister Bonaventura stuck pretty much to black, which she relieved with scarlet AIDS ribbons and a neat metallic badge denoting Labour Party membership. "Who do you think He would vote for, if He came back down to reclaim His Kingdom on earth?" she would ask when challenged about this. "The Conservatives?"

And Sister Teresa, whose mother had stopped measuring her against the kitchen wall at fourteen when she had reached five foot seven, was forced to make her own arrangements as the kind supply of cast-offs rarely matched her size. Regularly, she would bundle up a pile of pleated skirts and crimplene trouser suits and take them to the Oxfam shop, where she would exchange them for something more fitting.

Today, when Resnick met the sister by the entrance to the radio station where she broadcast charity appeals and dispensed advice, she was wearing a calf-length navy skirt and a plain white blouse with a high collar and broad sleeves. She wore no discernible makeup and her dark hair was pulled back from her face by a length of ribbon.

Recognizing Resnick, she smiled.

"Good program?" he asked.

"Oh, you know. Sometimes when the same people phone in week after week demanding the same answers, you get to wonder. But, no, once in a while I think it may genuinely help and, at least, it makes people aware that we're here. I'm grateful for the opportunity to do that." When she smiled again, Resnick noticed, not for the first time, the tiny lines that creased next to the green of her eyes. "It increases our visibility, that's what Sister Bonaventura says. And she's the one with the diploma in media studies."

"You don't think it makes you a little too visible at times?" After one helpline session during which Sister Teresa had advised a battered wife to go into a refuge, the woman's husband had been waiting for Teresa and had attacked her in the station's car park—which had been where Grabianski, unlikely knight errant, had leaped to her rescue.

"It is only radio, Inspector," Sister Teresa said. "It's not as if I were making a spectacle of myself on television. People don't point at me in the street."

"You'll not mind being seen with me, then," Resnick said. "I thought if you had time for a cup of coffee …"

"Were you thinking of going into the market?"

"Why not?"

"Then I'll have a strawberry milkshake. And pray for forgiveness afterwards."

The market stalls, selling fresh fruit and vegetables, dairy produce, meat and fish, had once done battle with the elements in the Old Market Square; for years after that they had jostled comfortably together in a covered hall near the now defunct bus station. When one of the city's railway stations was demolished to make way for a vast new shopping center, the food market moved again, finding space on the upper floor above the ubiquitous Dorothy Perkins, Mothercare, and Gap.

Resnick came here frequently to buy salami and rich cheesecake at the Polish delicatessen, ham off the bone, Jarlsberg and blue Stilton, and to perch on one of the stools around the Italian coffee stall, drinking small cups of strong dark espresso, which the proprietor dispensed with an extravagant flourish.

This particular afternoon Aldo's appraising eye traveled its politically incorrect way the length and breadth of Sister Teresa's body, resting finally on the ring which she wore, third finger, left hand.

"*Si bella, signora.* If you were not married already, I would fall to my knees this moment and propose."

"I'll bet you say that to all the nuns," Teresa said.

Rapidly crossing himself, Aldo withdrew behind the Gaggia machine.

"Jerzy Grabianski," Resnick began.

"What about him?"

"I wondered if you'd seen anything of him recently."

A slight frown passed across Teresa's face.

"It's not that I mean to pry."

"Of course."

"It's just I thought he might have been in touch."

"In person, would this be?" Turning her head a little to one side, Teresa smiled.

"Possibly."

"He's been here, then? In the city?"

"Possibly." Resnick's turn to smile.

"I've not heard anything from him since ... oh, several months, it would be. A postcard from Slimbridge, the Wildfowl Trust. Birding, I suppose." She tried her milkshake, drawing it up carefully through a colored straw. Oversweet. "I've always thought it was from him, though he didn't sign it, of course. It was a painting of a blue-winged teal. A rare visitor from America, apparently. He'd seen a

20

pair of them that day, checked them off in his little book, I expect. Quite the collector."

"Exactly," Resnick said. And then, setting aside his espresso, "He didn't mention anything about paintings by any chance?"

They were sitting in the narrow kitchen of the sisters' house, previously a vicarage and close alongside the community center that had once been a church. If you listened carefully, you could hear the click of pool balls through the wall.

Sister Bonaventura had greeted Resnick with an appraising stare and invited him inside. "Always bringing men home, our Teresa. Likes to think she's saving their souls."

Teresa scolded her and hurried upstairs to her room, leaving Sister Bonaventura to play hostess, which she did by thrusting a potato peeler into Resnick's hand and pointing him at the bag of King Edwards that sat waiting on the counter. By the time Teresa returned, a worn envelope in her hand, the sister had engaged Resnick in a discussion about New Labour and the pernicious spread of Social Democratic policies.

"When I read that Billy Bragg had torn up his party membership card," she said, "I had to fight hard to restrain myself from doing the same." She topped and tailed two washed carrots and chopped them into a pot simmering on the stove. "After all the work that young man put into the cause. You remember Red Wedge, Inspector, naturally?"

Resnick allowed that he might, though it was confused in his mind with Arthur Scargill and the miners' strike. He knew if he got onto *that* subject with Sister Bonaventura, he would be there long enough not just to share supper, but to wash the pots as well.

"Here," Teresa said, rescuing him. "Are these what you're referring to, I wonder?"

These were a pair of photographs, Polaroids, both of the later Dalzeil painting, one clearly showing the surround of Miriam Johnson's wall. Sister Teresa's name and address were on the envelope, the postmark too smudged to read.

"When did you get these?" Resnick asked.

"It would have been early May, the seventh or the eighth perhaps."

21

"As if you didn't know," Sister Bonaventura said.

Teresa ignored her.

Reflected in one of the photographs, Resnick could now see, was the blurred image of the man taking the picture—Jerzy Grabianski at work. Resnick remembered the camera they had discovered in his bag.

"Why are you so interested in him?" Teresa asked. "I mean, why now?"

"Two paintings—this and another by the same artist—they've been stolen."

"And you think Jerry ..."

"I think it's a strong possibility, don't you? Given his proclivities."

"As an art lover."

"As a thief."

"You didn't get very far with those potatoes," Sister Bonaventura remarked.

"You don't know for certain that it was him?" Teresa said.

Resnick shook his head.

"Of course. If you did there would be no need to be shilly-shallying here with me. You'd have him somewhere under arrest. But since presumably all you have are suspicions, if he had been here and made contact with me that would be—what would you call it?—circumstantial evidence."

"It might have helped to place him near the scene."

"Of the crime," Sister Bonaventura said.

"It would be my duty, then," Sister Teresa said a touch regretfully, "to help you if I could?"

"What is a crime," said Sister Bonaventura, "is that these paintings were ever in private hands in the first place. They should be on public view, available to all and sundry. Not just the privileged few."

"I don't see our friend Grabianski," Resnick said, "as some artistic Robin Hood."

"Don't you?" Teresa asked.

"Maidens in distress," Sister Bonaventura said, now peeling the potatoes herself. "A different legend, surely."

22

"I don't suppose you've got a number for him? Any kind of current address?" asked Resnick.

Sister Teresa said that she did not.

"Ah, well ..." With a sigh, Resnick rose to his feet.

"You're not staying for supper, then?" Sister Bonaventura asked.

"Maybe some other time."

Teresa escorted him to the door. "Do you need to borrow these?" she asked, glancing down at the envelope by her side. "If they'd be any help ..."

"I don't think so. Not now, at least." He looked at her handsome face, unflinching green eyes. "I doubt you'll be getting rid of them, throwing them away."

When he turned back near the street end, she was still standing in the doorway, a tall, solidly built woman in simple, straightforward clothes. Had she always wanted to become a nun, he wondered, one of those fantasies so beloved of little Catholic girls, one that most of them leave behind with their first period, their first real kiss? Or had something happened in a split second that had changed her life? Like walking into a room and finding yourself face to face with God?

Next time, he thought, crossing toward the Boulevard, he just might ask. Next time. For now there was a colleague he could contact down in the smoke, someone who kept his ear well to the ground. And the secretary of the Polish Club would have connections with his counterparts in Kensington and Balham. Small worlds and where they connected, Grabianski might be found.

Five

Hannah was wearing a Cowboy Junkies T-shirt, white with a picture of the band low over her waistline; if she hadn't been wearing it loose outside her jeans they would have been tucked from sight. The *Lay It Down* tour, is that what it had been called? She remembered the way Margo Timmins had performed half of her numbers sitting down, hands resting across the microphone, a voice that was clear and strong, stronger than on their recordings. Unhurried. Hannah had liked that. Liked, too, the way she had prattled on between songs, seemingly inconsequential stories she felt needed telling, despite the hectoring calls from young men on the edges of the audience. Beautiful, also—but then they always were—Margo with her sculpted nose and perfect mouth, bare legs and arms. Well, women were beautiful, Hannah knew that.

She reached out toward the mug of coffee she had made after she had showered and changed from school, but it had long grown cold. A handful of small boys, primary age, were playing football in the park, an elderly woman in a dark anorak was slowly walking with a lead but no apparent dog; the foliage was several shades of green. Beside Hannah, on the floor by her comfortable chair, were folders for her to mark and grade, fourth-year essays on soap opera—realism or melodrama? For tomorrow, there were lessons still to prepare, chapters of Hardy to reread, Lawrence short stories, poems by Jackie Kay, Armitage, and Duffy.

Hannah folded her arms across her lap and closed her eyes.

When she awoke, the telephone was ringing. Disorientated, she made her way toward it; although it had probably been no more than twenty minutes, she felt she had been asleep for hours.

"Hello?" Even her voice seemed blurred.

"Hannah? I thought perhaps you weren't there." It was Jane, husky and concerned.

"Has something happened? Are you okay?" She had seen Jane in the staff room less than two hours before.

"Oh, yes, it's this stupid thing."

"What thing?"

"This day school, what else?"

Alex, Hannah had been thinking, something's happened with Alex. Some monumental row. "I thought everything was in hand," she said.

"So did I. There was a message when I got home. The film we're meant to be showing—*Strange Days*—it looks as if it might not be available. Apparently the distributors saw some of the advance publicity about the event and got cold feet. They're worried we're setting it up as an easy target so it can be rubbished."

"Oh, Jane, I'm sorry."

"I wish I'd never taken it all on."

"It was a good idea."

"*Was* is right."

"Come on, it'll be fine. And, anyway, maybe they'll change their minds."

"I suppose so." There was a silence and then: "Hannah, would it be all right if I came round?"

"You mean now?"

"No, it's fine. It doesn't matter."

"Jane ..."

"Really."

"Jane."

"Yes?"

"Stop off at the off-license, okay?"

When Resnick got to Hannah's house a couple of hours later, the two women were sitting in the kitchen with the remains of a bottle of Chardonnay between them, plates pushed to one side.

"Charlie, sorry, we've already eaten. I wasn't sure if you were coming or not."

"I should have called. Let you know."

"No. No."

Resnick glanced across from Hannah to Jane, the patches beneath Jane's eyes suggesting she had been crying.

"I should go," Jane said, pushing back her chair.

"There's no need," Resnick said. "Not on my account."

Jane banged her hip hard against the table and stifled a cry.

"Are you all right?" Hannah asked.

"Uum. Yes."

"You weren't thinking of driving?" Resnick said, giving the bottle a meaningful glance.

"I was."

"I'll make coffee," Hannah said, getting to her feet. "Charlie, coffee?"

"Thanks."

"Jane, why don't you take Charlie into the other room? Tell him about your day school. You might be able to persuade him to come along. Represent the male point of view."

Resnick was looking at her carefully, uncertain from her tone how ironic she was being.

He found bits and pieces in the back of Hannah's fridge: a jar of black olive paste, three anchovies at the bottom of a foil-wrapped can, feta cheese; in a wooden bowl on the side were two sorry tomatoes and a small red onion. The bread bin yielded a four-inch length of baguette which, when he took the knife to it, shed crust like brittle paint. Five minutes later, he was sitting with a can of Kronenbourg and his sandwich and chewing thoughtfully, while Hannah made the last of her notes on Carol Ann Duffy's dramatic monologues, and music played in the background, light and pleasantly soporific.

"You staying, Charlie?"

"If that's okay."

Hannah grinned at him and shook her head.

"Don't take things for granted, that was what you said. Don't take *you* for granted."

"You don't," Hannah said.

"Good. I'm glad."

"Oh, Charlie …"

"What?"

She let her copy of the book slide through her fingers as she reached for him along the settee on which they were both sitting. Her cheek was cool against his mouth, her hand warm against his neck.

"What?" he said again, but by then she was kissing him and neither of them said a great deal more, not even is the back door locked or is it time for bed?

They had not been together long enough for familiarity to determine the when and how of making love. Sometimes—most often—their first movements would be gradual: slow, generally cautious kisses and manipulations; then, in the quickening of arousal, it was generally Hannah who rose over him, hips swiveling down, eyes closed, Resnick's hands or her own pressed hard against her breasts.

Later she would cry out, knees locked fast against his ribs, a cry that filled Resnick with a kind of aimless pride, even as it scared him with its abandon, its closeness to despair.

No longer inside her, he would fold himself around her, touch the roundness of her calf, the inside of her thigh; pliant, the sticky swell of her belly, fall of her breast against his palm; Resnick's mouth against her hair.

Leaning back against him, comforted by his size, the bulk of him, Hannah closed her eyes.

Resnick had slept and woken again. From the top of the chest of drawers, Hannah's clock told him it was shortly after one-thirty. He considered the possibility of sliding from the bed without disturbing her and going back to his own home. Why? Why would he do that? Was he still not really comfortable here?

He had almost reached the bedroom door when Hannah stirred and, waking, called his name.

"You're not leaving?"

"No." He pointed to the stairs. "A glass of water. Can I get you anything?"

"Water sounds fine."

Hannah bunched up the pillows and when Resnick returned they lay on their sides facing one another, Hannah supporting herself on an angled arm as she drank.

"What was the matter with Jane, earlier?"

"Oh, you know … When she got involved in this gender thing, I don't think she realized how much it would involve. One minute she was making helpful noises, the next she was half an organizing committee of two. Or so it seems. And she thinks it's important: she wants it to work."

"And what's the point of it again?"

"Oh, Charlie, really!"

"I'm only asking."

"For about the twelfth time. And you can stop that."

Resnick's fingers hesitated in the warm cleft behind her knee, looking at her face in the near dark, endeavoring to see if she was serious or not.

"All right," he said, "I'm listening. Tell me now."

"Women as victims of violence, sexual mostly. Only what they'll be looking at here are movies, books too—they're by women."

"And that's supposed to make it better?"

"Different, anyway. Sado-masochism, rape. The whole thing about violence and sexuality, but looked at from the woman's point of view." Hannah lay back down again, angling onto her side. "I meant what I said before, you know, when Jane was still here. You might find it interesting; you should go."

"Hmm," said Resnick sleepily. "I'll see."

After not so many minutes, Hannah heard the tone of his breathing change and in less time than she would have imagined, she was fast asleep herself.

Six

They overlaid into a gray morning. Not significantly, but enough to set them at odds with the day: Hannah concerned that her attempt to interest a bunch of lower-sixth physicists in contemporary poetry would evaporate into still air; Resnick troubled by a mangle of things the stubborn heaviness of his brain would not allow him to unravel or confront. One of those mornings you knew the toast would burn, and it did.

"Maybe," Hannah said, scraping the worst of the blackened bread into the bin, "we should go back and start again?"

Resnick swallowed his coffee, shrugged his way into his coat. "You really think that'd help?"

"With you in that sort of a mood, I doubt it."

"I'm not in any kind of mood, I just hate being late." Aiming for the corner of the table with his mug, he missed.

"Shit!"

Pale blue ceramic with a band of darker blue at its center, it lay in pieces on the tiled floor.

"It doesn't matter, Charlie. Forget it."

He looked on, helpless, as Hannah dragged the dustpan and brush from beneath the sink. The mug was one of a pair given to her as a gift. An old boyfriend, Resnick remembered, the peripatetic music teacher she was careful not to talk about too much.

"Look, I'd better get going."

"Yes."

Rear door open out into the small yard, he looked back: Hannah at the sink stubbornly refusing to turn her head. The way they had been last night and the way they were now—why was it always such hard work?

He was at the end of the narrow ginnel which ran between the backs of the houses when she caught him.

"Charlie."

"Um?"

"I'm sorry."

Relieved, he smiled and brushed a stray fall of hair away from her face. "No need."

They stood as they were, not moving.

"Is it the job? The promotion, I mean ..."

"Serious Crimes?" He shrugged and shuffled a pace or two away. "Maybe."

"There'll be other chances, don't you think?"

About the same as County have, Resnick thought, of getting into the Premiership. "Yes, I dare say."

With a small smile, Hannah stepped away. "Shall I see you later?"

"I don't know. I'll call."

"Okay."

At the corner opposite, where he had parked his car, particles of glass silvered up from the roadway like shiny sand. The wing mirror and off-side front window had been broken; nothing, as far as Resnick could see, stolen. He would not have been surprised if the engine had refused to turn, but it caught at the first touch of the ignition and, wearily, he pulled away from the curb, turning left and left again into the early-morning traffic.

Kevin Naylor had drawn early shift: a host of break-ins near the Catholic cathedral, almost certainly kids from what they'd taken, the mess they'd left in their wake; two BMWs and a Rover reported stolen from Cavendish Crescent South; one of the lock-ups back of Derby Road burned out, probably arson.

As part of an ongoing operation, Graham Millington was eagerly awaiting a further meeting with an informant on the verge of shopping the team of three who had knocked over the same post office in Beeston, three times in five days. University graduates, if the informant was to be believed, looking for a way of funding a trip across the States, paying off their student loans.

Lynn Kellogg, meanwhile, was due to interview three sets of

neighbors whose houses backed onto one another between Balfour Road and Albert Grove and whose animosity—so far involving dead rodents, broken windows, all-night sound systems, and human excrement—came close to constituting a serious breach of the peace.

Carl Vincent, aside from the cases of benefit fraud and receiving stolen property that were weighing down his case file, was continuing to check through local antique shops and auction rooms, just in case whoever had taken the Dalzeil paintings had done so without either a ready outlet or any real sense of their worth.

Resnick's regular early-morning meeting with the superintendent had been postponed; Jack Skelton was in Worcester, along with officers from forty-three other forces, attending a meeting to launch a joint investigation into the murders of some two hundred women, which, over the past ten years, had gone unsolved.

"This floater, Charlie," Skelton had asked, glancing through the file. "Beeston Canal. Anything to add?"

Not a thing.

Now Resnick wandered out into the CID room, spoke briefly with both Millington and Naylor, glanced over Lynn's shoulder at the report she was preparing, finally paused by Vincent's desk and watched as the list of auction houses scrolled up the screen of the VDU.

"Any luck?"

"Nothing so far. More than half don't seem to know who Dalzeil was. It's like giving art history lectures by phone." Vincent grinned. "Open University, strictly first level. But so far, no one's owning up to being approached. Nothing that fits our bill, at least."

Resnick nodded. "Okay. Stick with it for now. I'll follow up a few things of my own." He had a contact in the Arts and Antiques Squad at New Scotland Yard who might be able to help.

"Sir?" Lynn Kellogg swiveled round from where she was sitting. "I couldn't have a word?"

"Sure. Ten minutes. Just let me make one call."

Back in his office, Resnick was midway through dialing the Yard number when Millington burst through from the outer office, scarcely bothering to knock. Anxiety was clear in his eyes.

31

"Mark Divine, boss. Stupid bugger's thrown a fit by t'sound of it. Gone off half cock in some nightclub. Glassed someone for starters. And there's talk he had a knife. Right now he's banged up in Derby nick."

"Christ!" For a moment, Resnick closed his eyes. "All right, Graham. I'll get over there myself. You hold the fort here."

"Long as you're sure."

Resnick barely nodded, hurrying to the door.

"Sir ..." Lynn was on her feet, watching her chance for pinning Resnick down about her transfer go storming past.

I was right, Resnick was thinking, hurrying down the stairs and out through the rear exit to the car park: the whole damn squad's falling apart.

Divine sat slumped forward on the narrow bed, elbows on knees, head in hands. The interior of the cell had been painted a dull shade of industrial gray. The stink of urine seemed to seep through the walls.

"How's he been?" Resnick asked.

"You mean since he sobered up?" The custody sergeant was singularly tall, taller than Resnick by several inches, and most of those extra inches in his neck. When he spoke, his Adam's apple bobbed awkwardly above the collar of his uniform shirt.

"That's what this is then, drunk and disorderly?"

"He should be so lucky."

"But he was drunk?"

"Either that or popping Es. Regular one-man rave."

Resnick stood back and the sergeant slotted the key into the lock, the inward movement of the door surprisingly smooth. Divine didn't look up straight away and when he did the jolt of recognition twisted on his face and he punched the skimpy mattress with his fist.

"Mark ..."

Divine blinked and looked away. Bruising hung purple from his mouth and around his eyes; a cut that angled deep across his cheek had been held in place by steristrips.

"He's been to the hospital?"

"Doctor saw him here."

"What about an X-ray?"

The custody sergeant shrugged.

"And the injuries, they were sustained where?"

"Over half the city center, looks like. Two or three skirmishes in pubs before the nightclub where things really got nasty."

"Not here, then?"

"Eh?"

"I said, Sergeant, those injuries to the face, no way they could have been sustained when he was in custody?"

The sergeant held his gaze for fully ten seconds. "Didn't exactly come quietly. Meek and mild. Might've taken a bit of time, getting him subdued."

"Time?"

"And energy."

"Force then?"

"Reasonable force, yes."

Resnick's turn to stare.

"Police and Criminal Evidence Act, 1984; section one hundred and ..."

"I know the section, Sergeant."

"I'm sure you do, sir."

"And I'm sure whatever happened, whatever reasonable force was used in making the arrest, it's all been logged."

"Of course."

"Thank you, Sergeant, you can leave us now."

"Yes, Inspector."

When Resnick sat down on the bed, Divine flinched. All those months and the memory of it clear like burning, raw inside him. Cold sweats when his body turned against him, wrenching him. The shame. Like a knife inside him. Skin on his skin. Cunt and whore. Carl Vincent delicately covering him.

"Mark?"

Divine's voice so quiet, even that close, Resnick could not be certain he had spoken.

33

"Can I get you something? Cup of tea? Cigarette?"

When Divine looked back at him, his eyes were bright with tears.

Resnick's counterpart was bluff, busy, sandy haired. Working in cities less than twenty miles apart, they knew one another by sight and reputation, little more. To Barrie Wiggins, Resnick was a bit of an oddball, soft round the edges, not the sort you'd opt to sink a few pints with after closing, swapping stories. Wiggins, Resnick knew, enjoyed a reputation for being hard as High Peak granite, the sort who still liked to be out with the lads on patrol of a Sat'day night, roll up his sleeves and pitch into a bar-room fight. One of the best-known anecdotes about him, how he got hold of some ex-miner clinging to his right to silence, slammed his head down into a desk drawer and squeezed tight till the man changed his mind. It was an anecdote that Wiggins liked to tell about himself.

"Bloody mess, Charlie. No two ways about it. Your lad, got himself in a right bloody mess."

"Tell me," Resnick said.

Wiggins shook a packet of Benson Kingsize in Resnick's direction, raised an eyebrow at his refusal, lit one for himself and inhaled deeply. "Leaving aside the scraps he was into in half a dozen pubs beforehand, it's the ruckus at Buckaroos that's the dog's fucking bollocks."

Resnick had driven by the place several times in the past: a sprawling nightclub with a kicking stallion in pink neon over the door and bouncers who wore bootlace ties with their DJs.

"None of this corroborated, of course. Not fully. Not yet. My lads out asking questions now. But the way it seems, your lad was abusive to the bar staff right from the start; he asks this girl to dance and when she says no, drags her out onto the floor anyhow. She manages to pull away and when he comes after her, lobs her drink in his face. Your boy slaps her hard for her trouble." Wiggins tumbled ash from the end of his cigarette. "When security shows up, he sticks a pint glass in one of 'em's face."

"Provocation?"

34

"Like I say, we're asking questions. No problem there. More witnesses than you can shake a stick at."

"And the injuries?"

"Seventeen stitches in some other poor bastard's face. One lad with a cut across his hand, tendons severed, doubtful if they'll mend. When the first uniforms arrived, that was when he pulled the knife."

"What knife?"

"Stanley knife. Inside pocket of his suit."

"And he used it, is that what you're saying?"

Wiggins shook his head. "Not what we're hearing so far."

"Threatened to?"

"Apparently."

"It's not possible the officers misinterpreted, heat of the moment?"

"Come on, Charlie."

"It's possible, though? Couldn't he have been handing it over?"

Wiggins chuckled. "Blade first?"

Resnick was on his feet, hands in pockets, pacing the room. "Divine. You know what happened to him. A few months back."

"I'd heard something."

"He was raped. Smashed round the face with a baseball bat and raped."

"Doesn't excuse ..."

Resnick brought the palms of both hands down against the inspector's desk, flat and fast. "Reasons, not excuses. Reasons. This is a serving officer ..."

"Suspended ..."

"Sick leave."

"Same thing."

Resnick let that pass. "A detective constable with a commendation for bravery ..."

"And a knife in his pocket."

"He's frightened."

"Funny way to show it."

"Ever since he was attacked, frightened. Months before he'd go out at all."

"Ah, well, always find a reason, eh, Charlie. Search hard enough. Excuses for every fucking thing. I don't doubt but you could find him some psychiatrist, half an hour in the witness box, make it seem as if nowt ever happened."

Resnick shook his head. "I just want you to understand."

"Oh, I understand. One of yours, Charlie, you want to do your best for him, I can appreciate that. Respect it. Good management. Good for the team. But see things from my point of view; think how the papers'd look at it, bloody television, some copper runs amok with a blade and we pat him on the head and tell him to take it easy, dole out a few aspirin."

"That's not what I'm saying. Not what I want."

"What do you want, Charlie?"

"To think your people'd treat him with some understanding. And go easy when it comes to laying charges. Think about the whole picture."

"The whole picture," Wiggins smirked. "We're good at that. Noted."

"Don't keep him locked up longer than you have to. Whatever else, ask for police bail, don't let him fetch up inside on remand."

"Not down to me, you know that."

"You could help."

Wiggins stubbed out his cigarette and stopped himself halfway through tapping out another. "Filthy bloody habit." Thinking better of it, he lit up anyway. "All right, Charlie. No promises, but ..." He got to his feet, held out his hand. "You have another word with him before you go. Make sure he's going to play it right. Penitent and contrite. You've already fixed a decent brief for him, I dare say."

After arriving at Derby police station, Resnick had put in a call to Suzanne Olds. The solicitor was waiting for him in the corridor near the custody area and the police cells. Leather briefcase, tailored suit, legs long enough to turn heads.

"You've spoken to him?" Resnick asked.

"It's not easy getting him to say much at all. Except he doesn't care what happens to him, that's clear."

"About this?"

36

"Anything."

"You'll change his mind."

"I'll try."

Resnick shook her hand. "I owe you for this."

"I'll make sure you pay."

Seven

Lynn Kellogg was waiting for him in the corridor. Since passing her sergeant's board, she had taken to wearing more severe colors, this morning an austere mid-calf skirt and matching jacket, flat black shoes, and a blouse like sour milk. She had let her hair grow out a little, but it was still short. A little makeup around the eyes, a touch on the lips.

"My transfer, sir ..."

"I thought you might have been waiting for news about Mark. Or maybe you didn't know."

"Yes, Graham said."

"And you didn't care."

"That's not fair."

"No? Probably not." He started walking and Lynn followed, hurrying into step beside him.

"I know there wasn't any love lost between us, but that doesn't mean I'm not concerned about what's happened."

Just not high on your list of priorities, Resnick thought. He was surprised to be accusing her of anything less than compassion.

"He is all right?" Lynn said.

"No. No, he's not."

They were almost at the stairs, a dogleg that would take them into a second corridor, the entrance to the CID room immediately ahead.

"It is three weeks now," Lynn said, "since my transfer was supposed to have gone through."

"These things take time."

"I know, only ..."

"You can't wait to be away."

She found a thread, loose on the sleeve of her jacket, and snapped it free. A uniformed officer came along the lower corridor, taking his time of it, and they stood back to let him pass.

"Now I've made up my mind, I think it will be easier, that's all." She was not looking at him as she spoke, looking everywhere but at his face. "For both of us perhaps."

The daughter he had never had, the lover she would never be. It hung between them, largely unspoken, unresolved, so tangible that if either of them had reached out they could have touched it, grasped it with both hands.

"The Family Support Unit," Resnick said. "I'll give them a call. See what's holding things up."

"Thanks." Lynn standing there, arms folded tight across her chest.

There was a message from his friend Norman Mann of the Drugs Squad to contact him whenever he got his head above water, nothing urgent; another from Reg Cossall—a drink some time, Charlie, bend your ear. Set this bastard job to rights. Someone, Naylor's handwriting it looked like, had fielded a call from Sister Teresa, the time and a number and a promise to call again. Two routine faxes requesting information about young people gone missing: a fifteen-year-old girl from Rotterdam, last seen on the Dover ferry, a thirteen-year-old boy from Aberdeen.

The phone rang and, picking up, he identified himself. Miriam Johnson's clear but genteel voice was easy to recognize.

"It was your associate, Inspector, that I was hoping to speak with. I remembered something, you see, regarding the paintings."

"DC Vincent's not here at the moment," Resnick said. "Will I do?"

He could nip across to Canning Circus, pick up a double espresso, and take his time strolling down through the Park, breathe some air, stretch his legs.

She had rich tea biscuits waiting for him, symmetrically arranged on a floral plate, Earl Grey tea freshly brewed. "Milk or lemon, Inspector?"

"As it comes will be fine."

They were sitting in the conservatory at the back of the house, looking out over a hundred feet of tiered garden, mostly lawn. Near the bottom was a large magnolia tree, which had long lost its blossom. Inside the conservatory, shades of geranium pressed up against the glass, herbs, inch-high cuttings in small brown pots.

"I can't be certain this is relevant, of course, but I thought, well, if it were and I neglected to bring it to your attention ..."

Resnick looked at her encouragingly and decided to dunk his biscuit after all.

"It would be some time ago now, more than a year. Yes. I was trying to get it clear in my mind before. You're busy, of course, all of you, and the last thing I wanted to do was waste your time, but the nearest I could pin it down would be the early summer of last year." Her gaze shifted off along the garden. "The magnolia was still in flower. He made specific mention of it, which is why I can remember."

She smiled and lifted her teacup from its saucer; yes, the little finger crooked away.

Resnick waited. He could smell basil, over the scent of the Earl Grey. "Who, Miss Johnson?" he finally asked. "Who mentioned the magnolia?"

"I didn't say?"

Resnick shook his head.

"I could have sworn ..." She frowned as she issued herself an internal reprimand. "Vernon Thackray, that was his name. At least, that was what he claimed."

"You didn't believe him?"

"Mr. Resnick, if he had told me it was Wednesday, I should have looked at both my calendar and the daily newspaper before believing it to be so. Though it was ..." Her face brightened and her voice rose higher. "Isn't that interesting, it was a Wednesday. Maurice was here, tending the garden. I should never have let this Thackray into the house otherwise, not if I had been on my own."

"You didn't trust him? He frightened you?"

"My fears, Mr. Resnick, would not have been for myself, rather for the family silver. As it were. A metaphor. All the good things, unfortunately, had to be sold long ago."

"Then it was the paintings, that's why he was here?"

"Absolutely. From somewhere, obviously, he had heard about the Dalzeils and presented himself on my doorstep as a serious collector, imagining that I would be this dotty old maid, bereft of her senses thanks to Alzheimer's disease and happy to let him take them off me for a pittance."

Resnick grinned. "You gave him short shrift."

"I told him I appreciated his interest but that the paintings were not for sale. That was unconditional."

"How did he react to that?"

"Oh, by telling me how much safer they would be in someone else's hands, how fortunate I had been not to have had them stolen. At my advanced years—he actually said that, Inspector, that phrase, my advanced years indeed—wouldn't I be more sensible, rather than risk losing them altogether and ending up with nothing, to take what I could get for them and enjoy the proceeds while I was still able."

Indignantly, she rattled her cup and saucer down onto the table.

"When he was saying this, did you get the impression he was threatening you?"

"Oh, no. Never personally, no."

"But the paintings—was he implying, sell them to me or I'll get my hands on them some other way?"

Miriam Johnson took her time. "One could place that construction upon what he said, yes."

"You let him see the paintings?"

"Of course. His admiration for them was genuine, of that I am sure."

"And you heard from him again?"

"No."

Resnick uncrossed his legs and sat forward. "Did he leave you an address, a card?"

She had it ready for him, in the side pocket of her Pringle cardigan. *Vernon Thackray* in a slightly ornate purple font and with only a telephone number underneath. An 01728 code. Suffolk, somewhere, Resnick thought.

"You didn't contact him?"

"Nor he, me, Inspector. Not to my certain knowledge, at least." She smiled at him, bright eyed.

"How'd it go with Mark?"

Millington was at his desk, troughing into what looked suspiciously like an M & S chicken and mushroom pie.

Resnick was still filling him in when the duty officer phoned up to say that Suzanne Olds had arrived.

"Know more in a minute, Graham."

"Happen he should've stuck with seeing the shrink more'n the couple of sessions he did." Pausing, Millington eased a piece of something unchewable to one side of his mouth with his tongue. "Mind you, what with Lynn still trotting off for therapy rain or shine, only needs you to crack up and we can run the whole CID room from the psychiatric unit."

Me, Resnick thought. Why me? But then Millington was so much less likely a candidate. Disregard his avowed intention of happily resettling in Skegness and Resnick doubted a more unimaginatively sane man existed.

Suzanne Olds wrinkled up her nose at the offer of longmashed tea. She and Resnick had been crossing swords for years, Olds capable of raising her well-modulated voice in anger while rarely losing her cool; each respected the other's integrity, their underlying sense of what was right.

"They'll be ready to charge him this evening, push him through court tomorrow. Preliminary hearing. There's nothing I can say will talk them out of keeping him in the cells overnight."

"Charges?"

"Affray. Causing grievous bodily harm."

"And the knife?"

"If we're lucky, possession of an offensive weapon, nothing more."

"He'll get bail?"

"Given his police record, yes, I'd be surprised if he didn't. There'll be conditions, of course. It's difficult to know yet how stringent."

"And then Crown Court."

"Uh-hum."

"One month, two."

"Try two."

In that time, Resnick thought, who was to say what havoc Divine might wreak upon himself and other people?

"There's no way," Resnick said, "when it comes to trial, of defending him without hauling all that happened back out into the open?"

"And keep him out of prison? I doubt it."

Suzanne Olds shifted her weight from one foot to the other, back perfectly straight. In her teens, Resnick knew, she had been a prize ice-skater, county champion. "Divine's attitude might well have made him friends in the police canteen, but not many places else. Sexist, racist: just the kind the powers-that-be would love to see being held up as an example. Cleaning the Augean stables before the shit gets too high off the floor."

Resnick sighed. "You'll represent him all the same?"

"He needed to be taught a lesson, but not like that. I'll do what I can."

The number Vernon Thackray had left with Miriam Johnson was in Aldeburgh and was unobtainable. "Something must be wrong with the line," the BT official finally told him, having left Resnick to listen to endless repetitions of "Greensleeves." "We could have it checked."

Carl Vincent came back from his tour of the local auction houses empty of information, but carrying a nicely framed watercolor to give to his new boyfriend. Lynn's face showed every sign of an afternoon spent listening to people shouting abuse to and about their neighbors. Kevin Naylor had discovered two empty petrol cans on a piece of waste ground near the torched lock-up and submitted them for analysis. Only Graham Millington seemed due to end the day with optimism lightening his tread: a meeting with his informant arranged at the Royal Children for half-nine and every hope that names would be produced in exchange for a few pints and a nice little backhander.

Resnick was about to jack it all in and head home when Sister Teresa made her return call: another card from Grabianski had arrived, still without a return address—although this one did suggest a place in London where, if she ever traveled down, they might easily meet.

Eight

"You've got all this, all this tightness up here, the upper part of your body. The shoulders and … there, feel that. Can you feel that?"

Grabianski could feel it right enough, pointy tips of her fingers driving into him like sticks, the heel of her hand.

"Feel that now?"

It was all he could do not to call out.

"It's all seized up, blocked; all that energy blocked and we have to find a way of letting it out. It's because of what you do, the way you're always having to use your imagination, the creative part of you."

He had never told her what he did, not a thing.

"And here, of course. Down here. Feel that, in the chest? This is where it all stems from. See? That tension? Stiffness. That's where the source of the trouble is, that's where you're all clenched up. There, around the heart."

She tapped him on the shoulder and he could feel her leaning back from him, sliding away.

"Turn over now, okay?"

At first when he'd met her, Holly, met her on the street, Grabianski had thought she was just another pretty girl—that area he was now living in so full of them, sometimes he had to remind himself to look. But there she'd been, backing away from the window of this place selling second-hand designer clothing, Grabianski with his mind set on how he was going to find a buyer for a brace of nicely engraved solid silver pieces, eighteenth century, and the pair of them had collided, surprise and apologies. Holly wearing royal blue crushed velvet trousers, a cerise top that stopped several inches short of the plain gold ring in her navel. A

45

delicate oval face with brown eyes and browner hair. Not English, not entirely. Eurasian? They were yards away from the wicker chairs and tables set up outside the Bar Rouge.

"How about some coffee?" Grabianski had said.

Holly smiling; guarded, but smiling just the same. "I'm picking my daughter up from school."

Grabianski put her at late twenties, possibly thirty-one or thirty-two.

"Some other time," she said and he forbade himself from watching her walk away, crushed velvet tight over that neat little behind: Grabianski, a natural voyeur, practicing self-control.

He didn't see her for weeks and then he did, coming out of the post office across the street. Wearing a white dress today, simple and straight, hair pinned high, bare legs. Let it go, Grabianski had told himself, she won't remember you anyway.

She called to him from the pedestrian crossing, raised her hand and waved.

She ordered herb tea, camomile, and the waiter, recognizing Grabianski, brought him a *café au lait*. It was then that she told him her name, Holly, and, making conversation, he asked her what she did.

"Massage."

"Really?"

"Of course."

The elderly lady from the fruit and vegetable shop alongside where they were sitting was carefully arranging bundles of asparagus and Holly leaned toward her and lifted a plum between forefinger and thumb.

"Pay you later?"

"Like usual."

Grabianski watched her teeth bite into the yellow flesh. "What kind of massage?"

"Shiatsu. Shiatsu-do."

"Oh."

He was aware of her looking at him appraisingly, bulky beneath a pale blue shirt open at the neck. "You should come some time, it would do you good."

46

Whenever she saw him after that, every few weeks on average, differing times of the day, she would smile and remind him about the massage. Once she had her daughter with her, a freckle-faced child of no more than five who didn't look Eurasian at all.

"Here," and she gave him her card. "Make an appointment. Phone me."

He had already begun to think about lying there naked, just a towel across him, how his body would behave when she touched him. Visions of unguents and oils.

"Make sure you're wearing something loose," she told him when finally he phoned.

The address was close to where he himself was living, above a shop selling candles and hand-printed fabrics. "Take off your shoes and leave them there," Holly pointing to where several other pairs were lined up, her daughter's and her own.

In the low-ceilinged living room a white sheet was stretched out across the center of the rug; beyond it a cloth lay draped across a wooden chest, turning it into a kind of altar with fruit and pieces of dried wood arranged in metal bowls. Incense in the air.

"Lie down," Holly said, indicating the sheet. "On your tummy first. That's it, head to one side, so you can breathe."

But it had taken his breath away, the force with which she could press into him with her slight body, slim wrists and hands.

"Breathe in … and slowly out. All right, why don't you turn over onto your back."

After the first time, he had not gone again for almost a month and on their next meeting she had chided him gently on the street; since then, it had fallen into a pattern, he would visit her once every couple of weeks. She would work on him for nearly an hour, advise him on diet, assign him exercises which he forgot. Sometimes, squatting over his body, she would simply chat: something her daughter, Melanie, had done or said; once, mention of Melanie's father, who lived in Copenhagen, where he worked as an artist, computer graphics and videotape.

Now she eased herself back onto the balls of her feet and from there, in one smooth movement, rose to her feet.

"Have you been doing those exercises I showed you?" she asked.

Grabianski was afraid he might blush. "Maybe not as often as I should."

"You were really bad today."

"I was?"

"Across your shoulders again, your neck. I couldn't move it at all." Holly smiled. "It's stress, of course. You're worried about something, that's what it is."

What was worrying Grabianski, worrying him specifically, was that since he had acquired two rare Impressionist paintings on Vernon Thackray's behalf, of Thackray neither hide nor hair had been seen. That was without this business with the nun. Why, Grabianski was already asking himself, why had he succumbed to temptation, sent her another card?

He had first met Thackray some, oh, four or five years before, when he and Grice had been working a circuit that took them from Manchester in the West to Norwich in the East, Leeds in the North to Leicester in the South. It had been worth getting a yearly season ticket with British Rail.

His old partner, Grice, was still detained at Her Majesty's displeasure, and no substantial loss where Grabianski was concerned; a great third-floor entry man, one of the best, but unable to see beyond the newsagent's top shelf when it came to culture.

And Thackray—Thackray had been living in Stamford then: a mid-Victorian brick house with columns at the front and high arched windows looking out over a sunken pond and three-quarters of an acre of shrubbery and graveled paths. A gallery on the second floor, in which he could show off his select collection of British art. A small oil by Mabel Pryde aside—a self-portrait, dark, the shadow of her husband barely visible in the background—there was nothing that couldn't leave the premises for the right price, courtesy of Federal Express.

Thackray, meanwhile, had relocated to Aldeburgh on the Suffolk coast, drawn there by migrating poets and the annual music festival in honor of Benjamin Britten. Grabianski considered this a retrograde step. Thanks to a brief, early relationship with a middle-aged psychotherapist, he had once endured Peter Pears singing Britten's settings of English folk-songs—an experience so graphically engraved on his memory as to provide him with an instant definition of Purgatory. It also meant that Thackray was no longer calling distance away. Save by telephone, that is, and both of his lines—the one displayed in the directory and the other only available to select business acquaintances—were permanently out of order.

The last occasion on which Grabianski had seen him, it had been embarrassingly necessary to explain how it was that having broken into the house where the Dalzeils were kept, he had walked out again empty-handed.

They had been sitting in a hotel bar in Market Harborough, shaded through the long afternoon, dust prancing in the low shafts of steeply angled light. Thackray had been less than pleased: this left a good customer to be pacified, a matter of principle, of re-establishing trust.

"Tell him to be patient," Grabianski had said. "Tell him you always keep your word."

Which, in so far as his word to Grabianski was concerned, had since proved untrue. The paintings freshly acquired, he returned to the same bar and sat there for two hours, sipping wine, waiting in vain for Thackray to arrive. It made Grabianski uncomfortable: whatever else he was, Vernon Thackray was not a man to miss an appointment. Promptness, reliability, these were Thackray's cardinal virtues. But perseverance, patience—save for the occasional rush of blood, those were two of Grabianski's own. If one buyer could no longer be found, well, he would find another. Simple as that.

Even so, as Grabianski approached the southern edge of Hampstead Heath, it continued to nag at him, and he had walked beyond Parliament Hill itself and down into the first thickening of trees before the splendor of his surroundings eased it from his mind.

Nine

"Whatever sort of time do you call this?"

"Um?"

"I said, whatever sort of time …"

"Alex, please, don't start. Not the minute I get home."

"I'm not starting anything. I was merely worried …"

"You weren't worried, Alex, don't pretend. You just can't stand the thought that I might have been doing something on my own. Enjoying myself without you."

"Jane, why so hostile?"

"I really can't imagine. I must be premenstrual, that's what it usually is. Or else it's school. That's it, the stress of my job."

"I do sometimes wonder …"

"Yes?"

"Well, you know, whether you wouldn't be better off moving to part-time …"

"We're not going to start this again, are we?"

"I'm only thinking of you."

"Of course."

"If you did mornings, afternoons, maybe just three days a week …"

"Alex, we've been through all this; it just isn't practical."

"I don't see why not."

"Because it isn't, that's why. Because if I went part-time, always supposing that were possible, which as things are going it might not be—then I wouldn't be doing the same job."

"I would have thought it would be the same, essentially anyway. More time to yourself."

"Alex, I don't want more time, that kind of time. Time to get the shopping, do the washing."

"That wasn't what I meant."

"Wasn't it?"

"No."

"You know very well, I enjoy what I do and I certainly don't want to risk losing the little bit of responsibility I've got."

"I should hardly have thought getting kids to watch *EastEnders* in school time constituted responsibility. Quite the opposite, in fact."

"Very funny."

"I'm not being funny."

"No, you're not."

"All right, why don't we stop all this?"

"A good idea."

"Come here."

"No, Alex, I ..."

"Come here."

"Alex."

"Sweetheart, I shouldn't have shouted at you, I'm sorry."

"You didn't shout."

"Nag you, then. Get on at you, whatever."

"It's all right, just let me ..."

"Stay here for a minute, come on."

"Alex, the dinner."

"Bugger the dinner!"

"No, Alex, really. Besides, I've got to go out again afterwards."

"What d'you mean, go out?"

"A meeting. Finalizing the arrangements for the day school. It shouldn't take long. But I do have to leave at seven."

"Seven! It's a wonder you bother to come home at all."

"Oh, fuck off, Alex!"

"What?"

"You heard me, just fuck off. I can't do a bloody thing without you interfering, trying to make me feel guilty."

"All I did was make a remark. Is that so terrible?"

"Yes. It feels like I can't breathe without you standing over me, waiting to make some kind of comment."

"Some wives would be pleased ..."

51

"Would they?"

"At least I show an interest."

"In criticizing, yes, making me feel inadequate. Why didn't you do this, why don't you do that?"

"Oh, don't be so pathetic!"

"You see?"

"What?"

"You see what I mean. If ever I stand up to you, argue back, try to get you to see things my way, I'm being pathetic."

"Right."

"Poor, pathetic Jane, running around in circles, all the while fooling herself that what she's doing is so important when anyone with a modicum of intelligence can see it doesn't count for shit."

"You said it, I didn't."

"You didn't have to."

"Good."

"You're right, Alex, it was a mistake. I should have stayed at work, gone round to Hannah's, gone for a drink. Anything but this."

"Wait."

"No."

"Where d'you think you're going now?"

"Anywhere. Out. I'll be back around nine."

"You're staying here ..."

"Alex, let me alone. Let go of me."

"No! Don't you run out on me. Don't you dare."

"Alex, you're hurting. Let go."

"I warned you."

"Let me go!"

"I'll let go, you stupid bitch!"

"Alex, no!"

"Stupid, selfish bitch!"

"Alex, no. No. Oh, God, please no. Don't hurt me. No ..."

Ten

For once, there were no small children running full pelt between the tables, mean mouths and shrill little voices. The garden attached to the Brew House restaurant was mercifully devoid of mothers in long, flowing dresses from Monsoon, au pairs from Barcelona or Budapest who shopped at the Gap. Grabianski carried his tray, bearing filter coffee and an encouragingly large chunk of carrot cake, up the short flight of steps and across the flagstones to a table in the shadow of the far wall. With a flap of the hand, he scooted away a trio of blue-gray pigeons feasting on the remains of somebody's buttered toast. Sparrows jostled hopefully around his feet.

Quarter past the hour: he had no way of knowing whether Eddie Snow would be early or late.

On the low bench seats to Grabianski's right, two elderly men from Poland or the Ukraine were playing chess; a woman with startling white hair and spectacles that hung from a filigree chain was talking loudly to her companion about a recent visit to Berlin and the depressing legacy of the GDR; farthest from where Grabianski was sitting, a couple in their late thirties, wanly married but not to each other, held hands across the wooden table with the special hopelessness of those for whom happiness was the memory of damp afternoons in Weymouth or Swanage, hotel rooms that smelt of disinfectant and had a meter for the gas.

He was contemplating going for a second cup of coffee when a skinny man with thinning, short-cropped hair pushed through the door into the garden. Shiny leather trousers sheathed thin legs, a hip-length gray leather jacket hung loose over a black T-shirt bonded closely to his ribs. Despite the almost total absence of sun, he was wearing shades.

"Jerry?"

Half-rising, Grabianski reached out a hand.

"Eddie. Eddie Snow. Here, let me put this down."

His plate was loaded with sausages and bacon, grilled tomatoes, fried bread and scrambled egg that had been sitting too long. "Best meal of the day, right?" Snow used his teeth to tear open two sachets of brown sauce and dribbled the contents across the curling, crispy bread. "Between me and my arteries, eh?" Behind dark glasses, Snow winked. "You want to get something more for yourself, go ahead. I'm going to get stuck into this lot before it gets cold."

Grabianski nodded, pushed back his chair, and opted to wait.

The first time he had met Eddie Snow, himself and Maria Roy had been snapping at each other in the departure lounge at Orly Airport, a lunge toward romance that had been too calculated and too late. Eddie Snow had been drinking champagne and wolfing down packets of honey-roasted peanuts he had carried off from his last flight. "Couple of days in Cologne," he told them. "Just two days and I earned so much fucking money, it'd make your head spin to count it. Here, have some more of this bubbly, eh?"

"What is it you do?" Maria asked, careful to touch his wrist as she offered her glass. Money had always been a great aphrodisiac where Maria was concerned.

"Everything," Eddie Snow laughed. "Little of this and that. Just about everything. You know how it is."

He had shaken hands on a deal with a private collector, whose principal acquisitions up to that point had been twentieth-century American; a quarter of a million for a painting, oil on board, of a former hospital for the chronically insane in Dalston. One of the many the artist had sketched on his travels east and west along the North London line. Snow had picked it up cheap from an ailing British rock star, who had once had hits on the label Snow had set up in those heady days of love and commerce when Virgin Records was a warehouse off Portobello and a hole-in-the-wall shop on Sloane Square.

Eddie Snow was not quite as youthful as he looked; sunglasses aside, it showed around the eyes.

Midway through his meal, Snow took a packet of Marlboro from his jacket pocket and lit up. "So, Jerry, what happened to that TV guy's wife you were screwing? Arse on her like the Pope's pajamas."

By way of reply, Grabianski slid an envelope up onto the table and from it eased out two Polaroid photographs. Using middle finger and thumb, he swiveled them round for Snow to see.

"Straight to the business, eh, Jerry. I like that." The photo on the left showed a landscape painting, a typically rural English scene; sheep grazing under the careless eye of a straw-chewing youth, an avenue of trees angled behind.

The second was as singular as that was conventional. The sun, full and faint, lowered through clouds over an expanse of ground, purple and brown, that could either be moorland or field. Trees stood sparse on the indistinct horizon.

It was this picture that Eddie Snow picked up and angled to the light. After a long moment, his face broke into a smile.

"Had me there for a minute." He replaced the Polaroid. "*Departing Day*: study, isn't it? Not the real thing."

Grabianski waited.

"Eyesight'd started going by then, poor tosser. Either that or he'd got the DTs."

A sparrow, perversely brave, dipped its slate-colored head toward a piece of bacon rind and narrowly missed a backhander for its pains.

"So what you saying here, Jerry?"

"I'm not saying anything."

"Yeah, so I noticed." Snow picked up the photographs, first one and then the other, and studied them again. "You'll want to get shot as a pair?"

From Grabianski a nod.

"Two a penny these," Snow said, indicating the sheep.

"Not by him."

"Crap all the same. This first one. Pastoral bollocks. Whereas this ... Going for it, that's what he's doing there. Color. Light. All them gradations of blue in the sky. Whistler in a way, but Turner closer still."

"You like it?"

"Yeah, course I do, but that's not the point."

Grabianski smiled. "Your friend in Cologne ..."

Eddie Snow shook his head. "Strictly kosher. Never touch anything without it's got perfect pedigree, properly authenticated bill of sale, the whole bit." He lit a second cigarette. "I don't suppose you've got a bill of sale?"

"And you," Grabianski said, "have you got buyers who are less scrupulous?"

Using his tongue, Snow fidgeted a piece of sausage from between his teeth. "Let me know how to get in touch."

"Better I get in touch with you."

Snow scraped back his chair and stood up. "Legit business. I'm in the book."

"I know."

As Grabianski watched Eddie Snow walk, slim-hipped, away, he noticed that though the couple were still holding hands, the woman was crying. He restored the Polaroids to his pocket and moved the remains of Eddie Snow's breakfast to another table, where the birds could scavenge in peace. He would have another cup of coffee and then that second piece of carrot cake would go down a treat.

Eleven

She could feel it happening. The listlessness that crept over her, those evenings when he had neither arrived nor phoned; evenings which previously she would have used productively, reading, preparing work, enjoying the space and time before settling back downstairs at ten to watch whatever was on TV. *Northern Exposure. Frasier. ER.* Or she would be on the telephone to friends, arranging to meet for a drink, a chat, a movie perhaps. And there were those evenings when she would crawl home from school like someone who had been beaten, those days when for one reason or another the kids had left her exhausted and drained. But all of this was okay, this was what she could handle, it was her life: pleasant, controlled, contained. And she could feel what was happening with Resnick beginning to threaten that in so many ways and, much as she enjoyed being with him, it was hard not to resent him for it.

She recognized the feelings from before; first with Andrew and then with Jim. An Irishman who taught poetry and a musician who taught clarinet, oboe, and bassoon. Andrew aggressively and Jim by default, both men had made her dependent upon them. Not for money, stability; not, exactly, for love. Presence, that's what it was: need, the need of one person.

Outside a relationship she was fine, living on her own something she had learned, something she had earned the right to do. She had her job, her immediate family, her network of friends, some of whom she had known since university, a few since school. But once a commitment was made, however unclear or uncertain, then no matter how hard she tried to resist it, things began to change.

Hannah smiled to herself wryly, remembering the key she had slipped into Resnick's pocket—what?—six weeks ago, two months?

So casual a gesture, almost insignificant. Now it felt as though she had handed over part of herself, the part that allowed her to stand up straight, on her own two feet and clear-eyed.

She thought about her mother, abandoned in the dust-free suburban home in which she had lived for more than thirty years, Hannah's room still first left at the top of the stairs. Posters of famine and forgotten pop stars, teddy bears. Her father was living in France with a twenty-nine-year-old writer called Robyn who had just sold her first novel. Robyn with a Y.

"It won't last, Dad," she'd told him, cutting into her capricciosa in Pizza Express. "It can't. She'll leave you, you know that, don't you?"

Stupidly happy, her father had sipped his Peroni and smiled. "Of course she will. In time."

It was three and a half years now, shading up to four. And Hannah? Eighteen months with Andrew, a little over two years with Jim. The way her mother bit her lip heroically when the question of grandchildren came to mind. Birthdays on the calendar, challenging time. Did she really want to make herself vulnerable to all of that again, the disappointment, the pain?

When the doorbell rang, it wasn't Resnick, forgetting his key, but Jane, lines of sorrow plump around her eyes.

They sat in the kitchen while Hannah made tea, impatient for the kettle to boil; drank it at the table, Jane holding her cup with both hands, steadying it slowly to her mouth. Upstairs in Hannah's study, they sat in the bay window, Jane with her feet tucked up beneath her in the easy chair, Hannah on a cushion on the floor. Dark spread like a slow bruise across the park.

Three times Jane started to speak and each time she betrayed herself with tears.

Getting lightly to her feet, Hannah touched Jane's hand, and leaning over from behind the chair, kissed her gently on the head, gave her shoulders a squeeze. "I've got some things I should be doing downstairs. I'll be back up in a while."

Hannah organized the books and folders she wanted for the next day, wrote a quick card to her mother, rinsed the supper things. She was sorting some clothes, ready for the wash, when the phone rang.

"Charlie ..."

Resnick's voice was muffled, remote; strange to think he was no more than a mile or so away.

"No, I don't think so, Charlie, not really. Not tonight. It's just ..."

Resnick was quick to assure her she didn't need to explain.

"Tomorrow, then," Hannah said. "How about tomorrow? We could get something to eat; a movie, maybe. If you're feeling up to it."

Resnick told her he had to be in London, didn't know what time he would be back.

"Okay, no problem. And look, I'm sorry about tonight." She made hot chocolate, whisking the milk; upstairs, Jane's head lolled sideways in the chair and her eyes were closed. Hannah was about to turn around again and go back down when Jane stirred.

"I thought you were asleep," Hannah said.

"Just for a minute, that's all."

"Here."

Taking the thick white china mug, Jane sipped at it and laughed.

"What?"

"I haven't had this for years."

Hannah settled herself back down, cross-legged on the floor. One lamp was burning at the far side of the room, illuminating shelves of books, a segment of table, sanded boards, an orange arc of wall.

"Do you want to phone Alex?" Hannah said. "Tell him where you are."

"No, I don't think so. Thanks."

"We had this row, earlier. Before I went out. Alex had come home and I'd not been there. I mean, he was back sooner than I'd thought, an appointment had been canceled or something, I don't know, and I'd stopped off in town after school. Just looking round the shops, nothing ..." Jane looked across at Hannah and paused. "He'd only been in twenty minutes, half an hour at most."

"I don't understand."

"I wasn't there. He got angry, upset."

"But why? I mean, what does he expect, for heaven's sake?"

Shrilly, Jane laughed.

"You to be there at his beck and call? Rush home after school and get his dinner ready for him, warm his slippers by the fire?"

"No. No, it's not like that. That's not what it's about."

"What then?"

Jane took her time. "It's to do with …"

"Control, that's what it's to do with."

"He wants to know exactly where I am, what I'm doing, all of the time."

"That's ridiculous."

"Yes."

"Unreasonable."

"It's the way it is."

Hannah sighed. "He's got to understand, surely, you've got a life of your own."

"No."

"What do you mean?"

"According to Alex, we're married and that's that. We don't have lives of our own."

"Oh, fine …"

"He says that's the whole point."

"It's his point. That's the trouble. His rules, his timetable."

"He says it's the same for him."

"Except you don't start climbing up the wall if he's twenty minutes late getting home."

"No."

"So he can come and go as he pleases."

"But he doesn't. I always know where he is, what he's doing, every minute of the day. If he says he'll be in at five twenty-five, at five twenty-five there he is. So why shouldn't it be the same with me?"

"Come on, Jane. How many answers do you want? You're a grown woman doing a difficult job. You've got your own friends. Damn it, you married him; it wasn't an operation joining you both at the hip."

"Look, Hannah, I know it's difficult for you to understand …"

"Because I'm not married, you mean?"

"Maybe."

"Jane, I'm your friend. Married or not, I can see what's happening to you, how unhappy you are. I've got a right to be concerned."

"I know. I'm sorry. I am grateful. And I don't know what I'm doing, sitting here defending him."

"Habit? Duty?"

Jane shook her head. "I really don't know."

"Do you still love him?"

"I don't know that either."

Hannah leaned close toward her. "Have you thought about leaving him?"

Jane laughed. "Only all the time."

"And he knows?"

"Not because of anything I've said."

"But you think he does know?"

"He suspects, he must do."

"And you think that's why he's behaving like this?"

Jane stepped to the window, leaned forward until her forehead was pressing against the glass. Small bats cavorted outside, splintering the space between the house and the trees. When she turned back into the room, the ghost of her mouth remained, a blur of breath upon the pane.

"It isn't only … He's jealous, that's part of what this is all about. Just jealous."

"What of?"

"Oh," Jane gestured widely. "Anyone. Men. You. Our neighbor across the street. Anyone. It doesn't really matter." Slowly, she shook her head. "He thinks I must be having an affair."

"That's ridiculous."

"Of course it is."

"Then why?"

"Because … Oh, because … He says it's why I don't want him any more. Sexually, I mean."

"And that's true? Not wanting him, that's how you feel?"

"Yes, but that doesn't mean …"

61

"I know. I know."

Jane came to where Hannah was sitting and reached out her hand. "It's just a bloody mess."

"I'm sorry."

"And I don't know what to do."

Hannah squeezed her friend's hand and rested it against her cheek.

"I'm frightened. I really am."

"You'll be all right," Hannah said, encouragingly, and then she realized Jane was starting to shake. "Come on," she said, levering herself to her feet. "Come on over here and sit down."

"The light," Jane said.

"What about it? Is it too bright? I can turn it off."

"No, I want you to come with me, over to the light."

She pulled free her cotton top, pushed down the waistband of the skirt, and half-turned away: the bruise shone purple–black in the glow of the lamp, slick and fierce as a man's fist.

Twelve

Grabianski was thinking of his father; the half-sister, Kristyna, he had never seen. The family had fled Poland in the first year of the war—and a slow, cold fleeing they'd had of it, walking, occasionally hitching a lift, hiding beneath the heavy tarpaulin of a river barge: Czechoslovakia, Austria, Switzerland. Kristyna had drowned in the waters of Lake Neuchâtel; she had been eleven years old.

His father, a textile worker from Lodi, had flown as a navigator for both the French and British forces; parachuted out over the Channel, plummeting toward the black, unseeing water with images of Kristyna, her stiff, breastless body, trapped tight behind his eyes.

He had survived.

Jerzy Grabianski had been born in South London, his mother a nurse from St George's, his father sewing by electric light in the basement room in Balham, where they lived. Weekends, when his mother was working, his father would walk him on Tooting Bec Common, sit with him in the Lido, dangling Grabianski's flailing legs down into the shallow water, never letting go.

What would he think, Grabianski wondered, if he could be here now? His father, who had struggled with such tenacity, stubborn against almost overwhelming odds, each penny counted, every yard, each thread. And Grabianski, who, in contrast, had realized the profits on a stash of antique jewelry he had been saving and bought a spacious flat close to Hampstead Heath, where he was sitting pretty.

He remembered a film he had seen twenty years earlier in a down-at-heel flea-pit cinema in Uttoxeter or Nuneaton: a rancher talking to one of Jack Nicolson's ramshackle bunch of Montana outlaws. How did it go now? Old Thomas Jefferson said he was a warrior so his son could be a farmer, so *his* son could be a poet.

Well, maybe that's what this is, Grabianski thought. This careful, almost silent movement across other people's lives, a kind of poetry.

When the waiter brought him his *café au lait*, he ordered eggs Florentine, poached instead of baked.

He was dabbing a piece of French bread at the last of the yolk, lifting spinach on top of that with his fork, when a shadow fell across the door. Resnick, blinking at the change of light, steadying himself before stepping in.

"Charlie."

"Jerzy."

Grabianski waved a hand expansively. "Have a seat."

Resnick was wearing a gray suit with broad lapels, too warm for the changing weather. Taking off the jacket to drape it over the back of his chair, he was aware of perspiration rich beneath his arms, the cotton of his shirt sticking to his back.

"I doubt this is a coincidence," Grabianski said. "Day trip to visit Keats' house, the Freud Museum perhaps?"

Resnick shook his head.

"I was afraid not. A disappointment anyway. Especially Freud. Don't like to think of him here at all. Vienna. Fast asleep on his couch after an overdose of *sachertorte*."

The waiter fussed and fiddled with napkins and cutlery until Resnick asked for a large espresso and a glass of water.

"Sparkling or still, sir?"

"Tap."

"But here." Grabianski leaned forward, voice lowered, "This place."

"'If ever you're in sunny Hampstead,'" Resnick quoted, "'start your day at the Bar Rouge on the High Street. I do.'"

Grabianski sat back with a rueful smile.

"Postcards," Resnick said. "Not exactly high security."

"I didn't think you'd have people trawling the mail."

Resnick's espresso arrived, not yet the water, and Grabianski ordered another coffee for himself.

"Not quite."

Disappointment passed across the breadth of Grabianski's face. "I didn't know you and the good sisters were so hand-in-hand."

"Working in the community the way they do, we've things in common. Shared interests, I suppose you could say." The espresso was good, very good. Strong without a hint of being bitter. "Sister Teresa especially."

Grabianski nodded. "A keen sense of duty. In excess."

"She seems to have an interest in you. In saving your soul, at least."

Grabianski couldn't disguise the pleasure in his eyes. "And you? Is your concern for me spiritual, too?"

"I think it's your art collection I'm more interested in saving. Before it leaves the country."

"Ah." Grabianski held a cube of sugar over his cup, immersing a corner and watching as the coffee rose upward, staining the sugar brown. "Once learned, never forgotten."

"What's that?"

"Osmosis. Third-year biology."

"General science myself."

"When we've finished this," Grabianski said, "what do you say we take a stroll? That is, if you've got the time."

They walked a while without talking, entering the Heath across East Heath Road, then dropping down from the main path through a haze of shrubbery until they reached the viaduct. Half a dozen men and a couple of boys sat fishing at the water's edge beneath. Nobody seemed to be catching anything.

"You know," Grabianski said, "I heard a rumor about you."

Leaning on the parapet, head angled sideways, Resnick waited.

"Seems you've got yourself a woman. Serious. Is it true?"

"Probably."

Grabianski skipped a pebble down into the pond and watched the ripples spread. "I'm happy for you."

"Thanks," Resnick said. And then: "You heard this when you were in the city?"

"Was I in the city?"

"The Dalzeil paintings ..."

"Ah."

"You know they're missing?"

"I might have heard."

"Another rumor?"

"Something of the kind."

"And this rumor, does it tell you whether the paintings have passed on into other hands?"

Grabianski smiled, lines crisscrossing around his eyes. "Nothing so exact."

"And I don't suppose a search warrant would help to clarify ...?"

"A warrant? For where?"

"I'd have to fill in the details of your address."

"I'm surprised you think you'd have grounds, especially so far from home."

"We know you're interested in the paintings, why else the Polaroids? We know you broke into the house once before. Given your professional reputation, I'd say we had probable cause."

Grabianski grinned. "If there's anything to that reputation at all, I shouldn't think you'd find what you're looking for wrapped in brown paper underneath the bed."

"Maybe not."

A woman went by, running, a black baseball cap reversed on her head, black and white T-shirt, skin-tight black shorts; there was a small water bottle attached to her belt at the small of her back, a Walkman clipped to her side. Sweat shone on her perfect thighs.

Watching, neither Resnick nor Grabianski said a word.

"There's nothing you can do to help me then?" Resnick said, the runner now out of sight.

"Afraid not," said Grabianski, smiling. "You know I would if I could."

They walked on southwards, climbing between a scattered grouping of beeches and down through thickish grass until another path led them past a group of youngsters playing frisbee and up toward the hill where kites flew high and wild and the city could be seen clearly, stretched out beneath them. The Post Office Tower, King's Cross, the dome of St. Paul's; the pale columns of Battersea

Power Station away to the right, the transmitter blinking from the top of the Crystal Palace mast, the crest of Canary Wharf reflecting back the light in the east.

"Some view, eh, Charlie? Worth traveling a distance to see."

"Maybe."

"Didn't want it to have been altogether a wasted day."

"No fear of that," Resnick said. "Old friend of mine to see later …"

"Another?"

"Down there somewhere, Scotland Yard. Transferred into another section recently. Arts and Antiques."

Back in his flat, Grabianski made a quick and careful inventory of those few items he had still to dispose of and which it might be embarrassing to have found in his possession. Not that he really imagined Resnick and a cohort from the local nick were about to come barging in mob-handed, but there was nothing wrong with taking a little precautionary action. The paintings, of course, were not there and never had been; they were safely bubble-wrapped in the security vault of his bank.

Thumbing through the telephone directory, Grabianski wondered if Resnick had been bluffing about his contact at the Yard. Arts and Antiques—a growing area of expertise.

Eddie Snow, he could see, had not been lying: there was his number, highlighted in bold. More than half-expecting the answer-phone, Grabianski was surprised when Snow himself picked up.

"Eddie," Grabianski said, "sooner rather than later. We ought to talk."

"You know the Market Bar?" Snow sounded as if he had been interrupted in the midst of something else.

"Portobello, isn't it?"

"I'll see you there. Eight o'clock."

Before Grabianski could acknowledge this, the connection was cut. He wondered if eight o'clock meant dinner; he'd heard the first-floor restaurant was expensive but very good.

Thirteen

He hadn't seen it as a sightseeing tour, but that was what it was turning into. Instead of ushering Resnick up to the third-floor office which she shared with two other officers and a deficient air-conditioning unit, Jackie Ferris walked him through the narrow side-streets of Whitehall into St. James's Park. Beyond a heavy scattering of shirt-sleeved tourists, tufted ducks, and pink flamingos, the broad swathe of the Mall stretched from Buckingham Palace to Admiralty Arch.

"Any excuse to get out, Charlie, you know what I mean? Too much of the job spent in artificial daylight, staring into VDU screens."

Resnick nodded, noting the tones of the North East still lurking at the back of her now largely neutralized voice. Sunderland? Gateshead?

"Once around the lake and then we'll find somewhere to sit, that all right for you?"

It was fine.

He had first met Jackie when she was a sergeant in the Fraud Squad, seconded to help him out with an investigation into an insurance company scam involving two associate directors, one head of sales and three-quarters of a million pounds. She still wore the same glasses, round and steel-framed, the same or similar, but the Top Shop jacket and skirt had been exchanged for a Wallis suit with the faintest of stripes, a blouse the color of fresh chalk, shoes with a broad buckle and low heel.

"How come the switch?" Resnick asked as they were crossing the bridge over the water. "Arts and Antiques. Promotion aside."

"I'd been taking this Open University course. Humanities. One of the modules was History of Art. After all that time with ledgers, spreadsheets, it appealed. Figures still, but a different kind. Besides, me mam wouldn't let us sit down to us tea of a Sunday without the *Antiques Roadshow* was on tele." Seeing her smile, Resnick caught himself wondering why there were still no rings on her left hand. "More of a music man, aren't you, Charlie?" she said.

Resnick nodded.

"Jazz, isn't it?"

He nodded again, grateful that she made it sound more like an eccentric affliction than a disease.

There was an empty bench between a trio of stocky Germans poring over their map of London and a man of indeterminate years whose clothing gave off an aura of chronic alcoholic abuse.

From her shoulder bag, where they were jammed between mobile phone and electronic organizer, she fished a packet of Bensons and a slimline lighter. "Not entirely social, Charlie, that was what you said." She tilted back her head and let the smoke drift out onto the air.

Resnick asked her what she knew about Dalziel and she told him, ticking off his major influences and principal works along the way.

"These days, what are the chances of his stuff coming up for sale?"

"I wouldn't hold my breath."

"But if it did, there are people who'd be interested?"

She angled her head to look at him. "This is legit?"

"Not necessarily."

"Hmm. Less easy. Museums, galleries, count them out, of course. But private collectors, there'd be a few."

"Abroad?"

"Most probably."

The Germans brought over their map and asked directions to Shepherd's Market; Jackie told them, clear and precise, and they went on their way.

"How would I find them, these prospective buyers?"

"Through an agent, a dealer."

"Even though he or she would know, presumably, they were stolen?"

"Not many, but some. Supposing the money was right."

"And it's a specialist field?"

"Oh, yes."

Resnick nodded. "So here I am sitting with my Dalzeils ..."

"More than one, then?"

"A pair."

"You'd be looking to make contact with someone interested in late nineteenth-, early twentieth-century painting, Impressionism, British art in general."

"And how many ... I mean, are we talking a lot of people here or what?"

"Known to us, major players, half a dozen."

"You could let me have the names?"

Jackie Ferris pursed her lips and exhaled. "You know how it is, Charlie. These days especially. Nothing for nothing. But, yes, I'm sure we could do a deal."

The girl in gold leggings talking to Eddie Snow was so thin you could have sucked her up through a straw. Grabianski stood there for several moments watching, sharing the corner door-space of the Market Bar with a tall black guy sporting silver and lime green. The black guy looking out, Grabianski looking in.

Eddie Snow was sitting on a stool pulled up to the bar, the girl standing close beside him, Eddie's forefinger easing its way along the cleft of her behind. Above their heads, what looked like several generations of wax cascaded down from heavy iron candle holders. Today Eddie was wearing his black leather trousers with a black roll-neck top, the sleeves pushed back along sinewy arms.

The room was shaped like an L, high-ceilinged, tables ranging along both outside walls beneath windows opening out on to the street. Not late enough to be really crowded, the space between tables and bar was thick enough with drinkers that Grabianski had to excuse himself to pass through.

The old man in the corner aside, the mouth of whose white beard was stained ginger with nicotine, Grabianski thought he and Eddie Snow were the oldest in there by at least ten years.

"Eddie." Grabianski held out his hand but Snow ignored it, patting the matchstick girl proprietorially instead. "Later, babe."

Without giving Grabianski a second glance, she stepped away on the slenderest of high heels, and Grabianski leaned forward to order a pint of Caffreys at the bar.

"You know the kind of money she can get," Snow said, eyes following the girl, "few times down the catwalk, couple of fancy turns? You just wouldn't believe."

The bartender held Grabianski's twenty up to the light.

Snow readjusted his position on the stool. "I've been asking questions about you." He was drinking Pernod with a splash of lemonade.

"I should hope so."

"Word is, you and Vernon Thackray are like that." Snow cradled his long fingers together and squeezed tight.

Grabianski slipped his change down into his pocket; the cloudiness was slowly disappearing from his beer, leaving it light and clear. "I suggest you ask again."

"You saying it's wrong?"

"I'm saying it's stale news."

"Thackray, he's not interested in these Dalzeils?"

"Once upon a time."

"Oh, yes, how's that story go?"

"Look," Grabianski said, "never mind all that. Do you want to do business or not?"

Snow put on a show of being surprised. "Why all the sudden urgency?" he said.

Behind them the general conversation lulled and Grabianski recognized the music that was playing without being able to give it a name.

"Clapton," Eddie Snow said, "'Tears in Heaven.' Poor bastard. How d'you hope to get over a thing like that?"

"Let's just say I'd like to realize some profit, move on."

"Not anxious, then?"

"Anxious?"

"These friends of yours, police, not nosing uncomfortably around?"

"I don't have friends in the police."

"Not what I've heard."

Grabianski leaned closer toward him. "I've already told you, you're hearing wrong."

71

Snow caught the bartender's eye and another Pernod appeared. "Unnecessary chances," he said, "it's what I can't afford to take."

Grabianski drank some more of his beer, set the unfinished glass back down, and turned around. Snow detained him, a hand on his arm.

"No call to take offense."

"Offense nothing. Have you got a buyer or not?"

"Thackray and myself crossing swords, conflict of interest, I should want to avoid that."

"So you have?"

"Thackray ..."

"Forget him."

"I might have, yes. Overseas, of course. Percentages'll be high."

"But you can do the deal?"

Snow nodded. "I shall need to see the paintings, of course. And the buyer, he'll want verification. In writing. Too many forgeries about these days by half."

"So arrange it," Grabianski said. "Whatever's needed. I've done my part." The bar was more crowded now, jostling up against him where he stood.

"If I can look at the paintings tomorrow afternoon, bring someone with me, someone I trust. Long as that goes okay, I can start setting things up, putting out feelers, you know the way it goes."

Grabianski nodded. "Tomorrow then. I'll call you first thing."

"Right." Suddenly Snow was standing, fingers tight round Grabianski's wrist, the smell of aniseed sharp on his breath. "But if I find out you're setting me up ..."

"Tomorrow," Grabianski repeated. "First thing."

Back out on the street, Grabianski could feel the sweat, slicked over his body like a second skin.

Resnick had called Hannah three times and each time got her machine. Bored, he watched fully fifteen minutes' television in the hotel where he was staying, one of several fending off dilapidation close to Euston station. A bus took him through the low-rent ravages of King's Cross to the Angel, where Jackie Ferris had recommended a restaurant near Chapel Market. Cheapish and good.

It turned out to be French, the cooking done behind the counter in a space no bigger than a half-size snooker table. He settled for the onion soup, then lamb's liver, which was tasty and tender, a nice pinkish turn of blood drifting into the accompanying rice and courgettes.

The names Jackie Ferris had given him, printed out neatly on a single sheet, were folded inside the smart new notebook he had requisitioned from the stationery manager that morning:

Hugo Levin
Bernard Martlet
Maria Rush
Martin Sansom
Edward Snow
Vernon Thackray
David Wood

All with London numbers save Martlet, who lived in Brighton, and Thackray, whose address was in Aldeburgh. But Resnick knew that already: it was Thackray who had called on Miriam Johnson, offering to buy the paintings; Thackray whose line was now, seemingly, disconnected.

He struggled to say no to *crème brûlée*, accepted losing with a brave face, and asked for a double espresso and the bill. According to Jackie, the club he was going to was only a short walk away and he didn't want to miss the first set.

There was no way Resnick could have known, but Grabianski's grandmother—not the Polish one, but the English—had brought him here, to Chapel Market, on her rare trips north of the river. Cheap vegetables, stockings, birthday cards, and cheese, off they would go, staggering home, weighed down with bargains and with young Jerzy struggling to keep his string bag from dragging on the ground. But not before they had shuffled into the eel and pie shop for steak and kidney pie and mash, Jerzy's head just level with the counter and the edge of his white china plate.

The street that Resnick walked along was thick with refuse from that day's market, crates and boxes interlaced with bright blue paper, rotting oranges, grapes, onions oozing pus.

The Rhythmic was on the left-hand side, beyond where the market proper ended. The main room was large, larger than Resnick had anticipated, the half immediately facing him set out with tables for dining. He had time to buy a bottle of Budvar and find leaning space along the side wall before the lights dimmed and, after a brief announcement, Jessica Williams came on stage.

Tall, red-haired, and wearing a long, loose flowing dress, she sat at the piano and for a moment fidgeted with the height of the stool. Even before she began playing, fingers hesitating above the keys, Resnick had noticed the size of her hands. Then, without introduction, she launched into "I Should Care." Almost deferentially at first, brushing the tune around its edges, feeling her way freshly into a melody she must have played—and Resnick heard— a hundred times. Ten minutes later, when she had exhausted every variation, left hand finally rocking through a stride pattern that would have made James P. Johnson or Fats Waller beam with pleasure, she finished to a roar of disbelieving applause.

And paused, eyes closed, waiting for the silence to resume. This time it was a slow blues, building from the most basic of patterns to a dazzling display of counterpoint that recalled for Resnick an old album he had bought by Lennie Tristano—"C Minor Complex," "G Minor Complex"—bop meets Bach. After that, she clearly felt relaxed enough to talk, and played her way through two sets of standards and originals that held the crowd's—and Resnick's— attention fast.

By the time he walked back out into the London night some hours later, he knew he had been in the presence of something— someone—special.

I should care, the words came to him, *I should let it upset me.* When he dialed Hannah's number from the callbox on the corner, the answerphone had been switched off and it rang and rang and rang till he broke the connection with his thumb.

Fourteen

Resnick had been sitting there no longer than it took to prize the top off his first cup of coffee, when he saw Jackie Ferris approaching from the opposite corner of the square. This morning she was wearing a tan raincoat, open over a rust-red cotton sweater and blue jeans. Black and white Nikes on her feet.

It was a well-kept space surrounded by railings, flourishing shrubs, and trees; flower beds marked the perimeters of close-cut grass. The cafeteria was a low prefabricated building in the north-east corner, a paved crescent in front of it dotted with tables and chairs. On all sides, red or green buses trailed one another through the heavy morning traffic and the pavements were busy with people on their way to work.

"You found it okay, then?"

"No problem." Russell Square was less than a ten-minute stroll from Resnick's hotel.

Jackie nodded toward his cup. "Ready for another?"

"Not yet."

Resnick leaned back against the metal chair and waited; the coffee was slightly bitter but at least it was strong. Jackie re-emerged with a polystyrene cup of her own and two slices of toast on a paper plate. Before trying either toast or coffee, she lit a cigarette.

"So how was last night?"

"Fine."

"Enjoy the jazz?"

"Very much."

Watching Jackie Ferris take her first bite, Resnick wished he had ordered himself some toast.

"You know, I read something about her. Jessica Williams, right?

One of those magazines. Took her—what?—twenty years before she could get any sort of proper recognition. She'd play around these bars, California somewhere—Sacramento, I think that's what it said—just waiting for a break. Anyway, according to what I read, it wasn't just the fact that she was a woman held her back. More that she was gay." She looked across the table at Resnick, squinting a little behind her glasses. "Did she make anything of that, last night?"

Resnick shook his head.

"And you wouldn't have known, you couldn't tell from the way she played?"

"I don't see how."

"No."

Jackie stubbed out her half-smoked cigarette. "It's easy to get fooled sometimes, you know? You look at someone like k.d. lang filling Wembley Arena umpteen times over and you think things have changed, but really it's not true. I don't know, but how many jazz players are there, women who've really made it, got through to the top? Not singers, but musicians."

Barbara Thompson, Kathy Stobart, Marian McPartland—Mary Lou Williams, of course, Melba Liston—that Japanese pianist whose name he could never remember. "Not many," Resnick said.

"Man's world, eh, Charlie? Even now."

"Maybe."

"Like the police."

"I thought things were getting better."

Jackie Ferris laughed. "How many women, what percentage, inspector and above?"

"There's you for one."

"And don't think it didn't cost me, Charlie. What, you don't want to know."

Resnick finished his coffee and held up his empty cup. "Time for another?"

"Plenty."

This time, he remembered the toast.

"I've talked to my boss," Jackie said. "This is the way we'd like it to play out."

◆◆◆

The CID room was empty, save for Lynn worrying away at an electronic typewriter that should have been pensioned off a long time back. Resnick stood in the doorway, wondering how long it would take till she was forced to recognize that he was there.

"The Family Support Unit," Lynn said finally. "I went down to see them myself. They've given me an interview, Friday. Half-nine. If that's all right."

Resnick nodded. "That's fine."

He went into his office and closed the door. Before he could sit down, the phone rang; it was Suzanne Olds.

"Mark Divine," she said. "He got bail."

Resnick breathed a slow sigh of relief.

"They made a condition of residence, of course."

"The flat here in the city?"

"Yes. Banned from visiting Derby city center or any nightclub anywhere this side of the trial. Forbidden from contacting or interfering with any of the prosecution's witnesses. All pretty much what you'd expect."

"And Mark?"

"Said if they thought they could tell him what he could do with his own time, they had their heads up their arses."

"He'll calm down."

"Maybe." She sounded less than confident.

"I'll call round," Resnick assured her, "have a word. He'll see sense in the end."

From the tone of her reply, Suzanne Olds didn't seem convinced.

Resnick ran the gauntlet of traffic across to Canning Circus and haggled over which kind of mustard to have with a honey roast ham and Emmenthal sandwich, a generously proportioned dill pickle on the side. He was carrying this back into the building as Jack Skelton, shoes shining like there was no tomorrow, came hurrying down the stairs.

"Off to Central, Charlie. Something's come up with these Serious Crime appointments. Pow-wow with the chief. Ride with me, you can always get yourself a lift back."

Sitting next to Skelton in the back of the car, Resnick brought him up to speed on the situation with Divine, and outlined the details of his meeting with Jackie Ferris.

"Huh," Skelton grunted, "the Yard'll not be helping us monitor your pal Grabianski and dole out expert advice, without wanting plenty in return."

"A little information," Resnick said, not quite believing it. "Some forgery scam they're interested in. They've got the idea Grabianski might lead them to the people involved. Whatever we get out of him, they want us to feed back to them."

"And that's all?"

Resnick shrugged. "So far."

Skelton took a roll of extra-strong mints from his pocket and popped one into his mouth. "Well, run with it for now. But don't commit more than we can afford. And watch they don't give you the run-around. Smart bastards, the lot of 'em. Treat us like country cousins if we give them the chance."

Resnick still had his sandwich, more squashed than perhaps was comfortable but the taste would be pretty much the same. When he sat down on the bench across from Peachey Street, the winos who sojourned there daily, dawn to dusk, looked at him askance. He washed it down with a brace of espressos at the Italian coffee stall nearby and talked Aldo into letting him use his phone.

Just back from work, Hannah's spirits rose at the sound of his voice.

There was cucumber and dill soup in the freezer and they ate it with rye bread Resnick had picked up after leaving Aldo's; later, a mixed salad dressed with honey and olive oil, a chunk of Wensleydale cheese and narrow slices of plum tart. When Hannah went upstairs to work for a while, Resnick called Graham Millington at home and got his wife instead. The sergeant was out for the evening and wouldn't be back till late; seeing one of his informants, Madeleine thought, unable quite to disguise the distaste in her voice.

Resnick took off his shoes, put his feet up on the settee, and fell asleep listening to Bonnie Raitt.

"I thought you liked this?" Hannah said a little later, waking him with a glass of wine. Bonnie and Sippie Wallace were joking their way through "Women Be Wise."

"I do."

"And this?" leaning over him.

"Mmm," he said, recovering his breath, "I like that, too." In bed, after they had made love, she told him about Jane, about the bruise above her kidneys, the state she had been in.

"You're sure it was Alex?"

"Who else would it be?"

Slowly, Resnick rolled onto his side to face her. "And she hasn't said anything to you before?"

"No. I had no idea. I mean, I knew he bullied her, verbally—we talked about that—but not ... not this."

Resnick stroked her shoulder. "She should report it officially. Make out a complaint. And if she hasn't done so already, go to her doctor, or to the hospital, one or the other."

Hannah moved closer, her breast resting against the inside of his arm. "I think she's frightened of going to see anyone. What Alex might do if he found out."

"If she doesn't, it could be more frightening still." Hannah turned onto her back. "You couldn't talk to him? Unofficially, I mean?"

"It's difficult."

"But if he's hitting her, if you know he's hitting her ..."

"Unless she makes a complaint ..."

"He can do as he likes."

"I didn't say that."

"As good as." Hannah was sitting up now, legs drawn up to her chest.

He reached for her arm and she shook him off.

"Don't."

"Don't what?"

"Try and get round me."

"I wasn't trying to get round you."

"Patronize me, then."

"Fine!"

He had flung back the covers and was almost to his feet before Hannah grabbed hold of his hand and held it fast.

After a moment, Resnick knelt on the bed and kissed her forehead, the side of her mouth, her eyes.

"Oh, Charlie."

He lay beside her and they cuddled close, listening to the whine and hum of traffic from the road, the rough synchronicity of their own breathing.

"Why doesn't she leave him?" Resnick said eventually.

"Charlie, for the life of me, I don't know."

Fifteen

Divine's flat was above a butcher's shop on Bath Street: a couple of ramshackle rooms, one of which also served as a kitchen, and a bathroom back down the hall. Despite protestations in the shop window below that only prime Scottish beef was sold, the odors of something old and inwardly rotting seeped endlessly up through the boards.

It was the third place Divine had lived in as many months; trapped inside his surroundings, self-conscious in the face of others and, despite himself, afraid, he quickly grew to hate whatever walls kept him prisoner and lashed out, defacing and despoiling before he escaped. His previous landlord, an Asian entrepreneur in Sneinton, was pursuing him with a bill for damages that didn't fall far short of a thousand pounds. It had needed Resnick to stand surety before the owner of this building had agreed to take Divine on; a promise that the young DC had turned a corner, calmed down, and if that were not the case, Resnick himself would make whatever restitution was necessary.

So Divine spent his days with the ill-matched curtains drawn, the television playing in the corner of one room, take-out cartons piled precariously alongside the enamel sink, numerous beer cans, mugs stained orange-brown with the residue of endless tea. Night merged into day. When he ventured out, it was to walk the streets, hands in pockets, shoulders hunched, face turned away. Pubs he went into were those in which he could be certain his former colleagues would not be found, old spit and sawdust bars no one had bothered to rejuvenate, forever on the verge of closing down. Here Divine would sit with a slow pint, listlessly turning the pages of the *Post*, the *Mirror*, or the *Sun*.

Up until a month back, he would slide into a phone booth, dial the squad room number, wait for Millington or Naylor or whoever to identify themselves, ear pressed hard against the receiver, listening to the sounds of all that activity, sucking it in.

A few times, he had rung Naylor at home, once getting Kevin himself, otherwise Debbie—the chatter of a small child in the background, the whirr and blurt of an electric mower—Divine had broken the connection without speaking.

At first, the nurse he had been seeing at the hospital had been sympathetic, gone out of her way to be understanding, tried to persuade him to continue with the therapy, spent time with him, trying to get him to talk about what had happened. But somewhere along the line there had been one sullen, half-drunken silent night too many and she had stopped calling, stopped caring. Divine, sitting there hunched in his own morbidity, had scarcely listened to what she said by way of explanation, barely registered the sound of her footsteps, brisk and assured now, relieved, walking away.

He picked up a woman on the curve of Mapperley Road and paid her the usual to undress; when his erection disappeared, she laughed it off and made him a cup of tea instead, showed him photographs of her kids. It was a slow night, and cold: she had no desire to rush back out onto the streets.

A week ago, for the first time, Divine had gone back to the street where it happened. Several hours of aimless wandering had brought him down through a maze of narrow streets on the edge of Radford and there he was. The skin along his arms prickled cold and his legs refused to move. Lights burned, shaded, in the house; normal people living normal lives. Whatever normal meant. Divine's stomach clenched as he saw again in the corner of his eye a man moving fast toward him, sensed the heavy swish and swing of a baseball bat, the sound, brittle and clear, of splintering bone. And then his legs being kicked out from under him, forced apart. Hands tugging at his belt, his clothes. *Didn't I tell you it'd be me and you? Didn't I say I'd have you?* An arm around his neck, powerful, forcing back his head, fingers probing hard between his legs. *Cunt. Whore. This is it, this is what you want.* Teeth, as the man climaxed inside him, biting deep into Divine's shoulder, breaking the skin.

It will take a long time, the therapist had said, before you can expect to assimilate all of this.

The knuckles of Divine's hands, pressed back against the wall behind him, were grazed raw and yielding blood. What had he expected, coming here like this?

Sooner or later, the therapist had told him, you have to confront what happened to you, accept it even, only then will you be able to see it in some kind of perspective, move on.

Bollocks, Divine said. Accept it, bollocks. What I want to fucking do is forget.

And there were times now, when he'd drunk enough, sometimes when he slept, when forget was what he did. Those times when he didn't wake red-eyed and slaked in sweat, the sweet stink of blood and butchery sliding between lath and plaster till he could taste it on his tongue.

He was standing at the sink, head bowed beneath the tap when he realized someone was knocking at the downstairs door, likely had been for some time.

Resnick took him to a café on Bath Street and sat him down near the window, the market traders setting up their stalls on the uneven triangle of ground outside. Eggs, bacon, sausage, beans. Resnick liberally applied brown sauce, folded thin slices of bread and butter and dipped them into the yolk, wiped the juices from the edges of the plate.

"Eat," he ordered Divine. "You don't look as though you've had a decent meal in days."

Divine was unkempt, unshaven, his clothes had started to hang haphazardly from his rugby player's frame.

"Eat."

"Not hungry," Divine said, but little by little, grudgingly, eat was what he did. Ten minutes later, Resnick's own plate comprehensively cleared, Divine hurried through to the small toilet at the back and threw up. By the time he returned, wiping tissue across his pallid face, Resnick had a fresh mug of tea waiting, sweet and hot.

Divine lit a cigarette and almost as quickly stubbed it out.

"These conditions of bail," Resnick started.

Fidgeting back his chair, Divine looked away.

"There's not going to be a problem? Mark, there's not going to be a problem?"

"Why should there be?"

"Suzanne Olds came to see me ..."

"Stuck-up cow."

"Good at her job."

"Yeah, maybe."

"She came to see me because she was worried ..."

"Well, now she can stop worrying, can't she, 'cause you can see. Look. Look, what'm I going to do? Nip off down the South of France? Costa del Sol?"

"You went to Derby," said Resnick, almost smiling.

"Fucking Derby!"

"You had a knife."

"Yeah, well I haven't got it any more."

"Nor anything like it?"

Divine hung his head; his skin was itching and the inside of his throat felt like a length of tubing someone had been attacking with industrial cleaner. He brought the mug to his mouth and the tea burned. More than most things in the world, he wanted to pull off his clothes and lower himself into a hot bath, close his eyes.

"Tell her she doesn't have to worry. I'll keep clean."

"Good." Resnick reached into his pocket for money to pay the bill. "You okay for cash?"

Divine nodded: fine.

"Okay, I'd best be getting back. And Mark ..."

"Yes?"

"If ever you need, call me, work or home, it doesn't matter, understood?"

"Yeah. Yes, thanks."

Hesitating just for a moment, Resnick fished out one of his cards, bent from his top pocket, and wrote his own number and then Hannah's in biro on the back.

"Any time, right?"

"Right."

A quick handshake and Resnick left him sitting there, cradling the mug of tea.

Jack Skelton was loitering with intent in the vicinity of Resnick's office. Skelton, while not exactly back to the peak of fitness which once saw him running four miles each morning, had nonetheless lost the excess ten pounds the past year had seen him put on, and was looking spruce this morning in a light wool check jacket and tan slacks, hair brushed to within an inch of its life.

Following Resnick through into his partitioned room, Skelton closed the door firmly at his back.

"Announcement's being made any day now, apparently."

"Announcement?"

"Serious Crimes. Who's going to be in charge, here in the city."

"I thought Kilmartin."

"Kilmartin's dropped out. Rallied round up in Paisley, offered him something he couldn't refuse."

"Season ticket to Rangers, was it?"

"Could be."

"And you've no idea?"

Skelton shook his head. "Rumors, you know how it is."

Resnick knew.

"Should've put yourself up, Charlie, then we wouldn't have all this ..." The superintendent broke off, seeing Resnick smiling widely. "What? What's so bloody funny?"

"Marlon Brando. It was on the box the other night. Where he's a boxer, working down on the docks. *I could've been a contender, Charlie.* Sitting there with his brother in the back of a car."

Skelton was shaking his head. "Must've missed it."

Resnick, too, if Hannah hadn't nagged on at him. Charlie, you'll like it. Honestly. Just give it a chance.

"What about the other business?" Resnick asked. "This deal with the Yard."

Skelton patted his pockets for his cigarettes, remembering yet again that he'd given up. "Passed it by the powers that be. Fretting about possible expenses, overtime, you know the kind of thing, but basically, yes, just so long as you don't think they'll give us the run-around, take all the credit, you can move ahead."

Resnick nodded. "I thought I'd get Carl Vincent on board. He's been following up the original theft. Even knows something about art."

"Tend to, don't they, Charlie. His sort. That way inclined, if you catch my drift."

"Jackie Ferris," Resnick said. "I'll put her in the picture. Give her a call."

He finally got through to her at four thirty in the afternoon, Jackie busy following up several leads that had come her way earlier in the day.

"Good," she said briskly, when Resnick told her they could go ahead. "That's grand." And then, "Your pal Grabianski, my best infor-mation, he's been cozying up to a character named Eddie Snow. Could be using him to get shot of the Dalzeils."

"And Snow, you think he could be implicated in this forgery business?"

"It's a strong possibility, yes."

Resnick told her a little about Carl Vincent, his reasons for wanting to get the DC involved.

"Fine. Why don't I come up to you this time? We can go over the ground."

"You're sure?"

"Why not? You can show me round the castle. Introduce me to Robin Hood."

Sixteen

Carl Vincent was seventeen days shy of his twenty-ninth birthday; old enough still to be a DC, almost too old if you considered that he was bright, quick, good at what he did. Of course, it didn't help that Vincent was black. In Leicester, a city with a famously large Asian population where he had served for most of his career, it had been less than convenient that he was quite the wrong shade of black, the kind whose origins trace back to the Caribbean, rather than Bangladesh or Pakistan.

Strangely, one thing that didn't seem to have stood in the way of Carl Vincent's promotion was the fact that he was gay. It had not been a factor simply, because, until he had transferred the thirty or so miles further north, nobody inside the Job had known. From his first posting, Vincent had established a routine which kept his private life precisely that. On those rare occasions when he visited a gay club, he was careful to ensure there were no other officers present; the one time he was spotted and later challenged, Vincent passed off his visit as work, an undercover checkup on an informer, and his explanation was accepted. He had never had a relationship with another officer; he abjured cottaging; he was not a member of the Lesbian and Gay Police Association. There was nothing in the way he walked, stood, or spoke that was in any way effeminate or camp.

But almost immediately after he had joined Resnick's team, something occurred, a murder case they were working on, which necessitated him declaring his sexual preferences and then, more or less at Resnick's suggestion, coming out to the whole squad.

There was a nasty irony, he thought, behind the fact that the only officer who seemed to have problems accepting his gayness was Mark Divine. An irony compounded when it was Vincent who arrived first on the scene of Divine's attack and fought off his assailant; Vincent who covered Divine gently with a soiled sheet and held him, albeit briefly, in the cradle of his arms.

For this day's meeting, Vincent had chosen a loose, lightweight wool suit the color of pale sand and a dark blue shirt shading toward black. He wore no tie. Fashion-conscious, Skelton would have observed: trendy. That way inclined, his sort, if you catch my drift.

Jackie Ferris had opted to travel by train and divided her journey between reading printouts from the *Electronic Telegraph* about a hundred and sixty-one paintings that had gone missing from the Ministry of Defence collection and the new Stella Duffy. Of the two, the Duffy had quite the best sex.

She had been to see her read once, Stella Duffy, a bookshop somewhere in Covent Garden. All red hair and floating white cotton. When one of the audience had asked her if she was worried about reactions to the lubricious love scenes, her response had been to tell the story of her mother in New Zealand, who after reading *Calendar Girl*, had informed her that she was going to come back to earth as a lesbian because clearly they had more fun.

Well, Jackie thought, discarding her cup of complimentary Inter-City tea, it was a point of view not to be sneezed at.

Resnick had dispatched Carl Vincent to meet her at the station; he picked her out right away, a brisk figure in a brown and white button-through dress and broad-lapeled linen jacket, soft leather briefcase tucked under one arm.

"DI Ferris? DC Vincent. Carl. Local CID." He held out a hand and grinned. "Welcome to the city."

"Thanks. Jackie Ferris, detective inspector. Arts and Antiques Focus Unit, attached to the Yard's Specialist Operations Organised Crime Group. Not that I'm trying to pull rank."

"Absolutely not."

"And I usually get roses." She was smiling broadly.

"I'll bet. But for now it's a lift to the Castle Museum. The boss thought it'd be easier to talk there than in his office."

"Fine," Jackie said, Vincent steering her toward his car. "Give me a chance to look at their Bomberg."

"Sorry?"

"David Bomberg. I looked up the Castle's holdings. They haven't got a lot of modern stuff, but he's worth checking out."

Vincent held open the passenger door. "Don't know that much yet, I'm afraid."

"But you're learning fast."

"I hope so."

"Good."

Resnick had arrived at the Castle twenty minutes early and walked slowly around the grounds. On the southern parapet, he stood looking down at the canal: kids fishing, a man in a bright blue leisure suit cycling, couples taking a short cut to the supermarket or to Homebase, the sedate movement of a red and yellow barge through gray–blue water. In all probability, she had been dead by that point, the young woman whose body had floated toward the far lock and had never yet been identified, her blank, almost featureless face rising momentarily to the surface of Resnick's consciousness.

How many were there whose deaths still sought proper explanation and resolve? How many women in water, ditch, or hasty grave, their bodies spilled out at the sides of roads or in the stairwells of deserted buildings?

A hundred and ninety nationwide? Two hundred?

Half a dozen in his immediate area alone, and close enough in cause and means to think there might be a connection between them. But not his business, not any more. Serious Crimes: their affair. Turning, Resnick cleared it from his mind and watched as one of the uniformed attendants opened the gate on to Lenton Road and Vincent drove through.

"Teacakes," Jackie Ferris enthused. "Place like this, there's got to be teacakes."

Not any more.

They sat in the far corner of a surprisingly bright and spacious room, the café recently revamped with fresh paint, trendy but comfortable chairs, and overpriced but tasty gateaux and pastries. The waitress, young and alert, made her way purposefully between the three of them and a pair of retired ladies in serious hats.

"As scams go," Jackie said, "it's near classic. Basically simple and with the beauty of covering all the bases." Her first bite told her the apricot Danish was as delicious as it looked—she was in her element. "The perennial problem with selling forgeries, no matter how well they're executed, is attribution. Obviously, copying a piece that's already in a known collection is pretty much a waste of time. Choose an artist who has no reputation at all and there's little to gain. So ..." pausing for effect and to try her English Breakfast tea, "... the smart move is to paint in the style of someone who's bankable but not really famous, choose the kind of subject they would have worked on at a certain stage of their career and then provide it with unimpeachable authentication."

"Doesn't sound so easy," Vincent said.

"What they do is perpetrate a second forgery. Or set of forgeries. The archives at the Tate, for instance, are recognized as the main source of documentation for twentieth-century art. These people have gained access to the archives, not difficult in itself given the right accreditation, and somehow altered the information to include references to the forged painting."

"Highly specialiszd," Resnick observed.

"Absolutely. Whoever's responsible for this, they're very careful, very good. And they know their art history backward."

"What kind of things do they fake?" Vincent asked. "What kind of documentation do you need?"

"The clever thing—and that's why none of this was picked up on for, oh, five, or six years, possibly more—is that they've run the whole gamut. Forged letters from relatives or patrons, sometimes by the artists themselves. References in critical monographs. Additions made to catalogs. In at least two instances, they've had a whole catalog specially printed, purporting to come from a show which when you check back never took place. And the way information technology's developing, a number of these fake additions have already found their way onto CD-ROM."

"But we're not talking Picasso here," Vincent said. "So who?"

Jackie Ferris shrugged. "Ben Nicholson. Some of the Abstract Impressionists. Joan Mitchell and Adolph Gottlieb, for instance."

Resnick signaled the waitress for another filter coffee. "The ring behind this, there must be at least three, then. Someone to forge the paintings, someone else to handle the fake documentation, and a third party to sell the paintings."

"Exactly. Though in theory, each of those three could be more than one person."

"You mean," Vincent said, "they could have different painters slaving away in their attics or wherever, copying different artists."

"And more than one dealer, yes."

"You think that's likely?" Resnick asked.

Jackie Ferris wiped her mouth with a paper napkin and told herself she didn't really need a cigarette. "On the one hand, we don't consider it likely more than a small nucleus is involved; anything larger and something would have leaked out sooner. But because of the range and number of pieces, more than one dealer is a strong possibility. A small consortium, maybe. Two or three."

"Names you fancy?" Resnick asked.

Jackie smiled. "A few."

"Edward Snow."

"Absolutely."

"Thackray?"

"Possible. But less likely."

"This stuff in the archive," Vincent asked, "I assume you've vetted all the staff?"

"With the proverbial fine-tooth comb. No, we're positive it's an outsider."

"And this has only happened at the Tate?"

A quick shake of the head. "The British Council and the V & A, too, though on a much smaller scale."

"An operation of this kind," Resnick said, "all the preparation involved, expertise, it can't come cheap. What kind of profits are we talking here?"

"A Ben Nicholson watercolor, quite small, could easily fetch up to twenty thousand pounds. One of Mitchell's large canvases, especially since she died, find the right buyer and you could be looking at twice that."

"And how long would one of these forgeries take, the painting itself?" Vincent asked.

Jackie Ferris laughed. "Someone who knew what they were doing. Seriously skilled. Maybe a six-day week. Now can we take a walk outside so I can smoke?"

Below them, a few bikers were already enjoying a pint on the cobbles outside the Trip to Jerusalem; to the east, the flat roofs of People's College gave way to the more ornate buildings on the edge of the Lace Market, and beyond those, the sails of Sneinton Windmill showed white against the rising red brick and dark tile of terraced houses and the clustered green of Colwick Park.

"What I'm not quite clear about," Vincent asked, "is exactly how you see Grabianski fitting into all this. I mean, a couple of stolen paintings, that's what he's trying to get shot of. He's not a forger, he's a thief."

"And people like Snow and Thackray, show them an opportunity to make serious money, and they'll deal in whatever they can get. Selling a couple of Dalzeils to some collector who just wants to tick them off and keep them in his vault, that's easy money. Most likely helps to finance the rest."

"Grabianski, though ..." Vincent persisted.

"Look," Jackie Ferris laid her hand on his arm, "we've tried getting close to Eddie Snow before. It's never worked. Send in someone undercover and Snow smells them out before they've as much as shaken hands. Your Grabianski's already inside. We just have to keep him as close as we can. You do. At the very least, he can help us pull Snow in for receiving stolen goods. And who knows ..." a quick smile lit up her alert face, "... if we're lucky, we might get more. Okay?"

"Okay," Vincent smiled back. "Why not?"

"Whatever it is that's worrying you," Holly said, moving her hands over Grabianski's body, "I'm glad I don't have it on my conscience. Right across these shoulders, here along the neck, you're seized up as anything." She pressed down hard with her thumbs. "Feel that? I can hardly shift it at all."

Grabianski could feel it okay. Bright little shafts of pain biting into his upper body. But as for something worrying him, surely she had it wrong. Aside from the fact that since he had taken Eddie Snow to the security vault and shown him the paintings, he had not heard a thing. It'll take a while, Snow had said, setting things up. I'll get back to you soon as I can. And Resnick—nothing would convince Grabianski that the detective inspector had made the trip down to London merely to tease him with the possibility of picking him up for lifting the Dalzeil paintings. No, he knew Resnick: just didn't know yet what he had in store for him.

"Are you sure you've been doing those exercises I showed you?" Holly asked, driving a thumb into the space between collar-bone and shoulder-blade.

"Ummph," Grabianski mouthed into white cotton.

"Every day?"

"Uum."

"Well, when we're through I'll show you another one for the lungs. Forefinger and thumb together, big breath, throw your arms wide, and come forward hard on your bent front leg. It's good to do in front of an open window."

Do that in front of an open window, Grabianski was thinking, and I just might throw myself through.

Seventeen

"How many words d'you know for vagina, Charlie?"

Resnick spluttered with surprise and set the cold *penne arrabiata* he was snacking on aside.

Hannah was sitting in her customary position, feet drawn up beneath her on the settee, lamp angled down behind her head, reading. For a change, no music was playing. The house was quiet, sealed in by the dark outside.

"I suppose," Resnick said, "you've a good reason for asking?"

"Prudish, Charlie?"

"Probably."

After several months of sleeping together, they both knew that to be true.

"This book I'm reading." Hannah held up a slender hardback, the head and bare shoulders of a young woman filtered through blue on the cover, and across her skin, in red and lower case, the title, *in the cut*. "The woman in it, the one telling the story, she teaches English …"

"Like you."

"Not at all like me. At least, not a lot. For one thing, she's working in New York. Anyway, she's writing this book, academic, about slang, different dialects. Every time she hears a new word, a different usage, she notes it down."

"Like a word for vagina?"

"Exactly."

"And there are a lot of those?"

"Don't you know?"

"I mean in this book."

"A lot."

"Doesn't sound like your usual kind of thing."

"I'm reading it for this day school of Jane's, *Healing the Cut*."

"That's what it's called?"

"I thought you knew."

"If I did, I forgot. But that's where the name comes from, that book?"

"Yes."

Resnick nodded. "And that's one of those words, cut, the ones you were asking about?"

"Yes."

With a sigh, Resnick turned back to his supper, broke off a piece of bread, and dipped it into the sauce. "What's it like?" he asked a few minutes later. "I mean, is it any good?"

"Yes. I mean, she can clearly write ..."

"But?"

"There's so much violence. Not up front, but the threat of it, always there in the background. Women being violated, awful things happening to them. And she seems—the woman in the story—she seems attracted to it, almost. Excited."

"You don't like that?"

Hannah was thoughtful. "I don't trust myself for liking it."

"No one says you have to finish it."

Hannah smiled. "I want to find out what happens."

"Your friend, Jane," Resnick asked later as they were on their way up to bed, "that business with her husband, you haven't heard anything else?"

"No, not a thing."

Jane was sitting in the dining room, one of those awful bloody paintings Alex had insisted upon buying staring down at her from the opposite wall. Her watch, which she had taken off and laid on the table, told her it was not so many minutes short of twelve o'clock. Folders and papers and books were scattered in ragged piles across polished oak. Of course, she would be tired in the morning, but at least now, with Alex in bed, she had peace and quiet. And the work had to be done.

She was just thinking about going into the kitchen, making

another cup of coffee to keep her going, when she heard the faint creak of the stair.

Holding her breath, she tensed for the opening of the door, but after a pause, the footsteps continued on along the passageway. The sudden jet of water onto metal, the opening of a cupboard door, dull and low, the closing of the fridge. Jane allowed herself a smile: two minds, for a change, with a similar thought.

Alex would do this when he couldn't sleep, fix himself a warm drink and sit up in bed, pillows propped around him, reading some research article on dentistry with the World Service faintly churning in the background: our correspondent in Delhi, our correspondent in Dakar.

Alex surprised her by coming in.

"Still at it?"

"What does it look like?"

"Here, I thought you might like this." On a small tray, he had set out a cup and saucer, coffee, milk, an arc of biscuits. "I made decaf. I thought it best."

"Thank you."

"The least I could do."

He moved away—but only a pace—and stood behind her, Jane aware of his closeness, his breathing; on the page beneath her eyes words jumped and danced, suddenly unintelligible.

"Go on, then. Don't let it get cold."

"In a minute."

"It won't be the same."

With almost exaggerated care, Jane poured the coffee from its china jug and added milk.

"No sugar?"

"You know I don't …"

"This late at night, I thought for the energy maybe."

"No."

"No, of course. Sweet enough." She drank without tasting. "Alex …"

"Mmm?"

"Please don't stand there."

"What? I'm in your light?"

"No, it's just …"

"What?"

"Oh, nothing, nothing. It doesn't matter, really."

"Good."

Blinking her way into focus, Jane fought to concentrate. At her back, Alex started humming a tune, something vaguely classical and then, as if realizing what he was doing, abruptly stopped. Reaching forward, he grazed the knuckles of his right hand gently across her cheek.

Stifling a shout, Jane froze.

Slowly, Alex's fingers moved down inside her top, turning beneath her arm until they were touching her breast.

"Alex, what are you doing?"

"I should have thought you'd have known."

"Why are you doing this now?"

"You shouldn't have to ask."

With a sigh, Jane closed her eyes and leaned forward, trapping his hand between the edge of the table and her breast. Angling his head, Alex kissed the nape of her neck, ran the tip of his tongue around the curling edges of her ear.

"Come to bed," he said.

"Alex, I can't …"

"Come to bed."

Shaking her head, she straightened her back and shook him free. Black silk robe, bare feet, Alex stood looking at her, arms folded now across his chest.

"Alex, I'm sorry …"

"Yes."

"I have to finish this."

"Yes."

"Really, I …"

"Jane, I understand."

Slowly, she began to turn away. "Thanks for the coffee."

"That's okay."

When she heard him move toward the door and ease it open, one of the knots in her stomach slipped free.

"Jane …"

"Mmm?"

"When you come up, I'll be waiting …"

"Charlie!"

At the sound of Hannah's voice, Resnick broke from sleep, pushing himself up on one arm, Hannah already sitting up, bent forward, her body ploughed in sweat.

"Oh, Charlie!"

"What? What is it?"

Her hair was lank and damp and dark against her face.

"What happened?"

She grasped one of his hands between hers and squeezed. "Nothing."

"Nothing? It doesn't sound like nothing."

"It was just a dream. A stupid dream." Lowering herself back down, she kissed him on the cheek. "Just hold me a little, I'll be all right." And hold her he did, arms warm around her, drawing out the clammy coldness of her skin.

"Charlie," she said again a while later, speaking out into the darkness; but by then he was lost in sleep.

Eighteen

The face on the fax, as such faces tend to be, was blurred and darkened out of recognition. The details, printed below, were economical and sparse. The body had been spotted by a night worker on his way home, pedaling his bicycle along the towpath of the canal. Something yellow puffed up in the water, like a piece of tarpaulin, an old sack. These observations, grubbily poetic, did not find their way onto the fax. Extent of injuries, date, time, presumed cause of death. Yellow anorak aside, she had been wearing blue jeans, a turquoise polo shirt, gray canvas shoes. No purse or wallet found with the body; no other forms of identification. Dark hair. The tattoo of a hummingbird in three colors high on her right arm, a silver ring through the left nostril: no other distinguishing features or marks. Aside from the wound at the back of her head, a three-inch gash above the left ear.

Resnick picked up his phone and dialed the number at the bottom of the fax. Worksop was a small town to the north of the county, bisected by the Chesterfield Canal; one of those places where not a great deal seemed to happen, and when it did the rest of the world usually failed to blink. For a few days now, the media would focus on this, a young woman murdered, always the possibility of sexual assault. And then if there were no arrests, no startling revelations, the incident would flicker and fade from the news; a post-mortem would be opened and closed, details analyzed, shuffled, cross-checked, the file left open. Another set of statistics for Operation Enigma, the initial planning meeting of which Jack Skelton had recently attended in lieu of the city's yet-to-be-appointed head of Serious Crimes.

The north of the county had not been so cautious. Sandy Paul was the new DCI, fished out of the fast-track graduate pool, a first from Durham in politics, his masters in criminology. Rumor had it he was studying for a law degree in his spare time. Between feeding the ferrets and a spot of fishing, that's likely what I should be doing, Reg Cossall had observed; always assuming I'm not busily engaged in tupping the wife. Cossall, a DI who had joined the force the same month as Resnick, the pair of them raw-boned and idealistic behind the ears, was on his fourth wife; Sandy Paul only recently betrothed to his first, a barrister with chambers in Sheffield and a growing reputation in cases of misrepresentation and fraud.

"I'm sorry, Inspector," one of the civilian support staff announced with all the warmth of a British Telecom recording, "but Mr. Paul is attending a press conference at this moment. If you would like to log the details of your call, I'm sure Mr. Paul or one of his officers will get back to you."

Mr. Paul, Resnick thought, nice that, the Mr., makes him seem more approachable somehow, more like a bank manager or the head of a local double-glazing firm.

The sergeant who finally rang back was someone Resnick knew, a committed Chesterfield supporter who occasionally ventured down to the County ground and joined Resnick in bemoaning the absence of players like Armstrong and Chedozie, who had once graced their teams.

Resnick was surprised to find that Brian Findley had transferred into Serious Crimes.

"Made me an offer I could scarce refuse, Charlie. Sign on or get shifted out to the likes of Bolsover." He pronounced it Bowser. "Faced with that, not a lot I could do."

Resnick, who in an earlier life had enjoyed a brief but fiery relationship with a social worker from Bolsover, understood what Findley meant. It had been years before he could think of certain kinds of sexual activity without the scent of coke fumes seeming to drift, unbidden, through the air.

"You've not joined up yourself, then, Charlie? Still managing to keep pure."

"Not sure, Brian, if that's the word."

"Dragging their heels a bit down there, aren't they? Still to appoint a DCI."

"Any day now."

"Woman, isn't it? Favorite. What I heard."

Resnick had heard nothing of the sort.

"Any road up," Findley said, "whoever it is, I hope they've got a bit more experience than the boy wonder here."

"Problems, then?"

Findley moved the mouthpiece closer and lowered his voice. "Organization, management, public relations, he's a fucking marvel. But ask him to find his left armpit of a Sat'day night, I doubt he'd manage it with a flashlight and an OS map, large scale."

"This girl in the canal," Resnick said, "how much do you know?"

"Not a lot. Not soddin' enough. Somewhere between eighteen and twenty-two or twenty-three. Been in the water nigh on four hours when she were spotted."

"What's that make it?" Resnick broke across him. "Two thirty? Two?"

"Thereabouts."

"And this blow to the head ..."

"Would it have finished her if her lungs hadn't filled with water? Up to yet, no word."

"But your best guess?"

A hesitation, Findley clearing his throat, and then: "What's your interest, Charlie? Special, that is."

Succinctly, Resnick told him about the body that had been found the night of the Milt Jackson concert, though he kept the musical references to himself. As he remembered, Brian Findley's tastes revolved round "Apache" by the Shadows, "Diamonds" by Jet Harris and Tony Meehan. *Footwork, Charlie, that's what amazes me, the co-ordination. That Hank Marvin, all them intricate dance steps in his winkle-pickers and he's playing the tune on his guitar the whole time.*

"Similarities, then, that's what you're thinking," Findley said.

"Maybe."

"Computer's like as not spewing them out downstairs about now."

"How about sexual assault?" Resnick asked. "Any sign?"

"Still swabbing the orifices, Charlie. No official word."

"But unofficially?"

"Got to be quids on, don't you think?"

What, Resnick thought, had Hannah been saying? *Always there in the background, women being violated.* "You've got no farther with the identification?" he inquired.

"Reports of a young woman in town this last couple of days, asking for work. Casual, you know the kind of thing—pubs, burger bars. She was in the place on the canal yesterday evening, warehouse they've tarted up into some kind of disco, looking for a job there. Manager says he had nothing, had to turn her down. Sorry, though. Quite fancied her. Australian, apparently. One of these round-the-world tours they go in for all the time."

"How in God's name did she end up in Worksop?" Resnick asked.

"Go anywhere, don't they? Where the spirit moves them. Walkabout, isn't that what they call it?"

"Aborigines, I thought."

"Not this one. Whiter than the wife's mother's toilet bowl."

"You might keep me posted," Resnick said. "Anything develops as might tie in this end."

"Will do."

"Thanks. And the notes from down here, you want me to send them through?"

"Likely no need. If the computer's not picked up on it already, I can access them from here."

"Okay, Brian," Resnick said. "Keep in touch."

"You too."

A woman, Resnick thought, favorite to run Serious Crimes, which woman was that? He had bought his lunchtime sandwich and espresso at the deli near the station and carried them over into the cemetery, where he was now sitting, sharing his alfresco meal with several dog-eared angels and the spirit of Amy Maude Swinton, whose tenure on this earth had been less than twenty-one years.

A woman.

Since deciding not to apply for the DCI's post himself, Resnick had tried to seal himself off from the crosscurrents of speculation, informed and otherwise, which radiated between Central station and its various satellites. But of the hundred and nine serious applications, fifteen had come from women, somehow he had heard that. He had no idea how many, if any, had progressed onto the final shortlist, nor who they were.

He was just about to congratulate himself on getting through both halves of a ham and mozzarella with mustard and mayonnaise on rye without mishap, when he noticed an unsightly splurge on his right thigh.

Nineteen

"Listen," Resnick had said, Hannah beginning to make yawning noises behind her book and shift position at the other end of the settee, "you won't take this the wrong way ..."

"But you don't want to stay."

Resnick shrugged and smiled.

"Well," Hannah said, setting the book on the floor and getting to her feet, "the cats will be pleased."

"You don't mind?"

Hannah shook her head. "Of course not." She nudged the book with her foot. "I can go to bed with this."

"Another cheery tale?"

"A fifty-year-old man in prison for attacking little girls and a young woman who likes sex with eleven-year-old boys." She saw the frown darken his face. "It's life, Charlie, you know that better than most."

"All the more reason I'd not want to read about it." He was looking down at the book on the floor. *The End of Alice* by A. M. Homes. On the cover an old monochrome picture of little girls in ballet clothes had been artfully dismembered so that their bodies skipped and cavorted above the title, and their faces, shiny and alive, appeared below the author's name.

"Come on, Charlie," Hannah said, "I'll walk you to the car."

Take-away menus for Indian restaurants and pizza parlors were gathering dust behind the front door; any burglar who left a fingerprint on the hall table or the bannister of the stairs would fill Scene of Crime with delight. From a perch on the third shelf in the kitchen, Pepper stared down at him as at a stranger, a distant, faintly remembered relative at best. He was surprised Dizzy didn't take a bite out of his leg.

Something, Resnick thought, was going to have to change; it was difficult with his job to spend time enough in one home, never mind two.

He made supper for himself and the cats and carried the last few issues of the *Post* through into the front room. After the color, the coziness of Hannah's, the room was overlarge, heavy, almost unwelcoming. When he sat, his eyes were drawn to the Herman Leonard photograph of Lester Young framed on the wall; Lester looking tired, older than his forty-something years, either he had grown out of his suit, or his suit had grown out of him.

When, not so very much later, Resnick went up to bed, he left the stereo playing, Lester in his youth and glory, the sound of his saxophone, light and sinuously rhythmic, tracing him up the stairs: "I Never Knew," "If Dreams Came True," "I've Found a New Baby," "The World Is Mad" parts one and two.

So much for good intentions. Adrift in his own bed with only one of the cats for company, Resnick turned and wallowed the entire night, so that when the phone rang a little after seven, he was already up and showered, breakfasted, and feeling as if he'd scarcely slept at all.

Comforting at that bleary-eyed time of the morning to be greeted by Reg Cossall's cheery tones. "No need asking who she shagged to get the bloody job, Charlie, more a case of who she agreed to let alone."

Resnick hadn't the faintest idea who or what he was talking about.

"Siddons, Charlie. That bloody Siddons woman. More postings already'n pricks in a second-hand dartboard, an' now she's got this fucker."

"Helen Siddons?"

"Less you know any others."

"DCI, Serious Crimes?"

"Another stepping stone, most likely. Six month at most. Superintendent next. Bit of a leg up, all it is for her—or leg over. Any road, Charlie, thought you'd like to know. See you for that jar some time, right?"

"Right."

Resnick was left staring at the silent telephone. Helen Siddons had been attached to the local force a while back, already marked out for higher things; she had been enthusiastic, tenacious, nakedly ambitious; on the inquiry she and Resnick had worked together, she had proved disturbingly guilty of tunnel vision. And possibly more.

For all that Cossall's old-fashioned chauvinism could be taken with a pinch of salt, it was Resnick's experience that Siddons was not above making use of her obvious charms to cultivate friends in higher places. The clearest memory Resnick had of her was from a Christmas function almost two years before: Helen Siddons wearing an ankle-length dress in pale green and standing off to one side with Jack Skelton, the pair of them carelessly oblivious to the innuendo spreading about them as they leaned against the wall and talked, heads bowed, talked and smoked and smiled and talked some more. He remembered Skelton's wife, Alice, ignored and drunk and pawing at his knee. *What you have to see, she's not just fucking him, Charlie, she's fucking you too.*

Well, maybe ...

Graham Millington was waiting to waylay him inside the CID room. "Another triumph for fair play and the powers of positive discrimination."

"Something like that, Graham."

Resnick closed his door firmly behind him, the kind of firmness that makes good and clear casual interruptions are unwelcome. Until that morning he hadn't realized how much he had wanted the job for himself and now ... well, who did he have to blame but himself for not even trying, not applying? Helen Siddons would be a skip and a jump down the Ropewalk away, striding from room to room through the upper floor of the old hospital building that had been converted into the Serious Crime Squad's city office; likely as not, some civilian in overalls was carefully at work even now, adding her name and rank to the outside of her office door.

There was a note on Resnick's desk already: Jack Skelton's office at eleven-thirty, an informal get-together to welcome the new DCI into her post.

In Skelton's office, Helen Siddons was wearing a charcoal suit with a box jacket and a skirt that finished quite decorously a few inches below the knee. Her hair was attractively done in a French pleat, practical but not too severe, suggesting she could still let it down if the occasion demanded. Cigarette in hand, she was talking to an inspector from the Fraud Squad when Resnick came in. No more than a dozen people there so far, and among them Resnick noted Harry Payne from the Support Department, and Jane Prescott, newly promoted to inspector in Force Intelligence. Spotting Resnick, Siddons excused herself and came directly toward him, offering her hand.

"Charlie …"

"Helen, congratulations."

"Thanks." And then, adding a wry smile, "Bet you didn't think you'd see me again so soon."

"I wouldn't say that."

"Lot of things we wouldn't say, Charlie, doesn't mean they don't get thought. How many dicks did it take her to get where she is today, you know the kind of thing. Not that I'd assume that of you. I think I know you better than that."

Switching smiles, she turned as Skelton approached, the superintendent wearing his best suit too, and very smart, though his hand seemed to have slipped when he was shaving and he might have been too prodigal with the aftershave.

"Good to see you here, Charlie. There's coffee on the side. Sherry, if you'd like."

"Coffee will be fine." He didn't move.

"That spell Helen had with us a bit ago," Skelton said. "Just passing through, that's what we thought, eh? Good to welcome her back like this."

"You'll be going round all the stations, I dare say," Resnick said. "Letting them see your face."

"I dare say. Sooner or later. Coming here was different. You and Jack, people I know. Worked with."

"And will again, it's hoped," Skelton said, his hand barely brushing her sleeve.

"I wonder, Jack," she said, "that sherry you mentioned. Since this is something of an occasion …"

"Of course, right away."

"Charlie," she moved closer, filling the space Skelton had left, "I've a confession to make."

"Go ahead."

"This early visit, it's not purely social."

"I see." Resnick's mind was starting to race.

"Bit of a fishing expedition really. Poaching."

"Yes."

"Lynn Kellogg, she passed her sergeant's board a while back now, unless I'm mistaken."

Resnick tensed. "All set to join Family Support; she's got an interview lined up the end of this week."

Helen Siddons' face expressed clear distaste. "Come on, Charlie, she doesn't want that."

"Not what she says."

"A detective, Charlie, that's what she is, and a bloody good one. You know that better than anyone. What does she want with domestics and missing kids? Wiping noses and passing round the Kleenex."

"Ask her."

"I will. But with your permission, Charlie. Your blessing."

Resnick shifted balance. "Far as I know, nothing to prevent you approaching whoever you've a mind to."

"Charlie …" Now it was his arm, her fingers light on the back of his hand. "You've got to let her go some time. Fly the nest."

He pulled back, smarting. "She's not a kid, you know. I'm not her bloody father."

"No, Charlie. Not exactly that."

Twenty

The trouble with south London, Grabianski had long decided, it was flat as Kate Moss. All those times his mum had walked him from common to common—Tooting Bec, Tooting Graveney, Wandsworth, Clapham—unbuckling him from his pushchair and encouraging him to run: if he hadn't tripped across an upthrust root, looked away at the wrong moment, and smacked face first into a tree, he would have raced clear off the edge of the world.

Maybe that was why, Grabianski thought, ever since he had ceased to be a child, it was hills that drew him, mountains: the Lakes, Scotland, Snowdonia, the North Yorkshire Moors. His profits had gone on treks to the Tatra Mountains or Nepal, while Grice had been flirting with non-specific urogenital diseases in Benidorm.

And up here, high to the north of the city, Highgate, Hampstead, Muswell Hill, the open spaces were compounded of fold on fold of hills, sharp rises and sudden, unexpected declines, gullies and ravines. When he broke cover beyond the wayward thicket of tangled bush and trees and strode up toward the tumulus that marked the midway point between Kenwood and Parliament Hill, he truly thought he was Lord of All.

Another brisk ten minutes south, the sweep of the city below him, and he would be descending the thin diagonal path toward the bandstand and its attendant café, the D'Auria Brothers ice-cream and catering establishment, open all year round for quality food and fresh brewed coffee, pizza and homemade cakes a speciality.

When Grabianski, exultant, pushed his way in through the glass swing doors, Resnick and a young black man he didn't recognize were sitting at one of the center tables, the young man just starting on what looked like a cappuccino, Resnick, small cup of espresso to one side, taking a plastic fork to a generous slice of raspberry and redcurrant pie.

Part of Grabianski's instinct was to turn right round again and go back the way he'd come. But he knew that whatever that might achieve, it would be temporary, an exercise in deflecting the inevitable. Instead, he positioned himself at the end of the brief queue, ordered black coffee and a slice of pizza, waited while the pizza was microwaved, and carried his tray to where Resnick and Carl Vincent were sitting.

"Good walk?" Resnick asked.

Stirring sugar into his coffee, Grabianski assured him it had been fine.

Resnick made the necessary introductions and, not for the first time in his career, Grabianski wondered at the precise etiquette of shaking hands with someone who might well be about to arrest you and have you locked away for a generous five to ten.

"Carl's helping me on this," Resnick explained.

"This?"

"We thought, Jerzy, you might be in the mood to do a little, shall we say, trading? Man with your kind of interests—culture, ornithology—doesn't want to wither away inside."

Grabianski broke off a section of pizza. "Never was my intention."

"Exactly."

"Problem is ..." Vincent intruded.

"Is there a problem?"

"Those Dalzeils, clearly down to you."

Chewing, Grabianski smiled. "A little matter of proof?"

"We know you've been asking around, looking for a potential buyer."

"What? Snatches of overheard conversation? Scarcely illegal."

"How about possession?" Resnick said. "Two stolen paintings."

Grabianski laughed: this was speculation, pure and simple. They didn't have squit. "I've told you, Charlie, any time you like to turn up with a warrant, you can search my place from top to bottom. All you'll find are postcard reproductions, maybe the odd photograph."

"Fine," Resnick said, leaning forward, "but what about the safety deposit box?"

A piece of pizza crust found itself wedged uncomfortably at the back of Grabianski's throat; something about the expression in Resnick's eyes made him uncertain now if they were bluffing or not.

"And then there's always," Resnick added almost nonchalantly, "the paintings stolen from the MoD."

"What?"

"The Ministry of Defence."

"I know what it means."

"A hundred and sixty pieces missing altogether, though, of course, we're not suggesting they're all down to you." Resnick smiled. "Just one or two. Your trademark, I suppose you'd say. Neat, well-planned, careful. Someone who walked right into the Ministry building, Quartermaster General's office, large as life. One or two items walked out with him."

"*Coast Scene with Fishing Boats*," Vincent said, "that was one of them. "Nicholas Matthew Condy. Not a name to me, but worth close to twenty grand apparently."

"You know who the Yard's marked down as selling that painting, Jerzy?" Resnick asked. "Your friend, Eddie."

"Eddie?"

"Eddie Snow."

Grabianski picked up his cup of coffee and sipped at it cautiously, mind working overtime. At the table alongside them, four Asian girls from a nearby comprehensive were arguing over their German homework, filling the air around them with tobacco smoke and laughter. A middle-aged woman with the puzzled moon face of a child was sitting with her carer, twisting a narrow length of scarf in and around her fingers in a seemingly endless pattern, tea and toast beside her untouched. Beyond the glass, solitary men and women sat with their dogs or children, and a man wearing padded cycling shorts and a maroon sweatshirt shouted into his mobile phone.

"Jerzy," Resnick said, "we've got times, places, you and Eddie, not simply passing the time of day."

"Acquaintance, that's all. Someone I just met. Made his money in the music business, so I've heard."

"Made his money brokering the sale of stolen and forged works of art," Resnick said. "Arts and Antiques Unit at the Yard's got a list long as your arm. Big business. National treasures. Sort of thing that gets taken seriously. You can bet the Yard's been working on this for a long time. When they pull it all together—and they're close—someone will be going down for a long time."

Grabianski wished Resnick wouldn't keep going on and on about prison that way; he'd done prison and Resnick was right, he hated it like nothing else. The loss of most things he held dear, space and light and air.

"It's a fit up, Charlie," he said. "That's all this is." He didn't sound convincing, even to himself.

Resnick smiled, almost a grin, surprising Vincent by the extent to which he was enjoying the situation, savoring it even. "On our way down here, we called in on your pal Grice in Lincoln. Sort of early-morning wake-up call, though he'd been scrubbing out his cell a full hour by the time we were there. Asked to be remembered to you, naturally. Rot in hell, something along those lines, wasn't it, Carl?"

"Close. No love lost, that was clear."

"Always refused to sell you out till now, Grice. Even after what you did to him. That sort of villain, old-fashioned, it's in his water. Ingrained. Never grass."

"Kind you don't see much any more," Vincent said, "except on the TV."

"But now we've explained the situation, he might see his way to giving us a little help. Anything rather than doing the rest of his time; no parole, he could be looking at three more years." Resnick looked Grabianski square in the eyes and held his gaze till the other man blinked away. "He doesn't want that. And you know, Jerzy, the number of jobs he could set at your door. Dates, addresses, times. For all he's not the brightest of men, Grice's memory seems to work a treat."

Grice, Grabianski was thinking, that slimy little turd, he could see him doing everything they said and more.

"Eddie Snow," Grabianski said, "you want me to set him up."

Resnick and Vincent leaned back in their bright plastic chairs and smiled.

Twenty-one

Sharon Garnett was dressed to stop traffic: three-inch heels and a dark red velvet dress with serious cleavage. Red lipstick that showed bright against the rich brown of her skin.

When she stepped out into Victoria Street at the point where it met Fletcher Gate, the driver of a newly delivered, taking-it-around-the-block-for-the-first-time Porsche came close to gift-wrapping it around a convenient lamppost. Even the staff at Sonny's were impressed enough to set aside their usual sangfroid and stare.

Lynn, who had arrived early and stood for several moments feeling awkward before being shown to a table off the central aisle, smiled up at Sharon welcomingly and felt a hundred per cent less attractive than she had before.

"Sorry I'm late," Sharon said, the waiter pulling back her chair.

"That's okay."

"You look great," Sharon said, settling in, Lynn sitting there in the black dress she always wore for occasions like this, the one little black dress she possessed.

"Can I get you a drink before you order?" the waiter asked.

"I look like shit," Lynn said.

"Nonsense."

"I'll come back," the waiter said.

"No." Sharon caught his arm as he turned away. "I'll have a margarita."

"Certainly, will that be rocks or frozen?"

"On the rocks, and make sure they use a decent tequila, none of that supermarket stuff, okay?"

The waiter raised his eyes toward the ceiling, but not too far.

"Lynn?" Sharon asked. "How about you?"

113

"White wine. Just a glass."

"Would that be dry or …" the waiter began.

"The house wine's fine."

"Of course."

Sharon unclasped her bag and reached for her cigarettes. "I meant it," she said, touching the back of Lynn's hand. "You look fine."

Lynn smiled thanks. "As opposed to just sensational."

Sharon snapped her lighter shut and tilted back her head, releasing a stream of pale gray smoke. "If you've got it," she laughed, "package it as best you can."

When the drinks arrived, Sharon lifted hers in a toast. "Here's to us. To you. Success, right?"

"I haven't said I'll take it yet."

"No, but you will."

Sharon tasted her margarita, ran her tongue around the glass to get more salt, and tasted it again. "I should have asked him to bring a pitcher."

"You will."

"God!" Sharon said extravagantly. "Obvious or what?" Sharon Garnett had trained as an actress, worked as a singer, gone out on the road as one of three backing vocalists propping up a former sixties soul legend whose love of the horses and amphetamines had left him little but memories of past successes and a name which could still fill small clubs in Doncaster or Rugby on a Saturday night when there was nothing major on TV. Just over a year of motorway food and finger-snapping her way through the Ooh-Ahs of "Midnight Hour" and "Knock on Wood" was enough. Sharon took up with a group of mainly Afro-Caribbean actors and found out most of what there was to know about community theater. Which is to say it's a lot like touring with a third-rate band, the same transit vans and the same parched meals, but the pay is even worse and the audiences smaller still.

Quite what enticed her into joining the police, she wasn't sure. Maybe it was the way she'd observed the predominantly white, predominantly male officers operating in East London where she lived, or on the front line in Brixton; maybe she allowed herself to be converted by the agitprop plays she performed in community centers and church halls from Handsworth to Hyson Green. Then again, perhaps she was simply drawn by the adventure. There would be adventure ...

In London, they tried to turn her into some kind of uniformed social worker and made it clear that the pathway to CID was paved with more than hard work and good intentions. Sharon applied for a transfer out and, for reasons best known to the movements of the planets rather than any observable logic, fetched up in Lincoln, which was where she met Resnick, not Lincoln itself exactly, but a pig farm not so many hectares distant, the pair of them up over their ankles in pig shit and murder.

Soon after, Sharon moved again, this time to the East Midlands, and since there wasn't a vacancy in Resnick's squad at the time, joined Vice, where, at least, she got to operate in plain clothes and was allowed a certain degree of autonomy. Sharon had been made up to sergeant three weeks back, and this was the first time she and Lynn, close friends over the past couple of years—about as close as Lynn allowed anyone—had been free to celebrate. One disadvantage of working Vice, like soul singing and community theater both, it did mean working a lot of nights.

But this particular night there was a double cause for pushing the boat out—Lynn, after all, had just been head-hunted to join Serious Crimes.

"How many other detective sergeants?" Sharon asked, touching her knife to the last surviving piece of her rack of lamb.

"Four altogether. Why, you thinking about applying?"

Sharon grinned and picked up the meat with her fingers. "Give it a little time."

"That Asian bloke, Khan, the one who worked the Bill Aston investigation, he's already in."

"DS?"

Lynn shook her head. "DC." There was little left to show that the salmon she'd ordered had been served with a cream and dill sauce, sautéed potatoes, a fennel and watercress salad: clean plate, Lynnie, that's the way her mum had brought her up in the raw comforts of rural Norfolk.

"Khan," Sharon said, chewing thoughtfully, "he's the good-looking one, right?"

"I suppose."

"Oh, yeah, I forgot, you don't notice these things."

"That's not true."

"Isn't it?"

"Not necessarily."

"Yes? How long is it since you went out with a bloke then, tell me that?"

Shifting the knife and fork together on her plate, Lynn shrugged.

"How long since you …" Lamb bone between her lips, Sharon mimed a gesture that made Lynn blush.

"Is everything finished here?" the waiter inquired, hovering at Sharon's shoulder.

"Almost," Sharon said, deftly tweaking away the last scrap of sweet meat between her teeth.

"Shall I bring the dessert menu?"

"Not for me." Lynn shook her head.

"Yes," said Sharon.

"Any coffees?"

"Black," said Lynn.

"Later," said Sharon.

They split the bill down the middle and ordered a cab to take Sharon home; Lynn could walk to her flat in the Lace Market in a matter of minutes.

"Seriously," Sharon said, her taxi at the curb. "You haven't got any doubts?"

"Not really, only …"

"Only what?"

"Helen Siddons."

"What about her?"

"I'm just not sure; working under her, I mean."

"She's keen enough on you."

"I know, I know, but …"

"It's not because she's a woman? You're not one of those who doesn't like taking orders from other women?"

"I really don't know. I don't think it's that, no. It's just … all the time she was talking to me, Siddons, trying to persuade me, buttering me up, I never quite believed what she was saying."

The taxi-driver gave a short blast of the horn and Sharon shot him a look that stilled his impatience. "That's not Siddons," she said, "that's you. You're just not good at taking praise. Anyone tells you how good you are and you think they must be lying."

Lynn took a step out onto the pavement. "Anyway, I promised her an answer, first thing tomorrow."

"Okay, don't let me down." Sharon gave Lynn a hug and left a faint smear of lipstick across her cheek. "Either way, you've got to let me know, right?"

"Right."

Lynn waited while Sharon climbed into the back of the cab, gave the driver his instructions, and then settled back, waving through the glass. Then she walked briskly down toward Goose Gate, heading home.

Lynn recognized Resnick's car before she saw him, leaning in the half-shadow of the courtyard around which the flats were built. Her first reaction was that it was trouble, an emergency, something serious, work. But seeing his face as he moved toward her, she was less sure: Resnick, hands in pockets, the faint beginnings of a smile, which quickly changed into something more apologetic.

"Good night?"

"Fine, yes, why ...?"

"Kevin said something about you going out for a bit of a do, celebration."

Lynn's hand wafted air vaguely. "It was just me and Sharon. Anything more, I'd've invited everyone."

Resnick nodded. They stood there in the half-light, the evening humming round them, the ground, Lynn thought, tilting beneath her feet.

"You are taking the job?"

"Yes, I think so."

"Good."

"Is that really what you think?"

"Of course."

"Before, when I was trying to get into Family Support ..."

"Not the same."

"No."

Foolishly, Resnick looked at his watch. "I just wanted to be sure. Didn't want to think there was any reason, anything to do with me, you and me, why you wouldn't agree."

"No. No. I don't even think ... I mean why ...?"

Resnick didn't know either. What was he doing there? "You're going to accept, then?" he asked for the second time.

Lynn blinked. "Yes."

Resnick shuffled his weight from one foot to the other, a step he'd forgotten how to make.

"Do you want to come up?" Lynn asked. "Coffee or something?"

He was almost too quick to shake his head. "No. No, thanks."

Lynn hunched her shoulders, suddenly aware that she was standing there with just a linen coat over her short black dress. "Okay," she said.

"Yes," Resnick said. "Okay."

By the time she had climbed the double flight of stairs to her landing, his car was reversing round, red brake lights flaring for an instant, before heading forward beneath the brick archway and away from sight.

Lynn opened the door and double-locked it fast behind her, sliding home the bolt. Kicking off her shoes and shucking her coat onto the nearest chair, she padded into the bathroom and began to run the shower. Three more days and then she would be reporting for duty at the far end of the Ropewalk, close to where she had been based these past four years. Almost five. Slipping the catch at the back of her dress, she pulled down the zip and let the dress fall to the floor. Moments later, naked, she looked at herself in the mirror, never quite liking what she saw. Breasts too small, hips too large. As if, she thought, it mattered, stepping into the gathering steam. As if it mattered any more.

Twenty-two

They started the day with the shower scene. Poor Janet, a good girl really, regular and law-abiding, though not above the occasional sex and tumble with a married man in her lunch hour, succumbing to a momentary temptation and stealing forty thousand dollars. Pursued, suspected, she clings to her last vestiges of calm and is almost clean away. Then in the storm she takes a wrong turn and checks into the Bates Motel.

The day school audience responded the way audiences were programmed to do: the insistent, keening music, stabbing at the ears, the slash and cut of blade, the absurd figure of the attacker, all-powerful, unreal; shot after shot of the woman's body, naked, falling, cut after cut; blood on the shower curtain, blood on the tiles; her face, unmoving, the open, staring eye; blood merging with the flow of water, running away.

Poor Janet.

The lights came up on sixty, seventy people sitting there, the smaller auditorium; some with notebooks opened on their laps, some with cups of coffee cooling in their hands. Mostly women, young to early middle-age, a scattering of men: teachers, media students, specialists from the caring professions, academics, a phalanx of hard-core lesbian feminists, the obligatory few crazies, lost already in their own impenetrable agendas, a shaven-headed young woman exhibiting a fetishistic interest in body piercing and tattoos, a nun.

"What we've just been watching," the first speaker pronounced, "is the classic scene of ritual punishment, ritual cleansing. The female protagonist has transgressed the laws of her male-dominated world. The camera, while delighting in her sexuality—remember the first shots in the film, almost like a contemporary advertisement for Wonderbra, the way they emphasize her wantonness, the size and shape of her breasts, lying there on the bed while her lover gets dressed—the camera still punishes her for it. And us, as audience. Having pried on her, involved us in her secret activity, aroused us with her sexuality, it becomes her attacker, the movements of the camera becoming those of the knife, taking us, whether we want to or not, deep down into the cut.

"But Hitchcock being Hitchcock, extreme chauvinist that he was, these extremes of punishment that we witness, and in which we are forced to participate, are not carried out by a man. As the end of the film makes clear, it is only when Norman Bates is taken over by the other half of his divided personality, the mother half, that these murderous impulses come to the surface. Norman didn't kill the Janet Leigh figure, Norman's mother did. It is the female, the feminine side of our nature that is the site of evil here, the blood is on our hands."

It was some seven minutes short of eleven o'clock. Before the first break at noon, they would see brief extracts from *Hellraiser*, *Dressed to Kill*, and *Hallowe'en*. In the afternoon there were separate seminars, running simultaneously, one on women's fiction—*In the Cut*, *The End of Alice*, and Joyce Carol Oates' *Zombie*—the other devoted to sado-masochism and the fetishization of the female body in high fashion. Everyone would come back together at the end of the day for a screening of Kathryn Bigelow's *Strange Days*, followed by a final question and answer session and discussion.

Sister Teresa had brought sandwiches and a thermos of tea and sat on one of the low walls outside the media center, talking to a lecturer from Trent University and an earnest young man with a disturbing look of Anthony Perkins about him, who was in his first year of studying video and film. The person she really wanted to talk to was the bald woman with the wonderful tattoos.

"Aren't you the one who does that radio program?" the lecturer asked suddenly, her eyes brightening. "Sister something-or-other, is that you?"

Teresa smiled apologetically and did her best to deflect the question.

Why was it, she thought, people were always so fascinated with

120

nuns? Especially today, when there was all that sex and repression up there on the screen? At least they weren't showing *Black Narcissus*, that was something to be grateful for. Although in a rash moment a year or so back, Sister Bonaventura had confessed that it was Kathleen Byron's portrayal of a nun in that film which had persuaded her into holy orders, the messianic look of jubilation in her face before throwing herself to her death.

Sister Teresa's other colleague from their order, Sister Marguerite, would be attending that afternoon, specifically to go to the seminar on fetishism and fashion; after prayers that morning, she had threatened to break with protocol and go along wearing her traditional habit. See what they have to say about that!

Hannah and Jane were sitting just inside the Café Bar, sharing a crowded table with Mollie Hansen and several other members of the Broadway staff.

"So what do you think?" Mollie asked, spooning chocolatey froth from her cappuccino toward her mouth. "The turnout. You pleased?"

"Why, yes," Jane said, excited. "Aren't you? I mean, I never thought ... I suppose fifty, you know, that would have been terrific. Saturday, people away. But this, well, there must be getting on for eighty, don't you think?"

"Sixty-nine." Mollie matter-of-fact, chocolate or no chocolate.

"Are you sure? I would have thought ... But, well, it's still good; it is, isn't it? Okay? I mean, you are pleased?

"Oh, yes. Yes, it's fine."

"I thought it got us off to a good start," Hannah said. "The first session. She had some really interesting things to say. Don't you think that's right?"

"I thought she was great," enthused Jane. "Really, really good."

"She was all right," said Mollie, who had heard it all before and was wondering if she would bother going back after the break.

Jane had decided to go to the session on fashion, and since Hannah had done all of the reading for the fiction seminar, she would go there. Arriving slightly late, Hannah found herself sitting next to Sister Teresa, who had positioned herself midway along the back row, and immediately behind the young woman with the shaven head.

The group leader, a journalist and published writer herself, kicked things off with some observations about writer and reader, killer and victim, male and female, the weapon and the wound. She referred to an article on slasher movies which talked about the Final Girl, the one woman strong and resourceful enough to defeat the serial attacker, rather than becoming his victim. "The same," she said, "in books. Books by men. Think about *The Silence of the Lambs*. But here, in these books we've been reading by women, this doesn't happen. There is no escape."

She paused and looked out at her audience.

"Now is this because these women writers are more bloodthirsty than their male counterparts, want to scare us, chill us more? Or are they simply being more realistic, more serious, more concerned with the truth? If we become, as some of the female characters in these novels do, fascinated by violence, especially by a combination of violence and sexuality, then there is a price to pay. If you stick us—as someone, as far as we know not a woman, once famously said—do we not bleed?"

She sat down to the sound of coughing, furious scribbling, and some generous applause.

The questions were not all as productive as they might have been; as was often the case, too many people were concerned to state their given positions instead of opening out the discussion. But Sister Teresa asked a quiet, well-formed question about the absence of any wider spiritual morality within which to contain a more individual, sexual one, to which the shaven-haired young woman, who turned out to have a soft, Southern Irish accent, responded by comparing the sexual wounds received by women, the often ritual nature of their bleeding, with the Christian tradition of the piercing of the body of Christ.

At the end of the hour, Hannah's own question, about women asserting their right to explore the nature of their own fascination with violence and domination, remained unasked.

Time for tea, a quick cigarette or two for some, a degree of female bonding, and then back in for the main feature. Teresa barely had time to catch up with Sister Marguerite, her face aglow from good strong argument; for Hannah, a few moments in which to observe Jane's continuing elation that the project on which she had worked so hard was proving such a success.

As she was slipping back in through the front doors, Hannah passed Mollie Hansen, slipping out.

"Not staying for the film, then?"

Mollie shook her head. "I've seen it already."

"And?"

Mollie smiled her oddly invigorating smile. "It's bollocks. If you want an informed opinion." And, sports bag slung over her shoulder, hurried off to her workout in the gym.

Some hundred and thirty-nine minutes later, stumbling somewhat numbed out into daylight, Hannah wondered if Mollie might not have been right. For all those around her who spoke with admiration of the director's control of the big action sequences, or Ralph Fiennes' beauty, there were others who were appalled by the inclusion of a lengthy rape sequence, shot almost entirely from the point of view of the male aggressor.

"Talk about ending the day where you started off," said one of the group, hollering her exasperation. "You expect that kind of thing from someone like Hitchcock, but this is a woman, for fuck's sake!"

"Well, I'm sorry," said another. "But I loved it. Every minute."

Sister Teresa had remained in the cinema some sixty seconds into the scene in question before leaving.

Hannah looked around for Jane, to give her a final hug of congratulation, but failed to pick her out in the crowd that was milling around the service area in the Café Bar. Tired, stimulated, Hannah headed along Goose Gate in the opposite direction to that taken by Lynn Kellogg the night before. She would phone Jane later.

When she rang Jane's number at twenty-five past seven, Alex answered abruptly that she hadn't yet arrived home; at half past nine, there was no answer, and Hannah left a brief message on the machine. It was past one in the morning, Hannah alone in her bed and not quite able to sleep, when Alex phoned her: Jane had still not returned, nor been in touch; he had seen nothing of her, neither hide nor hair.

Twenty-three

Narrow, 1960s modern, the blip of gray-bricked houses presented their backs to the tightly curved sweep of road and the fenced circle of grass on which a rough-coated pony improbably grazed. Trees hung green across broad pavements in need of some repair, and in the gardens of neighboring, older properties, shrubs sat fat and prosperous on swathes of lawn. Sunday morning, less than fifteen minutes brisk walk from the center of the city, still too early for the milkman or the paper boy or the first church bell. The background hum of traffic vied with the sweet, intermittent racket of birds.

The interior of the Peterson house was less parsimonious than its exterior suggested, the rooms surprisingly broad and light, a central stairway opening onto glass. Save for a grandfather clock, clumsy and tall in the space opposite the front door, the furnishings were quite contemporary, blacks and whites and grays in wood and chrome. The walls were cream, a roughish matte finish at one with those places where the exposed brick had been allowed to show through. Paintings hung sparingly, vivid abstracts whose colors seemed to move.

Kitchen and dining room led off the entrance hall on the raised ground floor, spare room, laundry room, and bathroom below; the living room spanned the second floor, opening onto a wide balcony, the main bedroom and en-suite bathroom above.

Alex Peterson unfastened the sliding glass doors that led onto the balcony and stepped outside. For a moment, his body shivered deeply and he reached forward to steady himself, and Resnick, watching from the comfort of a brown leather chair, saw it as a pose and wondered why he felt the need to impress.

Normally a matter that would have been looked into by a junior officer, at this stage at least, Resnick had come out to the house in response to Hannah's mounting distress about her friend, and from a sneaking interest of his own. There had still been no call from Jane, no explanation; the routine inquiries to hospitals and the like had come up blank.

Peterson was wearing mid-blue trousers and a beige V-neck sweater, deck shoes, sockless, on his feet. His hair was suitably awry and he hadn't shaved. Blue eyes, pale, pale blue, showed their concern.

"Are you sure there's nothing you could have forgotten?" Resnick said. "Someone she was going to visit? A friend where she might have stayed?"

"And never phoned?"

"Isn't it possible she forgot? Simply didn't think?"

"Inspector—Charlie—you've got to understand. Jane and I, we make a point of staying in touch." He sat on the settee, angled away from the side wall. "We're very close."

"The day school," Resnick said, "you didn't go?"

Peterson allowed himself a smile. "It's no secret—we talked about it that night at dinner—I don't think time spent on that kind of thing's particularly worthwhile. Dress it up whichever way you like, they weren't exactly going to be discussing *Othello* or *Madame Bovary*. But, no, it was Jane's day. She'd worked hard to see it succeed. I didn't want to intrude."

"You think that's how she would have seen it, if you'd gone along, an intrusion?"

Peterson touched fingertips to the nape of his neck, below the neat line of hair. "Sometimes, and quite wrongly, Jane felt as if her work wasn't really important. She'd seen me build up a successful practice, become, I think it's fair to say, something of an authority, whereas she ..." He leaned forward, earnest in his stare. "No matter how much I encouraged her to think otherwise, Jane always under-valued what she did."

"Does," Resnick said quietly. "What she does."

"Of course. And yesterday, I wanted her to have all the glory. Prove to herself what she could achieve on her own." With a swing of his legs, Peterson was back on his feet. "More coffee?"

Resnick shook his head. "This list of friends," he said, "family. People Jane might have been in contact with. If you could check through it once more, there might be someone who didn't occur to you first time round." He looked at his watch. "I dare say you'll be making some more calls yourself. The next hour or so, you'll hear something, I'm sure."

At the door, Peterson shook Resnick's hand. "Thanks for coming. Handling things yourself. I appreciate that, I really do."

Jane's parents, Tim and Eileen Harker, lived in Wetherby, her father the head teacher of a local primary school, her mother an ex-midwife who baked cakes for the Women's Institute and Mothers' Union, took her turn staffing the Citizens' Advice Bureau, and wrote impassioned letters at the behest of Amnesty International. There was an elder brother, James, who worked as a systems analyst and lived with his wife and three children in Portsmouth, and two sisters. One older, Margaret, married to a sheep farmer in the Dales; the youngest, Diane, unmarried, lived with her two young children in Whitby on the North Yorkshire coast.

By noon, Resnick had spoken to all save Diane, whose number rang and rang unanswered. They were perturbed, confused, unable to supply a satisfactory explanation. The most recent to have spoken to Jane was her mother, who had talked to her on Thursday evening and done her best to allay her daughter's fears about the event she was organizing.

"She was distressed, then?" Resnick said.

"Worried about what might happen, yes. Oh, you know, the usual things—what if one of the speakers didn't arrive, or the film broke down, or ... well, you would have to know Jane to under-stand she could work herself into a lather about any little thing. Usually, without good reason."

"And you think it was this day school that was upsetting her, rather than anything else?"

"Why, yes."

"She didn't seem concerned about anything more personal, Mrs. Harker?"

"I don't understand."

"Nothing between herself and Alex? No big rows, disagreements, something she might have confided to you as her mother?"

Eileen Harker's voice stiffened. "Had my daughter felt the need to confide in me, Inspector, I doubt that I would betray that confidence unless I thought it truly necessary. But let me assure you, nothing of the kind passed between us."

Resnick held the next question for a moment longer on his tongue. "Your relationship with your daughter, Mrs. Harker, would you characterize it as close?"

"I am her mother, Inspector."

"And her marriage, you'd say, for the most part it was happy?"

"It is a marriage, Inspector, like many another."

Resnick understood that for the present that was all the answer he was going to get.

Sections of the *Independent on Sunday* and the *Observer* lay, barely ruffled, in various rooms. Dar Williams' soft, slightly mocking voice drifted out along the hallway.

"Have you get any news?" Hannah called, the moment Resnick set foot in the hail.

"No, nothing."

"Shit!"

When Resnick moved to kiss her, she turned her face away.

"What about Alex, Charlie? What's he got to say about all this?"

"He's no idea where she is."

Hannah laughed, abrupt and loud.

"You think he's lying?"

"Of course. Don't you?"

"I don't know. I'm not sure."

"For God's sake, Charlie, it's your job to be sure."

"Hannah, come on, let's sit down. Have a drink …"

"I don't want a bloody drink!"

"Then let's sit anyway."

"Christ, Charlie!" She glared at him angrily. "Why are you always so fucking reasonable?"

127

The recreation ground was a flat, open space bordered by three roads and a railway line. The far end from Hannah's house was given over to a crown bowling green and a children's playground, a thick hedge separating them from an expanse of trimmed grass circled by well-set shrubs and trees and the path around which Resnick and Hannah slowly walked.

Raucous across Sunday morning, a group of six- to nine-year-olds, white and Asian, vied to see who could reach highest on the swings.

Parents sat on benches, read newspapers, rocked prams. "You haven't said anything to Alex about what he did to her?"

"No. Not yet."

"Why ever not?"

"I'm not sure how far it's relevant."

"God, Charlie! A woman disappears, out of the blue, no apparent reason, no warning, you know her husband's been beating her up and you don't think it's relevant."

"Look." Resnick stopped walking. "Most people who disappear do so of their own volition. A situation, no longer bearable, they're running from; another, more desirable, they're running to. In very few cases is foul play actually involved."

"Except in this case," Hannah said, "we know very well that it was. Alex was beating her up."

"Once."

"No."

"That's all we—you—have proof of, once. And only your word for that."

"You think I'm making it up."

"Of course not."

"Then why won't you act upon it?"

Resnick resumed walking and, almost reluctantly, she fell in step beside him. "I still reckon, the most likely thing, she's gone off somewhere. Maybe just to clear the air. You said, that thing at Broadway, she was excited at the way it went. Buoyed up."

"And that made her run away?"

"Maybe it convinced her that she could."

Hannah shook her head.

"When we get back," Resnick said, "you could make a list of people she worked with at school, talked to; anyone other than yourself she might have confided in. You never know, sometimes it's just a chance remark …"

"Yes," she said a little stiffly, "of course."

There were fourteen names, for almost all of which Hannah had been able to supply addresses or telephone numbers or both; those Jane would have spent the most time with, members of her department, had been neatly asterisked in red. Resnick read through the list twice slowly, eight women, six men. The coffee that he'd made while Hannah was making the list sat, almost finished, by his side.

"You don't think," he asked, "she could have been having an affair?"

Hannah shifted a little in her seat and smiled a wry smile. "With Alex breathing down her neck the whole time, logging her every move? I don't see how she could."

Back at the station, mid-afternoon, Resnick tried Diane Harker's number again and she picked up on the second ring. It was soon clear that, unlike the others Resnick had contacted, this was the first she had heard of Jane's disappearance.

"I thought perhaps you'd already spoken to Alex," Resnick said.

"He'd not phone here. Not if hell were freezing over."

"You had a row?"

"You could say that."

"Can I ask what it was about?"

"My lifestyle, that's what he'd call it, I dare say. Irresponsible. Getting myself pregnant and scrounging off the State."

In the background, Resnick could hear a small child calling, the voice more and more insistent. "You haven't heard from Jane, this weekend?"

"I haven't heard in a good three months."

"You've not seen her?"

"I just said …"

"She's not there with you now?"

"You don't take no for an answer easily, do you?"

"It's important. I need to be sure."

"Well, no, I haven't seen my dear sister and no, I don't know where she is, but one thing, if after all this time she's come to her senses and left that prick of a husband I shall hang out of the upstairs window and cheer."

Twenty-four

Hannah carried the small radio into the bathroom and let Radio 4 voices mill around her as she soaked. It was only when the sound of the telephone interrupted with a new urgency that she realized she had also slept. Clutching a towel against her and dripping water liberally, her hand was reaching for the receiver as the ringing ceased. She immediately punched 1471, but the operator's voice informed her that her caller had exercised his or her option to keep their number to themselves.

Hannah swore, dialed Resnick's number, and got no reply.

She was almost at the bathroom door when she heard the front gate swing closed, the tread of feet, heavy upon the path. Grabbing her robe and hurrying downstairs, she had the latch turned back almost before there was time for the bell to sound.

"Charlie, I ..."

But, no, it was Alex, white-faced, strained, standing there at her door.

"Hannah, I'm sorry, I ... I didn't know where else to go."

She looked at him, those light blue eyes appealing out of the half-dark, and despite wanting to say no, she was sorry, but she was busy, too tired, this wasn't a good time, she found herself taking a step backward and inviting him in.

"Alex, has something happened? You haven't heard from Jane?"

"No. No. Nothing. Nothing at all."

They were standing in Hannah's kitchen at the back of the house and suddenly it seemed cramped and small, the ceiling unnaturally low, Hannah conscious of her nakedness beneath her robe.

"Sit down, Alex. Here. I'll just run upstairs and get changed."

131

"It's okay, I won't stay, I …"

But she pulled out an upright chair from the table and waited until he was sitting, elbow on the table, shoulders slumped.

"Just one minute, right?"

Passing the first-floor living room, she denied an impulse to try Resnick's number again, even have him bleeped from the station. What did she think was going to happen there in her own house? However many times had Alex been there before, Alex and Jane? She knew this was different. In the bedroom, she dressed quickly in functional underwear, a dark, three-button top, loose and shapeless, and blue jeans.

Alex seemed scarcely to have moved, save that his head was resting in his hands. He sat up and turned as she came in. "Look, Hannah, I'm sorry. I probably shouldn't have come."

"Nonsense. Here, let me get you a drink."

"Not a good idea, really. Most likely had too much already." He smiled at her quickly, his eyes searching for sympathy. "My way of getting through the afternoon."

"She'll be in touch, Alex. Really."

"You think so?"

"Yes, of course. She'll phone, make contact somehow. A letter, maybe, first post tomorrow."

"But from where? Where? Where the hell is she?" Surprised to see tears in his eyes, Hannah was tempted to reach out for his hand. "I don't know," she said quietly. "But I'm sure it will be fine." Why was she saying these things, these banalities, words she didn't truly believe? She didn't know a thing, couldn't think, except in dark imaginings, what might have happened to Jane, where she might have gone.

"There's one thought, Hannah," Alex said, "keeps going round and round; this one thought I can't shake. Whatever it is Jane's up to, you must know."

"Alex, I don't. I can assure you."

"She's your friend."

"I know."

"This is where she comes running, any time she's upset, any little disagreement we might have had. Spilling it all out to you."

"Alex, it isn't like that."

"Isn't it?"

Hannah gasped, surprised, as he seized hold of her wrist. All tears had gone now: this was the old Alex, staring at her with the same blue eyes, his fingers biting tight against the bone beneath her skin.

"She made you promise, didn't she? Promise not to tell."

"No."

"Hannah, you've got to tell me."

Straining, Hannah prized back first one of his fingers, then another before wrenching herself away. "Alex, listen to me. I've no idea where Jane is, not a clue where she might be. I'm as much in the dark as you."

He slumped back, his breath accelerated by the effort of holding her.

"Believe me, Alex, I only wish I did."

With a sigh, he bowed his head, hands trapped tight between his knees. "I'm sorry. Really sorry. I didn't mean … I don't know what else to do."

"It's all right. You're upset. I understand. But now I think you must go."

At the door, she watched as he hesitated halfway along the path and turned toward her, his face a rough oval of light. Uncertainly, he raised a hand and then walked on. Hannah stood there several moments longer, gazing out across the empty recreation ground, its gradations of dark.

Inside, she locked the door and slid the bolts across; checked the windows, front and back. In the bathroom, she cleaned her face, tied back her hair, and brushed her teeth. Naked in the attic room, the moment before slipping on the T-shirt in which she slept, a wave of cold ploughed through her, head to foot, the imprint of Alex Peterson's hand clear as daylight on her skin.

Twenty-five

"He attacked you, is that what you're saying?"

"Not attacked, no. That's too strong a word."

"Well, what then?"

"He grabbed hold of me. Here. My arm, wrist. That's all it was."

"Assault, that's what it was."

"God, Charlie ..."

"What?"

"When I told you what he'd done to Jane, it was as though it hardly mattered at all. Now because this has happened to me you're taking it so seriously."

"Of course I am. What else did you expect?"

Sliding her fingers between his, she leaned forward against him, her face smooth against the breadth of his shoulder. "I don't know," she said. Rarely, if ever, had she seen him show so much anger.

Hannah had arrived at Resnick's house early, dressed for school, her reddish hair swept tidily back from her face. Only when chunks of dubious-looking meat and jelly had been forked into the four cats' bowls, coffee brewed and toast made, had she told him of Alex's visit the night before.

Resnick listened carefully and then made her go through the whole thing again. This time he was calmer, more under control.

"I think he's worried, Charlie, genuinely worried. All that business, tears and everything, of course I could be wrong, but I don't think he was acting."

"Then you've changed your mind? The other day, what you seemed to be suggesting was that he'd done something to her. Alex. Harmed her in some way. Now you're less certain?"

Hannah eased her chair away from the table and immediately Miles sprang up into her lap. Only a month ago, she would have pushed him away. "Yes, I suppose so," she said.

Resnick got up and fetched the coffee pot, topping up his own cup and Hannah's as well.

"What I think is," Hannah said, "he's so used to being in control, the minute he loses it, he just doesn't know what to do. So he lashes out, uses force." She glanced again at the purple finger marks on her arm. "And he's strong, Charlie. He really is."

Hannah was reaching for her coat, Resnick piling the pots into the sink, when the phone rang.

"Charlie? Brian Findley. This girl, Charlie. The canal. The one you were interested in."

"Go on."

"Australian was right. Well, Tasmanian. All part of the same thing nowadays, I dare say."

Hannah was standing anxiously in the doorway and Resnick gestured to show that no, it was nothing to do with Jane, no news good or bad.

"Miranda Conway," Findley continued, "that's her name. Twenty-one. Dental charts confirmed the identification. Her parents are flying over now, though it's not clear what we can do about releasing the body. Anyway, thought you'd like to know. And Charlie ..."

"Yes."

"About your Serious Crimes post—right, wasn't I? That Siddons woman." Findley laughed. "Well out of it, mate, that's my way of thinking. My DCI may be a prick, but at least he's got one."

By shortly after half past nine, they were gathered in the CID office: Kevin Naylor in brown cords and a blue cotton shirt, tie loosened at the neck, top button undone; Carl Vincent, sitting across from him with a can of Diet Coke in his hand, wearing a gracefully crumpled linen suit and a white poplin shirt that had come all the way from India via Wealth of Nations; Lynn Kellogg's top was maroon, her skirt a serviceable black and not so tight as to make it difficult for her to run if the occasion demanded; off to one side, Millington sat hunched at a desktop, the jacket of his St. Michael suit folded alongside. Resnick's own suits had for the most part been custom-made by a tailor–uncle, according to patterns fashionable in Krakow circa 1939, broad-lapelled, double-breasted, and, fortunately, generous in cut; they had been in and out of fashion countless times and this one would have been fashionable still, were it not for the irremovable stain of paprika goulash and the presence of a safety pin which prevented—just—the striped lining falling down below the cuff.

"First things first," Resnick said. "It's been confirmed Lynn's taking up her promotion as sergeant within the Serious Crime Squad, where she'll be working under DCI Siddons. She starts at the end of the week."

Vincent and Millington applauded, while Naylor looked on, his pleasure for her tinged with envy. Little more than a year ahead of him in service and he had still to sit for his boards, never mind pass.

"I know we're all pleased, Lynn, a promotion long overdue, but that doesn't mean we won't miss having you around. Right now especially." At which Lynn, feeling herself beginning to blush, turned away at her desk and sent a set of papers skimming to the floor, causing her to blush more deeply still.

"The second thing," Resnick went on, no longer looking directly at Lynn, sharing a little of her embarrassment, "is Mark. I don't know how long it is since any of you have seen him, but I spent some time with him the other day and he was in a bad way. It's a good while yet till he's up in court and it's important he holds himself together meantime. So if there's anything you think you can do—drop round, phone, whatever—now's the time. Okay?"

Nods and half-spoken promises; each of them had made some attempt at getting close to Mark Divine in the weeks following his attack and each had been rebuffed.

"Right," Resnick said, "what's outstanding?"

Millington cleared his throat. "Them post office raids, I've got three names now, likely involved. Best information says they're revving up to try again, Gedling this time out. Must've got sick of Beeston."

"Don't blame them," Lynn said acidly. She had spent an uncomfortable six months rooming there before moving into her present flat.

Millington went on, ignoring her. "Liaising through Central. Harry Payne's got half a dozen from Support Department on stand-by. Any luck, we'll take 'em as they leave."

Resnick nodded and turned his attention to Kevin Naylor, who was fumbling his notebook from the inside pocket of his jacket, draped across the back of a nearby chair.

"These incidents of arson," Naylor said, continuing to flick through pages, "one of the blokes involved ... Cryer ... that's it, Cryer, John Cryer ..."

"Auto theft, isn't it?" Millington interrupted. "His speciality. The Cryer I'm thinking on? Gone down, oh, twice now."

"Cryer and this other feller," Naylor continued, "Benny Bailey ..."

"I knew a Ben Bailey," Vincent chipped in. "Leicester. Credit cards, though, that was his thing."

Resnick had known a Benny Bailey, too, known of him: a bopper whose first job had been trumpet with Jay McShann. He didn't suppose that was the same Bailey either.

"Anyway," Naylor was saying, "seems Cryer and this Bailey had an arrangement, lifting high-end motors, and shipping them across to the continent."

"Enough to bring them in, Kevin?" Resnick asked.

"Waiting on a fax from the ferry company. Copy of their manifests."

"Okay, keep me posted. Lynn, what about these warring parties back of Balfour Street?"

"Pretty much calmed down now. Court injunctions helped and getting the eldest youth from the one family shut away on remand's been no bad thing, either."

"Good. Have a word with the local uniforms, ask them to keep an eye. Meantime, we'll be getting an official report today," Resnick said, "woman gone missing. Jane Peterson. Mid-thirties, teacher at that comprehensive by the Forest. Not been seen since late Saturday afternoon. Husband claims no knowledge of her whereabouts, where she might be. I've spoken to him. Relatives, close friends, they've all been checked."

137

"Boyfriend?" Lynn asked. "Lover?"

"Not as far as we know."

"What did she take with her?" Vincent asked.

"Pretty much what she was standing up in."

"Bank account, credit cards?"

"We're checking that today. There's a list of colleagues at work needs following up on, another of more casual acquaintances, friends. Lynn, I thought while you're still here, you might drop by the school. Phone the head first, usual thing."

"Okay."

"Carl, just as long as that business in London's hanging fire, maybe you can pitch in as well?"

"Right."

"What with that woman we found floating in the Beeston Canal," Millington said, "and this recent job out Worksop way, you're not reckoning that's what we've got here?"

"Let's hope not, Graham."

"'Cause if it is, it'll be out of our hands. Just the kind of thing Serious Crimes'll want to cut their teeth on."

Everyone looked across at Lynn, who was busy searching inside her desk for a new notebook, any old biro.

Twenty-six

Since Resnick had last been in the building, Mollie Hansen had moved office. No longer squeezed into a shoebox room where her desk was overlooked by a near life-size poster of k.d. lang, Mollie now shared the top floor of the narrow building with her assistant, a large photocopier, and a fax, the assistant at that moment being occupied elsewhere.

"Hello," she said brightly, as Resnick's head and shoulders appeared above the top of the stairs, "what are you doing here?"

For answer, Resnick held up two polystyrene cups of cappuccino and a paper bag containing a brace of toasted teacakes.

"Ooh, bribery and corruption," Mollie grinned, "I thought that usually worked the other way round."

Setting the cups on the desk and depositing the bag, dark where the butter had leaked, onto an old copy of *Screen International*, Resnick swung across a chair and sat down.

"It's too much to hope this is purely a social call," Mollie said. She was wearing a short slate blue dress and bright blue plimsolls with stars on their heels.

"Not exactly."

"How about not at all?"

He smiled and levered open his coffee, only spilling a very little onto the top of Mollie's desk.

"Don't worry," she said, "it'll just merge in with the rest." Her teacake was excellent, slightly spicy, and generous enough with butter for it to run down the outer edge of her hand, causing her to dip her head and lick it away. All that was left to consider now was the etiquette of using her tongue on the chocolate nestling inside the lid.

"Jane Peterson," Resnick said.

"What about her?"

"How well d'you know her?"

"Not very. She was helping to organize this day school last weekend, we met quite a few times because of that. But, you know, meetings, agendas, they don't give you a lot of time to chat. And she wasn't one to hang around after in the bar."

"You didn't know her socially, then? You never talked about anything personal? Husband, family, anything like that?"

"Sorry, not really, no."

Resnick nodded. "And Saturday, how did she seem?"

Mollie drank some more coffee, thinking back. "She was fine. A bit worked-up, but you'd expect that. I don't think she'd been involved with anything like this before. But when everything was more or less okay, she was pleased. Lively, like I say." Mollie set down her cup and looked at Resnick steadily across her desk. "Now I don't suppose you'd like to tell me what's going on? Has something happened to her or what?"

"Why d'you say that?"

Mollie angled back her head and laughed out loud. "Come on! You're up those stairs first thing in the morning—well, first thing for some of us—first time you've gone out of your way to see me in ages. And bearing gifts. Which I can hardly get round to, because of all the questions about Jane Peterson you're firing at me. And you want to know why I think something's happened?"

"She's gone missing," Resnick said. "Since the end of the day school on Saturday."

"Right," Mollie said, "I see." And then: "She wasn't at the end of the day school on Saturday."

They were walking along Stoney Street, toward St. Mary's Church on High Pavement; the Ice Stadium was away to their left. Just as Mollie had been about to continue, her assistant had returned; the fax machine had begun chattering and then the whirr of the photocopier. It was quieter on the streets.

"You're sure she wasn't there till the end?" Resnick said. "Positive?"

"I was looking for her when the film came out. Aside from anything else, I had this free Friends membership to give her, a few comps, just a way of saying thanks. When I didn't see her, I asked around in case she'd come out early or whatever. Everyone I spoke to—I don't know, half a dozen, maybe—they all swore she'd not been in to the film at all."

"There's got to be a possibility they were mistaken, surely? It is dark in there, after all."

"Yes, but not that dark. And one of the women I spoke to had been at the seminar on fetishism earlier. According to her, Jane had been there and left halfway through."

"Which would have been when?"

"Half-two, quarter to three."

"And as far as you know, nobody saw her after that?"

"Not at Broadway, no."

Resnick's mind was racing between possibility and wilder speculation; he slowed himself down, making minor adjustments, adding as much as four hours to the time Jane had been missing, the opportunity she had had to get clear. But clear to where?

"If I come back to the office, you can get me a list of everyone who attended?"

"No problem."

"Good. We'll need confirmation."

As they went up the worn steps to the small graveyard that surrounded the church, he asked Mollie if she'd noticed any changes in Jane Peterson's manner during the weeks they'd been meeting.

Slowing her pace, Mollie thought it over. "She was a bit up and down, that's all. Positive most of the time, but then any little thing could throw her into a panic." Mollie smiled a sideways smile. "Not exactly your classic cool."

Resnick nodded: he couldn't imagine Mollie panicking over anything.

They passed around by the front of the church, where a lank man in a cassock was arguing with a homeless youth and his spindly dog, who were trying to make their bed in the covered porch.

"We'd best turn around," Resnick said.

"Yes," Mollie agreed, "I suppose we should."

Fascinating, Mollie thought, walking on at Resnick's side, how going out with Hannah had changed him. Not simply that Hannah had dragged him along, more or less willingly, to see movies quite a few times, and foreign art movies at that. It was something about the way he was with women that had altered, the way he was with her. Before, whatever the reason, he had always seemed on edge, as if never knowing quite how to respond. But the few times she'd run across him in the Café Bar lately—and now—he seemed more at ease, able to relax in her company. Which was true for her too.

Odd, wasn't it, Mollie thought, this big, slightly shambolic man with whom she had practically nothing in common, how she could feel drawn to him as much as she did.

By late that afternoon, Lynn and Carl between them had spoken to most of those members of staff who had any close connection with Jane. There was almost unanimous agreement that she was a good teacher, a little scatterbrained occasionally perhaps, not always totally on top of things where her preparation was concerned, and she had been known to be late; but she cared about what she was doing and, most important, had a good relationship with the children in her care. Most knew that she was married to a dental surgeon, quite a few knew his name was Alex, but not many had actually laid eyes on him. Alex Peterson was not one for attending school functions. Come to that, neither was his wife. Not unless her presence was mandatory. It was the one other area in which she had come in for a little mild criticism. But then, as Jane had apparently said not a few times, her husband worked hard, long hours, and when he did get home he liked her to be there. Old-fashioned, maybe, hardly likely to endear her to the school's few remaining militant feminists, but by and large people respected what she said and did. It was her life, after all.

The few friends and acquaintances Alex had listed who were not from the school had been more widely dispersed and hence more difficult to track down. Those Lynn or Carl were able to speak to only confirmed the prevailing picture of a rather highly strung woman with a bright mind who was happily, closely married to an articulate, intelligent, caring man. The kind of man, it was suggested, you didn't let go of easily.

Only one person, an osteopath whom Jane had consulted some eighteen months before, and whom she and Alex had met socially a few times since, suggested anything different. His automatic response, when questioned by Lynn, was to assume that Jane had left her husband, and gave her decision a seal of approval by adding, "Not before time."

When Lynn asked if he would care to explain what he meant, he first declined, then agreed to speak to her in person at eight forty-five the following morning. His first appointment, he explained, was at nine.

Resnick had noticed Sister Marguerite's name on the list of people who had attended the seminar on fetishism and fashion, and he made the short journey down to the sisters' house in Hyson Green himself.

When he arrived, a red-faced Sister Bonaventura was hauling great loads of washing out of the machine and sorting it for hanging from the crisscross of lines they had set up in the small back yard.

"Every dozen things we peg out," she complained, "two get swiped by the kids from the youth club next door."

Sister Marguerite was sitting in the front room, calculator in one hand and pencil in the other, figuring out that month's accounts on the backs of several envelopes before transferring the figures into the triple-entry ledger that lay nearby.

"Wouldn't you think, Inspector, people in holy orders should be exempt from paying VAT?"

Resnick waited until she had double-checked the household expenses column, before asking her about the day school.

"I was only present for the one seminar," she explained. "Fashion, dress, the meanings we attach to them; it's always been a subject that's interested me greatly."

"Isn't it true," Sister Bonaventura called from the other room, "you'd have been a model if you weren't a nun?"

"It's true," Sister Marguerite agreed, "it is a calling I felt very responsive to."

"You and Naomi Campbell on the catwalk at the same time, no one would know where to look." Sister Bonaventura set a mug of strong-looking tea in Resnick's hand. "PG Tips, it's all we can afford. Biscuits are out of the question."

Resnick thanked her and asked Sister Marguerite whether she had realized who Jane Peterson was and if she had seen her at the seminar.

"Sister Teresa pointed her out to me when I arrived, as one of the organizers, you see. And yes, she was with us, but not for long. Until the questions started, I think that's when it was."

"Roughly how long would this be after the session had started?" Resnick asked.

"Oh, forty minutes, no more. Certainly not as much as an hour. I assumed she had popped into the other seminar to see how they were getting on."

But Resnick had already checked that this was not so, and he did so again when Sister Teresa arrived, back from visiting a residential home for the elderly and infirm. "No," she stated confidently, "the lunch break was the last time I saw her, I'm positive about that. She certainly didn't come in to us."

Teresa walked with Resnick along the side passage and out onto the street. Traffic was heavy in both directions, backed up from the lights, and youths with squeegees and tattered ends of chamois leather darted in and out between the cars, prizing back windscreen wipers and furiously polishing at the glass, hands thrust out for small change.

"Our mutual friend," she said, "have you seen any more of him?"

"We paid a visit," Resnick said.

"We?"

"A colleague and myself."

"He's in trouble again, then, is he? He'll go to prison?"

"That's very much up to him."

Teresa glanced up at him, narrowing her eyes against the fading sun. "Repent, is that what he has to do? Confess his sins and be cleansed?"

"I think," Resnick smiled, "something in the way of restitution might be involved."

"A little penance, too?"

"Rather more than ten Hail Marys, the Stations of the Cross."

Sister Teresa took a step back toward the house. "I have it in mind to travel down to London shortly; there's an exhibition I very much want to see. Degas."

"And you were thinking you might ask Jerzy to join you?"

"It's so much more pleasurable, looking at paintings with someone who knows more than you do."

"I'm sure."

"And you'd have no objection?"

Again Resnick smiled. "You might want to let me know when it is you're going. Just in case there's a message it might be advantageous for you to pass along."

"Advantageous," Teresa asked, "to whom?"

When Resnick got back to the station, Alex Peterson was waiting for him, the expression on his face making it clear he had heard nothing from his wife. "Come on up to my office," Resnick said, "we can talk there."

A message from Hannah lay on his desk: called four thirty-five, ring back. He would as soon as he got the chance.

"Have a seat," Resnick said pleasantly enough, but for now Peterson preferred to stand.

"I'd like to know," Peterson said, "precisely what it is you've been doing."

Resnick waited, allowing the anger in the man's tone to fade out on the air. "Following the usual procedures."

"Which are?"

"Making contact, asking questions, establishing when and where the missing person was last seen."

"Christ, we know all that. We've known it since Saturday night. Seven o'clock that evening. Six thirty or seven."

"Half past two," Resnick said.

"What?"

"As best we can tell, she left the building at half past two. There's no report of anyone seeing her since then."

Alex Peterson sat down. Resnick waited for him to put his face in his hands and he did. When he looked up, it was to say, "There's got to be something else you could be doing."

"Not at this stage."

"At this stage? What do you have to do, wait until someone finds her in a bloody ditch?"

"Is that what you think's happened?"

"Of course not."

"Then there's little more we can do besides wait for her to get in touch."

"Surely you can ask at the station, the airport, wherever? She had to leave somehow. Maybe she hired a car."

Resnick leaned forward in his chair. "Mr. Peterson—Alex—I'm afraid in a way you're right. Unless we have reasonable cause for suspecting foul play, I simply can't commit more personnel."

"Jesus!"

"What you might consider doing is taking a photograph to one of those quick print places, getting some fliers made. There's nothing to stop you asking questions of your own accord."

"Aside from time."

I thought this was important, Resnick thought, more important than a few lost fillings and the odd wisdom tooth. It worried him that he felt this bristling animosity toward the man, made him wonder for a moment if he would do more if he felt otherwise. But, no, at this stage he was doing all that was possible.

"Look," Resnick said, "Jane's a grown woman, an adult person, perfectly responsible for her own decisions. There's not a single thing, at present, to suggest that wherever she's gone, wherever she is, she's not there of her own accord."

"I could go to the paper," Peterson said, "offer a reward."

"You could. Though in my experience you might be buying yourself more trouble than it's worth."

"At least it would be doing something."

"Yes." He wanted Peterson to leave so that he could phone Hannah; it wasn't beyond question that Jane might have contacted her. But there Peterson continued to sit, staring at Resnick through resentful, accusing eyes. Resnick remembered the bruises on Hannah's wrist.

"I have to ask you again," Resnick said, "you've no inkling where she might have gone?"

"Of course not."

"No special place, special friend …"

"No."

"And there was nothing between the two of you, nothing that happened prior to Saturday that might have led to her leaving?"

Peterson was half out of his chair. "That would just suit you, wouldn't it?"

"I don't understand."

"Making it my fault. Then you could wash your hands of the whole bloody affair."

"You were the one, wanted me to do more. What I'm looking for is motive."

"What you're looking for is to lay blame."

Peterson was leaning forward across Resnick's desk, hands gripping the sides. Sweat was blotched across his face and a vein was standing out, blue and strong, to one side of his temple.

"Do you always," Resnick asked, "lose your temper this easily?"

"Only when I lose my fucking wife!"

"Or ask questions that people can't answer."

Peterson blinked and blinked again. At first, he didn't know what Resnick was alluding to.

"It's not a good idea," Resnick said, "to lay your hands on anyone. Certainly not in anger. Do I make myself clear?"

Peterson straightened, the color drained out of his face. "I was worked up, anxious. I'd scarcely slept. Waiting round all that time for Jane to call. Maybe I wasn't quite in control."

"Exactly."

Peterson hated having to back down, but he did. Awkwardly, he brushed the sweat away from his eyes, wriggled inside his clothes. "I don't normally lose my temper, Inspector. It's not how I am."

Resnick stared back at him and didn't say a thing.

Twenty-seven

It was the same dream Lynn had experienced so many times: the same sense of fear mixed with exhilaration, terror mingled with release. Her arms were tied, chained, she was handcuffed behind her back, the man standing over her, now kneeling, face blurring in and out of focus, changing identity. Michael's soft voice with that faint Irish tinge she had never been certain was real or assumed. Michael Best's voice and then her father's; her father's and then Resnick's face. Whose mouth? Whose arms? She rolled out from the knotted sheets, the damp pillow halfway down the bed.

What had the therapist called her when she'd gone back to seeing her for the second time? A textbook case. Powerlessness and control; authority, domination; fear of the father, need for the father; passivity and penetration; absolution and guilt.

Lynn switched on the shower, waited for the water temperature to settle, then stepped into the spray. Michael Best was serving life imprisonment for the murder of one woman and the kidnapping of another, herself. It was doubtful that he would ever be released. Her father was even now stalking the runs of his Norfolk chicken farm, smoking the same wafer-thin hand-rolled cigarettes as he had for more than forty years and coughing up golden spitballs of phlegm. The cancer that had hospitalized him two years before was still in abeyance, held there by sticky tape and prayer. And Resnick … Lynn opened her eyes beneath the water and tilted back her head. Just a few more days and then she would be walking into a different office every morning, fresh voices, different faces. Not his. She should have done it a long time before. Either that or something else.

◆◆◆

Alan Prentiss began each day with twenty minutes' meditation, fifteen minutes of simple exercises, a bowl of rolled oats mixed with skimmed milk, nuts, dried apricots, and chopped banana. Alternately, *The Times* or *Telegraph* crossword. Four letters, ending in L and beginning with A, the word his wife had scratched into the leather of the raised couch where he treated his patients, the one morning she got up earlier than him and left.

Not before time, his own words, unguarded and instinctive, when he'd understood that policewoman to say Jane Peterson had left her pompous shit of a husband.

Not before time, the tongues loosened behind his back when Cassie had caught the early-bird flight from East Midlands to Edinburgh and the man she had met at an Open University summer school the year before. She was married now, remarried, not to her fellow student from the OU, but to a furniture upholsterer who, like Prentiss—the only way in which he was like Prentiss—lived above his place of work. They all three lived over his place of work, Cassie and the upholsterer and their child.

Prentiss capped his Parker ballpoint, looked at his watch and, automatically, checked it against the clock. She would be here in ten minutes, the woman from the police, always assuming she wasn't late.

He washed and put away the breakfast things, went up to the bathroom and cleaned his teeth, assiduously rinsed his mouth, watered the house plant on the landing which needed refreshing every other day, and neatly refolded his copy of *The Times* with the front page uppermost. There was a scene at the end of *Damage*, a film Prentiss knew a lot of people derided, in which Jeremy Irons, returning from the little shopping expedition he clearly made each morning, took the paper bag in which he'd carried home his loaf of bread, folded it neatly once and then folded it again, before adding it to the precise pile of similar bags on one side of his small kitchen. To Prentiss, there was nothing strange about such behavior, nothing obsessive. It was simply what one did.

Before he could look at his watch again, Lynn Kellogg was walking up the three steps to the front door, finger pointing toward the bell.

◆◆◆

They sat in the long downstairs room where Prentiss saw his patients, the room formed from taking out the middle wall and running what had previously been two smaller rooms together. Two certificates authenticating Prentiss' rights to practice hung framed on one wall; they were the only decoration among the purely functional: desk, treatment couch, lamp, table, chairs, stool. Lace curtains hung inside plain, heavy drapes, guard against the prying eyes of any West Bridgford neighbors.

"I'm sorry if this is rather rushed," Prentiss said. "It's only that ..."

"You have a patient."

"Yes."

"Osteopathy, that's what you do?"

Prentiss nodded.

"You manipulate, then, is that right? Bones?"

"Bones, yes. Other parts of the body, too."

Lynn clicked open her bag and took out her notebook. Left tired by her disturbed night, shadows deep beneath her eyes, her skin, despite makeup, was, for her, oddly pale. She'd intended to wear the new outfit she'd bought that weekend at Jigsaw, break it in before starting the new job, but this morning it would have been, she felt, a waste. Instead, she had pulled a pair of blue jeans back out from the laundry basket, an old pink shirt, badly faded, from a pile of things she scarcely ever wore, and finished off with a baggy cardigan her mum had bought for her in Norwich BHS two years before. She looked a state and she didn't care.

Alan Prentiss thought she looked rather nice. He wished now he'd suggested half past eight, thought to offer coffee, make tea.

"That was how you met Jane Peterson," Lynn asked, "she came to you for treatment?"

"The first occasion, yes. After that, I think possibly I may have said on the phone, we met socially a few times ..."

"You and Jane?"

"Jane and Alex. Dinner, whatever, it was always Jane and Alex and, well, I was seeing somebody then, a friend of Jane's actually, a colleague. Patricia. She'd recommended me."

"A foursome, then."

"Yes."

"And you got on? All of you together."

"No. Not really, no. I mean Jane and Patricia were okay, they had something in common, at least. Teaching. The school. But Alex and I …" Prentiss shook his head. "When Patricia and I stopped seeing one another, that was it."

"No more contact."

"That's right."

"Not socially."

"No."

"How did you feel about that?"

"To be honest, I was relieved. We'd never really hit it off, not all together."

Lynn began to write something in her book and thought better of it. "But you liked her, Jane?"

"Felt sorry for her might be closer to the mark."

"Sorry, why was that?"

"You've met Alex Peterson?"

Lynn shook her head.

"You should and then you'd know. Oh, he's charming—I suppose he's charming—good-looking, in the kind of way some women think of as good-looking—undoubtedly intelligent. But arrogant, of course, intellectually. Always spoiling for a fight."

"A fight? What kind of a fight?"

"One that he can win."

Footsteps hesitated outside and Lynn hoped it wasn't Prentiss' nine o'clock come early. She noticed him glancing at his watch.

"Why did she consult you in the first place?" Lynn asked.

"She was having pain here …" Stretching, he illustrated the back of the neck at the left side, where it runs into the shoulder. "She'd been to her GP, had pills. No good. She wondered if there was anything I could do to help."

"And was there?"

"A little. Very little. After one or two sessions, some of the soreness had gone, there was more freedom of movement. If she'd carried on attending regularly, I might have been able to do more."

"She stopped, then?"

Prentiss checked some calculation behind partly closed eyes.

"Offhand I would say she came to me six or seven times; if it's important, I could look it up."

Lynn raised a hand, gesturing for him to sit back down. "What did you think," she said, "was the source of the problem?"

Prentiss drew in breath sharply through his nose. "Him."

"Her husband?"

"I shouldn't say that, I suppose. It's probably unfair, but after meeting them, seeing them together, yes, that's what I think."

Lynn was leaning forward in her chair, elbows on her knees. "What was it," she said, "about him?"

"I've said. He was a bully. Always shooting her down. If she sat saying nothing, he'd taunt her, tease her. And when she did open her mouth, in his mocking, superior way, he'd tear her to shreds."

"And this was causing the problems with her back?"

"Her neck, yes. I think so. Stress. It affects us, you know, the way we are physically. It isn't always a case of overstraining, of bad posture."

Lynn sat straight, leaning her spine against the back of the hard chair. "Did you say any of this to her?"

Prentiss was slow to reply. There were steps now, approaching the door. "Not quite directly, no. But I think I implied the answer might be, well, elsewhere."

"How did she respond?"

"She stopped coming. Cancelled one or two appointments at first, always with good reason, but then I realized she wasn't coming back at all."

"And were you still seeing her and her husband together at this time?"

He shook his head. "No, that was after Patricia and I ..." He let the sentence hang.

Even though both of them had been anticipating it, each jumped at the sound of the bell. Standing, Lynn closed her notebook. "I'd just like to be certain. The problems Jane was having, it is your professional opinion that her husband was to blame?"

"Professional, I don't know. Perhaps I should never have said it so strongly. I'm sorry. It was indiscreet."

A smile edged its way around Lynn's lips. From this one meeting, the look of his house, everything plain and proper and in its proper place, indiscreet wasn't a word she would have readily associated with Alan Prentiss. "Perhaps it was just an honest reaction; you said what you felt. There's nothing wrong in that."

"Some people wouldn't necessarily agree."

Lynn hoisted her bag onto her shoulder and thanked him for his time.

At twelve thirty that day, Resnick received a phone call from Suzanne Olds' secretary: Mark Divine had missed his noon appointment, the second time this had happened. Ms. Olds had thought the inspector might like to know.

Resnick caught up on some paperwork, grabbed himself a sandwich from across the street, and finally snagged Millington in a slack moment, the sergeant just back from a lunch-time pint and a pie with the boss of the Support Group, and they drove out to Divine's together.

Ragged and ill-matched, the curtains were drawn across the windows of the first-floor flat, but in Divine's current state of mind, that didn't have to mean a thing. Neither the butcher nor his assistant could remember seeing Divine leave that morning, though for that matter, they couldn't swear to having clapped eyes on him since before the weekend.

On the landing, first Millington, then Resnick tried the door. The sound of the TV could be heard distinctly from inside. That didn't have to mean anything either. One, then another, then both together called Divine's name.

"Maybe sloped off for a few days," Millington suggested. "Change of scene."

And maybe, Resnick was thinking, he's inside there now, unconscious, taken an overdose or worse. "Check back downstairs, Graham, see if there's a spare key."

There was, at least there was in theory; Divine himself had borrowed it, having lost his own, and it had never been returned.

"You thinking what I'm thinking?" Millington asked, eyeing the door.

"Likely, Graham."

It only took one shoulder charge to soften it up, and then a foot, flat and hard, close to the lock.

The interior stank of rotting food, stale beer and cigarettes, unflushed urine but, thankfully, nothing worse. Of Divine there was no sign.

"Not scarpered, look. Not 'less he's leaving all this stuff of his behind."

Resnick scribbled a note, asking Divine to get in touch. Once again, he left his own numbers and Hannah's as well. Millington, meantime, used the butcher's phone to call a locksmith he knew and arranged to have the door fixed before the end of the day.

"I'll keep an eye," the butcher said. "Do me best to make sure no bugger slips up there, fills the place with needles and worse."

"Right," Resnick said, "thanks. And if you do spot him coming back himself, you might let us know. Graham here, or myself."

"'Course. Can't do you a deal on some nice chump chops, can I? Seeing as you're here. Take one of these home," he said to Millington, "put a smile on your missus's face and no mistake."

"Thanks," said Resnick, shaking his head. "Not right now."

Unwrap one of those within sniffing range of Madeleine, Millington was thinking, she'd get a look on her face, turn milk sour over a five-mile radius.

Twenty-eight

At first sight, he had taken it for a kestrel, but as it came closer, hovering above the shimmer of grass, the reddish underside and rounded wings marked it clearly as a young sparrowhawk.

Up here, from one of a number of wooden benches strategically placed around the area of some ancient burial ground, Grabianski could look down across a swathe of land that had been left to grow like meadow; the drying tops of grass blurred orange to bluish-brown and back again and, as Grabianski watched, alert, the sparrowhawk marked out its territory between an irregular triangle of oaks, firm against the occasional forays of crows.

At Grabianski's back, purple foxgloves twined out of the sparse undergrowth, and two benches to his right a young woman with almost white hair lay on her back, eyes closed, a copy of Emily Dickinson open on her naked chest. The engraving on the bench against which Grabianski himself leaned read: *Ethel Copland Campbell 1897-1987. Vegetarian. Socialist. Pacifist.* It was that kind of a place.

He was trying not to think about paintings, forged or otherwise, not to think about his dealings with Vernon Thackray, Eddie Snow. And Resnick, a man whose word he trusted, who, on certain levels, he admired—someone whom, had their lives but shaken down differently, Grabianski might have been pleased to call a friend— how seriously did he have to take the threat of being fitted into a frame and locked in tight?

He watched as the hawk rode the air with the smallest movement of wings and then dropped, almost faster than he could follow, down into the grass and away, a vole or some such fast in its grasp.

Marvellous, Grabianski thought, as the bird was lost to sight between the branches of the farthest tree, how life did that, offered up those little scraps, parables for you to snack on, inwardly digest.

The lower reaches of Portobello were lined by barrows selling fruit and vegetables at knockdown prices, stripy watermelons sliced open, lemons tumbling yellow inside blue tissue. The same black guy, wearing a wide white shirt with a gathered yoke, winked at Grabianski from the doorway of the Market Bar and stepped aside to let him through.

Moving slowly toward the bar, letting his eyes become adjusted to the filtered light, Grabianski saw Eddie Snow seated in the far corner, talking earnestly to a youngish man with shoulder-length hair. The woman Grabianski had seen him with before, the model, was perched on a stool close by, flawless, bored.

Grabianski ordered his pint of beer and waited, certain Snow would have seen him; now it was a matter of form, of etiquette, waiting to see when and how that recognition would be acknowledged.

What happened was that the young woman leaned forward at a sign from Snow's beckoning finger and after a brief discussion, got down from her stool and came to where Grabianski was standing, one arm against the surface of the bar.

"I'm Faron," she said, and Grabianski nodded pleasantly, wondering if some of the things he'd read about her were true. He hadn't recognized her before, not really, a face, thin and feral, like so many that stared out at him, big-eyed, from the fronts of glossy magazines. She was wearing shiny silver tights, clumpy thick-heeled shoes, and either a dress that was really a petticoat or a petticoat that was really a dress.

"Eddie says he's busy."

"I can see."

"It's important he says, like business. Is it okay for you to wait?"

Grabianski assured her that was fine; she made no move to walk away and when he offered her a drink she asked for an Absolut with ice and tonic and a slice of lemon not lime. According to her press releases she had been born and brought up in Hoxton, East

London, one of five children, none of them named Faron nor anything like; the fashion editor for British *Vogue* had noticed her behind the till at a garage in Lea Bridge Road when she called in for petrol on her way back from a photo shoot in Epping Forest. Wearing one of those awful pink overalls, of course, oil and the Lord knows what underneath her fingernails, but those eyes, those tremendous waiflike eyes.

Not so many months later, after numerous makeovers, a spot of minor surgery, and a name change, there she was in grainy black and white and bleached-out color, wearing price-on-application designer clothing in some industrial wasteland, staring empty eyes and legs akimbo. Since when, affairs with movie stars of both sexes, private clinics, smoked-glass limousines; rumor was she'd turned down a cameo part in the new Mike Leigh—or was that Spike?—and recorded a song for which Tricky did the final mix, but which had yet to be released. Rumor, juiced with money, will say almost anything.

Grabianski wondered if she were yet nineteen.

"What d'you do, then?" she asked.

"I'm a burglar," Grabianski said.

"Go on, you're winding me up."

"No, I'm not."

"Yeah? What you burgle then?"

"Houses, apartments, the usual thing."

She laughed, a giggle, brittle and fast. "You burgle Eddie, then?"

"Not yet."

She leaned a little away from him, uncertain. "Great security, Eddie, alarms and that, all over. Well, he has to. Paintings and that. Worth a fortune. It's what he's interested in, art." For a moment, she glanced round. "That bloke with him, Sloane, he's an artist. Painter. You know him? He's good. Galleries and that. I've never been, museums, they're boring. Well, I'm a liar, not since I was a kid. School trip, down the Horniman. Lost my knickers, coming back."

Grabianski was looking past her, past those famous eyes and over her shoulder at the man she'd identified as Sloane. His head in profile now and Grabianski could see he was nowhere near as young as he'd first thought. The build, style of the hair had deceived. The nose was full, patrician, etched here and there with tiny broken violet lines. The hair, full at the front too, had grown white above the temples; the lips, narrow and wide, were cracked. Sixty, Grabianski thought, sixty if he's a day.

"I'll tell you how good he is," Faron said. "We was round his place one day, his studio, you know, and I made some joke about Van Gogh, about him slicing off his ear, and Sloane, he got this painting off the wall, turned it round right where he was and done these sunflowers on the back. You never seen nothing like it. They was just like the real thing. Better. But then that's me, I wouldn't really know."

Grabianski nodded and filed it all away.

When Sloane walked past them and around the angle of the bar, Grabianski saw that he'd been right about the age. Sixty-two or sixty-three, he wouldn't have minded betting. Wearing nothing, nothing Grabianski could see, beneath a pair of paint-patched denim dungarees. Clear blue eyes that saw Grabianski even as they saw right through him. The same eyes that fixed on him now in the fly-specked mirror over the urinal. Sloane's voice, a stony South London shot through with a brace of New York American, saying, "This isn't going to be one of those pick-up scenes, is it? You show me yours if I show you mine."

Grabianski assured him it was not.

"Thank Christ," Sloane breathed, piss continuing to stream between his fingers, bouncing back from the shiny enamel. "I'm too old for that will-he, won't-he, kind of shit."

"You a friend of Eddie Snow?" Grabianski asked.

"Eddie doesn't have friends," Sloane said, buttoning up, "just mates he uses whenever there's a need."

Rinsing his hands beneath the tap, ignoring the hot-air drier in favor of wiping them on his dungarees, Sloane walked back out into the pub and when Grabianski followed, not so many necessary moments later, he had gone. Faron was sitting alongside Snow and she had taken what remained of Grabianski's pint with her, placing it across from them, by the place Sloane had vacated.

"Interesting fellow," Grabianski said, sliding into the empty seat.

"I don't like it," Eddie Snow said, "when people come sniffing round after me like dogs after a bone."

"You were supposed to be getting in touch with me."

"And I am."

"A couple of days ago."

"Ah, well," Snow said, "like the man said, all relative, time."

Faron looked at him suspiciously, in case he might have said something clever. Eddie Snow dressed today in his trademark leather, white tight trousers and a black waistcoat over a gray ribbed T-shirt, silver Indian bangles in the appropriate places.

"I just want to know," Grabianski said, "if you're still interested in the Dalzeils or not."

"Shout it from the housetops, why don't you?"

Swiveling as he rose, Grabianski cupped one hand to his mouth. "I just want to know ..."

"All right, all right, you've made your point," said Snow tugging at the sleeve of Grabianski's coat, "sit your bloody self back down."

Faron was giggling, pretending not to, and when Snow shot her a glance, she transmuted it into a cough.

"Run along," Snow told her affably enough.

She ran all the way to the bar.

"As it happens," Snow said, stretching an arm, "there is a fair bit of potential interest. Qatar. Arab Emirates. Monaco."

"What are the chances," Grabianski asked, "of translating this potential into something approaching cash?"

"Good, I'd say. Pretty good."

"And even while I might take your point about the uncertainty of time, you wouldn't like to hazard a guess as to when ..."

"Couple more days." Snow shrugged.

"Of course, I should have known, a couple more days."

Snow exchanged a further piece of private semaphore with Faron, who spoke to the barman and brought over fresh drinks.

"So how's old Vernon," Snow asked casually, "seen anything of him lately?"

Grabianski shook his head.

"Gone to ground a bit, I hear," Snow said. "Place out in Suffolk. Warbleswick. Snape. One of those. Like Siberia in the sodding winter and you can't turn round without squashing some turd in green wellies underfoot—so nice to get the dust of the city off of one's feet, don't you think?—but if you're into samphire or asparagus, oysters, of course, can't do better."

When Grabianski walked up the Hill toward his flat, clutching a bag of cherries from Inverness Street and a copy of *Mariette in Ecstasy* he'd picked up in Compendium, there, smug and unmistakable, was Vernon Thackray's dark blue Volvo estate, parked right outside.

They went up onto the Heath: Grabianski didn't want Thackray in his home. The sun was behind them, broken shafts of it still bright through the scattering of trees that lined the south side of the Hill. They were sitting on a bench, looking down over the running track and the pale brickwork of the Lido, Gospel Oak. Squirrels flirted with fear across dusty ground.

"I was beginning to think something had happened," Grabianski said.

"Happened?"

"To you."

"Hoped, then, that's what you mean. Hoped."

Grabianski didn't reply. Up to a point, let him think what he wants.

"This business," Thackray said, "it's necessary sometimes. A low profile, you understand. Minimum visibility." He was wearing a pale blue Oxford shirt that shone almost violet when it was caught by the sun, beige twill trousers with a definite crease, tasseled shoes. In certain parts of Suffolk, Grabianski mused, it was probably *de rigeur.*

"The paintings," Grabianski said, "the ones you wanted. They're available, you know that."

"Still?"

Grabianski half-turned on the bench toward him. "Japan, you said there was a buyer in Japan."

Thackray made a small gesture with his shoulders, too indefinite to be called a shrug. "Things fluctuate, change."

"Such as?"

"The yen against the dollar, the dollar against the pound."

"One of the beauties of art," Grabianski said, "I thought it maintained its price."

"I may not be able to get as much now."

"How much?"

Thackray smiled, rare as frost in July.

"How soon can you let me know?" Grabianski asked. "A definite price. And don't tell me a couple of days."

"Is that what he said?"

"Who?"

Thackray's hand alighted on Grabianski's leg behind the knee, squeezing tight. "You know the line, 'Human voices wake us, and we drown'? Listen to Eddie Snow, that's what happens. Eddie's hand on your head, holding you down." Relinquishing his grip, Thackray patted Grabianski gently on the thigh, a caring gesture, designed to reassure; learned, Grabianski imagined, from Thackray's housemaster at school. "The kind of things he's into, Eddie, in the end all they'll bring are grief and aggravation. Take my word, Jerzy, it's not what you need."

"What I need is to get these Dalzeils off my hands."

"Exactly. And now we've resumed an understanding, that's where I'll direct my attention: making sure that happens." He was on his feet, brushing dust, real or imaginary, from his clothes. "Nice here; you've done well. You'll have to drive out and see my place some time. Stay over. There's a guest room. Two. You could bring a friend. Lie in bed at night and listen to the waves lifting the pebbles from the beach, setting them back down." He gripped Grabianski's hand. "Early-morning swim before breakfast, quite safe as long as you stay in your depth, don't fight against the tide."

Twenty-nine

Closed for Private Function read the sign, chalked to a board near the top of the stairs, an arrow pointing down. In the main bar, an early-evening crowd was preparing itself for a night of Old Time Music Hall; rumor had it that Clinton Ford was making the journey over from the Isle of Man. Not paying too much attention, Sharon Garnett missed the sign and walked straight ahead, pushing her way through the reproduction Victorian glass doors to find herself face to face with mine host, decked out for the occasion in purple shirt, striped waistcoat, and raffishly angled straw hat. Behind him, forty or so punters, set on an evening of tepid beer and nostalgia, nibbled peanuts and Walkers crisps and, first one and then another, turned their heads and stared. Sharon, her hair spiked out around her face like a seven-pointed star, stood there in a body-hugging lime green nylon dress and smiled back.

"I think what you're looking for, me duck, it's downstairs."

"Quite likely," Sharon said. Then, with a cheery wave to all and sundry, "Nice to meet you. Have a good night. And remember, don't do anything you can't spell."

"Comedy night," the landlord said, "it's Sat'day. You're a day early."

"Better than being the usual four days late." Sharon had had two large gins and the residue of a bottle of New Zealand Chardonnay before leaving home and she wasn't about to take prisoners.

Lynn met Sharon at the foot of the stairs and gave her a quick, welcoming hug.

"You look amazing," Lynn said, stepping back for the full effect.

"So do you." It was a lie and they both accepted it; in fact, Lynn, in a cream high-neck dress and heels, looked fine. She'd had her

162

hair done that afternoon at Jazz, and for once had thought about her makeup for more than five minutes.

"The bar's free," Lynn said, "for now."

Sharon grinned and made her way in search of more gin.

Half an hour ago, Lynn had been in the same throes of panic experienced by anyone who ever threw a party of whatever size; she had been certain no one would turn up. And then, suddenly it seemed, they were all there—the team she was leaving, the squad she was joining. Even her new boss had put in an appearance, shaking hands with Lynn, as she looked round the room to check who else was there.

Helen Siddons had planned to bring her present affair with her, scotch any persisting rumors and spell it out for Skelton at the same time; but the man in question, an assistant chief constable from a neighboring force, was due to deliver the keynote speech at a Masonic dinner and could only offer to meet her afterwards. Knowing that meant he'd be snoring red-faced on her pillow within fifteen minutes, Siddons had declined.

The sound of conversation was already sharpening, voices liberated by alcohol; laughter, raucous and short-lived, rose up from around the room like a Mexican wave. The buffet was laid out along the rear wall, between the toilets and the bar, the usual quartered sandwiches and slices of yellow quiche, though the pakoras and samosas were less expected and going down a treat.

Helen Siddons was settling a prawn *vol-au-vent* onto her paper plate when Skelton appeared beside her, tobacco on his breath, his hand heavy upon her arm.

"You're here on your own," Skelton said, not a question.

"And Alice?"

Skelton shrugged.

"I don't know, Jack. It's not a good idea."

"It always was."

"Yes, well, that's as may be."

Watching them from across the room, Resnick wondered whether he shouldn't go over and interrupt, play chaperone. He decided it was none of his business, and went in search of Hannah instead, finding her sharing a table with Carl Vincent, Anil Khan, and

Khan's girlfriend, Jill, a receptionist at Central TV. He was about to join them when he spotted Divine, swaying a little maybe, but as yet still on his feet.

"Mark," Resnick greeted him, concerned but genuinely pleased. "Glad you could make it. How've you been? All right?"

"Yeah, yeah. Never worry."

"Well, take it a bit easy, okay?"

"Right."

Divine tugged at the knot of his tie and headed for the bar. Moments later, lager in hand, he collided with Sharon Garnett, carrying a tray of drinks toward a corner table. The crash momentarily stopped most conversation, Sharon squatting down among the broken glass, the front of her dress dark and wet.

"Here, let me," Divine said, lowering himself shakily onto one knee.

"Tell you what," Sharon said. "Why don't you fuck off instead?"

"Black bitch," Divine said, the words out of his mouth without hindrance or thought.

The back of Sharon's hand caught him full across the face, the edge of her ring opening a cut alongside his left eye. For a moment, he was stunned and then he lashed out, one of his feet kicking her hard in the thigh, a fist whistling close by her head.

"Hey, Mark! Enough." Naylor had been the first to react, pulling Divine back, Resnick quick to seize hold of his other arm, the pair of them hustling him over toward the door and through onto the stairs.

"Are you all right?" Lynn asked, shepherding Sharon toward a seat.

"Stupid bastard," Sharon said. And then to Lynn, dredging up a smile. "Yes, I'm fine."

"I thought," Khan said, "things were a little on the quiet side."

Vincent looked at his watch. "Early days."

Out on the street, Resnick propped Divine up against a wall, while Naylor called for a cab.

"I'll go with him," Naylor said, "make sure he gets indoors okay. Tell Debbie I'll not be long; I'll get the driver to wait."

"You're sure?"

"No problem."

164

"Good lad, thanks."

Resnick was scarcely back in the room before he saw Helen Siddons headed straight toward him. "Just got a call. There's a body, Charlie. In the canal. Not far from here. I thought maybe you'd want to come along."

After a quick word with Hannah, Resnick followed the new DCI from the room.

Someone had moved fast. Already the section of Wilford Road that ran into Castle Boulevard had been closed to traffic and the foot-path along Tinker's Leen had been roped off as far as the entrance to the new Inland Revenue buildings. Officers from the Technical Support team were rigging up lights. Jack Skelton talked to the uniformed inspector directing operations from above the lock, while Resnick followed Helen Siddons down the steps toward the water. She was wearing a stone-colored topcoat, loosely belted over her dress, and somehow she had found the opportunity to change into flat shoes. Two young PCs stood guarding the body, neither one looking as if they should legitimately have left school. They stood back and murmured "Ma'am" as the DCI approached.

Just as Resnick had done not so many months before, she lowered herself down and lifted back the plastic sheet. In the glare of artificial light, the face shone white, opaque as ivory. Borrowing gloves, Helen Siddons gently turned the head aside; a deep gash ran from behind the left eye to the inner edge of jaw, tissue and bone laid bare. She had not been in the water long, hours at most. Skelton was walking along the towpath toward them, the police surgeon in his wake. Siddons lowered the sheeting back into place and stood.

"You haven't got a cigarette, have you, Charlie?"

Resnick shook his head.

"Poor cow."

"Yes."

"How many's that now? No clothing, no ID. If anyone steps forward to claim the body, I'll be surprised."

But Resnick knew that wouldn't be the case: he had recognized Jane Peterson the instant Helen Siddons had exposed her face.

Thirty

Hannah wept.

It was not that she and Jane had been so close, not close like sisters, but she had known her as we often do those we work with, socialize with occasionally, as though through a prism, so much else unknown, hidden. Hannah had seen Jane angry, exhausted, hurt, excited: alive. Now she had to think of her as dead.

Resnick made fresh coffee, toast. Sounds of life filtered in from the houses on either side. By now the official identification would have been made, the preliminary medical examination over and done, a post-mortem arranged; an official murder inquiry set up, with Helen Siddons as senior investigating officer in charge. By midmorning, a new database would be in place, linked through the national HOLMES computer to other similar investigations, importing and exporting information. Files, begun in the wake of the newly formed nationwide operation and examining the unsolved violent deaths of women, would automatically be accessed. Those instances where the bodies had been discovered in or near canals and waterways would be prioritized. In addition to the normal CID personnel, there would be a researcher, a receiver, an indexer and reader, an action allocator. Helen Siddons would supervise all of this activity, set parameters, and after consultation with the detective superintendent overseeing all three squads in the authority, decide policy. Murder was a Serious Crime.

When Hannah came down, she was red-eyed but alert. "Charlie, I can't believe you're not going to be handling this. It just doesn't make any sense. You were the one that knew her, after all."

"I already had a quick word last night. I'll speak to Serious Crimes again today."

"And that's all?"

"Hannah, it's all I can do. It's not my case."

With a sign of impatience, she moved away.

"It'll be all right, you'll see," Resnick said. "It'll get sorted."

She turned slowly, the room not so dark he couldn't see her eyes. "Really, Charlie? Like all those others? That girl out at Beeston, like you sorted her?"

"Maybe I should go," Resnick said.

"Maybe you should."

Neither moved.

Resnick rang the Serious Crime Squad from his office at eight fifteen, eight fifty, nine, nine thirty, a quarter to ten, a quarter past. DCI Siddons was in a meeting, at a press conference, due to see Chief Superintendent Malachy, talking to BBC Midlands TV, plain busy.

Finally, he was able to speak to Anil Khan. Khan was wary, very much his nature, Resnick suspected, wary but not unfriendly. The medical report suggested that the cause of death was a blow or blows to the head, and that Jane Peterson had already been dead for some hours when her body was introduced into the water, although the water itself rendered establishing an exact time of death difficult, if not impossible. Preliminary estimates suggested she had been in the water for between six and twelve hours, possibly less. There was some evidence of recent bruising low on the right side, almost certainly dating from some time before the fatal injury. So far, none of her clothing or personal effects had been found. No witnesses had come forward, other than the dog walker who found the body; there was no information yet that filled in any of the time between the last known sighting of her on the previous Saturday and her death. No suspects.

"You've talked to the husband?" Resnick asked.

"I think we're talking to him again now."

"But not as a suspect?"

A pause. "Not as far as I know."

"And the bruising?"

"Waiting on more information, the post-mortem. I'm not sure."

Resnick didn't want to place him in an awkward position, push him too hard; he thanked him and broke the connection. Almost immediately, the phone rang again. "Look," Hannah said, "I think I'm going to drive over and see my mother. Spend a little time with her. I'll probably come back late Sunday night."

"Okay, it sounds like a good idea."

Resnick searched about in the kitchen until he found an aging scrubbing brush, some J-cloths, and a plastic bottle of Jif whose cap had broken off. After half an hour in the bathroom, he went down to the local newsagents and had a card put in the window: *Cleaning person wanted, hours by arrangement, must be good with cats.*

The only pub within easy walking distance of the Serious Crime Squad offices was a heavy metal hangout where the windows were routinely replaced every few days by sheets of hardboard. Which left two decent hotels and, at a stretch, the Playhouse bar. Helen Siddons was in the nearest of the hotels, still smarting from a session with Malachy, in the first minutes of which it had become clear that the superintendent imagined he was going to sit around and dictate the direction of the inquiry, leaving her to do all the running around, the majority of the work. It had taken all of her energy, everything from wide-eyed wheedling to stroppy insistence, to disabuse him of that, but in the end she thought she'd made her case. For the present, at least. As long as she was seen to be getting results, staying ahead of the game.

Now she was sitting at the first-floor bar, talking to her office manager and two other detectives Resnick could have put a name to if he were pushed. He went on past them to the far end of the bar, ordered a Budvar, and took it over to an easy chair by the window. A copy of the *Telegraph* lay open on the low table and Resnick turned to the sports pages and glanced from column to column as Siddons' voice rose above the rest. "Pressure," Resnick heard, and "thirty-six hours," "waiting for us to fall flat on our faces," and "nail this bastard to the floor." Bored by sport, Resnick scuffled through international news, business, obituaries. Helen Siddons picked up her drink, lit a fresh cigarette, and walked over to where he was sitting.

"Join you?"

"Please."

She was drinking whisky, a double; aside from a certain reddening around the eyes, she could probably drink it without visible effect until it drained down to her toes.

"So how's it going?" Resnick asked.

"Checking up on me, that what this is?"

"Why ever would I do that?"

"Jack Skelton's boy, sniffing out the land?"

The bottom of Resnick's glass hit the table with a smack that made faces turn.

"I'm sorry, I didn't mean that. Sit yourself back down." Reluctantly, he did.

"Bastard of a day! Everyone from the chief constable designate to the *Sun*. And Malachy behaving like I was his little windup doll." She breathed smoke out through her nose. "Well, he'll learn."

It's what you wanted, Resnick said to himself, what you bought into. Maybe you'll learn something, too.

"How was the press conference?"

"A zoo. You know what they're like when they sniff serial killer on the air."

Resnick swallowed another mouthful of his beer. "Is that what this is?"

The DCI stubbed out her cigarette half-smoked and lit another. "Three murders, no more than months apart, radius of thirty miles, what would you say?"

What Resnick said was, "Alex Peterson, you've had him in?"

"Of course."

"And?"

Siddons turned her face aside and lofted smoke toward the ceiling, a perfect ring. "His wife was just found with her head bashed in. He was a mess, what d'you expect?"

Somehow, Resnick thought, not that. "He's clean, though?"

"What?"

169

"The bruising to the body ..."

"He's not a fucking suspect. Charlie, get that into your head. Forget it."

"But surely ..."

"And this isn't your fucking case!" Back on her feet, she stared at him angrily, left the cigarette, took the drink.

Resnick watched her walk, tense, back toward the bar. Terse words and sullen laughter, heads turned momentarily in his direction. Resnick drained his glass, stubbed the smoldering cigarette out in the ashtray, and crossed toward the stairs. He was well on his way to Hannah's before he remembered she had left town.

Thirty-one

Helen Siddons thought about Peterson on the walk back to her office, the way he had held it together until one of the officers had bent low and exposed his wife's body, that was when he had lost it, catching hold of Lynn's arm and crying open-mouthed into her shoulder, Jane, Jane, the name, muffled, repeated again and again. After that, black coffee, aspirin, he had answered their questions cogently enough, told them nothing new.

Door closed, she brought the details of the other cases up on the screen. That Tasmanian girl out at Worksop, the still-unidentified body fished out of the Beeston canal; a woman with the tattoo of a spider's web on her left breast who had been dumped on the banks of the River Anker, where the M42 crossed it east of Tamworth; Irene Wilson, a known prostitute, whose partly decomposed body had been found in an allotment shed near the Trent and Mersey canal, south of Derby. Females aged between seventeen and twenty-five; all discovered in or near water with serious injuries to the head or upper body.

Don't get dragged too far down that track, Malachy had warned. Well, what the fuck did he expect her to do? Ignore it?

There was a knock on the door, deferential, and there was Anil Khan, blue plastic folder in his hand, studied concern marring his handsome face. "Post-mortem report, ma'am. I thought you should see."

"Of course I should bloody see." She slid the stapled pages from the folder, flicking them through without really looking. "Tell me."

"Evidence of bruising ..."

"Of course ..."

"To the body, ma'am. Chest and abdomen. Some of it fairly

171

recent, some quite old. Looks as if maybe she was being beaten fairly regularly."

"Christ!"

"Of course, it doesn't invalidate what we've said, I suppose there needn't be any connection at all."

"I know, I know." Helen's mind was spinning. "Listen, get hold of Peterson, bring him in. There's been a development, tell him. That's all. No details, right?"

"Yes, ma'am."

"And Anil?"

"Ma'am?"

"This report … for now, no one else need know about it, understood?"

Khan nodded and hurried off.

In her office, Helen pushed open the window and let in a raft of warm air. Cigarette on the go, she settled down to read the report. The clearest signs of bruising were at the back of the abdominal cavity on the right side, the presumed cause one or more heavy blows with a blunt instrument, possibly a fist. From the extent to which the bruises had faded, it was reasonable to suggest that the incident in which they had occurred had taken place not more than four, not less than two weeks ago. There were some faint signs, difficult to date, of residual bruising in a similar area but on the opposite side, as well as to the lower chest wall. What was certain was that at some point in the past year, one of the vertebrocostal ribs, the second from the top on the left side, had been broken and allowed to heal of its own accord.

What had Alex Peterson replied when she'd asked if he and his wife had ever argued? Sometimes, doesn't everyone? Well, yes, she thought, but there was argue and argue. She wondered what he would say now.

"We may have come up with something," Helen said, soft-pedaling. Peterson was alone with Khan and herself in the room. "It may be nothing, at this stage it's difficult to tell …" She broke off to light a cigarette.

"You can tell me, though," Peterson said, "what it is?"

"There is evidence of bruising, quite severe, on your wife's body."

"Of course, the fall into the water, the …"

"This is different."

"I'm sorry, I don't …"

"Some of this bruising is quite old, stretching back over as much as eighteen months, two years." She stared at him through cigarette smoke. "Some is more recent, inside the last month."

"What … what kind of bruising?"

"Oh, the kind that might result from being struck. Being punched. In, say, an argument. An argument that had got out of hand."

Peterson stared back at her, expressionless now.

"You wouldn't be able to offer any kind of explanation as to how these bruises came to be caused?"

Peterson's blue eyes slowly blinked. "Perhaps she had a fall."

"A number of falls."

"Possibly."

"Went riding, did she?" Siddons asked. "Climbing? Winter skiing?"

Peterson shook his head.

"Then perhaps," Helen said, "you could offer some other explanation?"

He held her gaze. "None. I'm sorry, none at all."

Stubbing out her cigarette, Siddons leaned back. "If you do think of anything," she said, almost carelessly, "you'll be sure to let us know."

He continued to sit there, uncertain. "You've finished with me? I can go?"

"Yes, I think so. Anil, perhaps you could show Mr. Peterson out."

When he was on his feet, she said, "You won't be going anywhere, leaving the country, nothing like that. Not with funeral arrangements to be made."

Peterson looked back and then walked away. He's good, Helen thought, guilty or not, he's very good. And guilty of what? Hitting his wife to end an argument? Join the club.

The phone was ringing as she walked in the door and she knew it would be either Jack Skelton or Maxwell Bowden, the ACC from Derbyshire, whose idea of sweeping her off her feet had been some decidedly tired-looking roses and a bottle of Drambuie in a paper bag.

"Max," she said, less than enthusiastically. He hated it when anyone called him Max. "What can I do for you?"

Wrong question.

"Actually, Max," she said, interrupting, "I've had a shit of a day. I'm going to take some paracetamol and crawl into bed."

Setting down the phone, she lit a cigarette and drew in deeply.

"No, I'm sorry," she said, receiver back in her hand. "Appealing as it is. Yes, I'll call you. Bye."

Carefully divesting herself of her new best suit and blouse and hanging them inside the ghastly flush-fronted fitted wardrobe, Helen kicked off the rest of what she was wearing and went to do battle with the shower.

She was drying her hair when the doorbell sounded and didn't hear it at first over the noise of the drier. There was a generous glass of scotch close to hand and a Marks & Sparks salmon and something-or-other waiting patiently by the microwave.

When she realized there was somebody persisting at the door, she tightened the belt to her pale green robe and padded her way into the hall. Through the security peephole, Jack Skelton's face looked more intense, more absurd than ever.

"Five minutes, Jack, all right? And don't let this thing ..." she tugged at the lapels of her robe, "give you any ideas."

"Halfway there already," Skelton grinned, but he was only going through the motions. "A drop of scotch'd be nice," he said, spotting Helen's glass.

"I dare say." She made no effort to pour him one and Skelton took a freshly washed glass from beside the sink, the bottle of Famous Grouse from between the salt and the Fairy Liquid.

"Not going to be a habit this, is it, Jack? I thought we had all that settled before I agreed to take the job."

"It's the job I've come to talk to you about."

"Not another lecture?"

"You had a run-in with Malachy."

"Are you asking, Jack, or telling?"

"He told you what to do and you told him to fuck off."

"Something like that, yes." She held the packet out toward him and when he shook his head, lit up herself. "Afraid she'll smell it on your breath, Jack?"

"Like she used to smell you?" His voice was easy and insinuating and for a moment, as his hand ran the length of her thigh, she could remember what she had allowed herself to see in him.

"Something about the job, Jack, I think that's what you said." She stared at him until he stepped away.

"Malachy, you know he was never your biggest fan from the off. Now he's wondering aloud if it's not the best thing to get shot of you before any real damage is done."

"How exactly is he proposing to do that?"

"Ride you out of town doggy-fashion, I believe that was his suggestion."

"Pathetic sexist bastard!"

"Possibly. But your immediate superior, none the less."

Helen rested her cigarette on the edge of the sink and took a good swallow at her scotch. "Don't worry, Jack. I've already figured out how to deal with this. Malachy gets his way and I get mine. And you've got two minutes to down that scotch, or you'll be taking it back to Alice in a paper cup."

Skelton laughed a sour laugh. "Just about the only way I'd consider it these days."

Resnick had wandered into the Polish Club midway through the evening, a quiet night, quite a few families with older children, and, after chatting to the secretary for a short while, taken up a position toward the end of the smaller bar. He was there, making his second or third bison grass vodka last and listening with half an ear to Marian Witzcak's somewhat alarmed recounting of a Glyndebourne production of Berg's *Lulu* on Channel Four, when Helen Siddons was ushered in.

"Charlie," she said, "we've got to talk."

Thirty-two

The entire squad was assembled, two dozen individuals variously standing, sitting, leaning, staring at bitten-down fingernails, recently buffed shoes, casting their eyes back over the canal maps tacked to the walls, before and after photographs of Jane Peterson, Miranda Conway, Irene Wilson, and two still-unidentified women; twenty-four officers, men and women, but mostly men, mostly white, aged between mid-twenties and late thirties, motivated, bright, carefully chosen, keen to do well, succeed, get the bastard who did these sorted and sorted fast.

Helen Siddons, smart and businesslike in a gabardine safari dress, was coming to the end of that morning's briefing. The team initially working the Worksop murder had passed on details of two potential suspects, one a brewery salesman whose regular run took him through most of the sites where bodies had been found. Details were on their way round.

"That aside, what I want us concentrating on is this period between the first two murders and the last three. If we are looking for the one man, what was he doing during this time? My gut feeling tells me he was locked away, maybe for something dissimilar, but equally it could be for some kind of sexually orientated crime. So, let's use the technology, chase down what we can."

She stepped back a moment, taking one deep breath and then another, amidst general coughing and clearing of throats.

"All right, all right, there's one more thing. The postmortem suggests that Jane Peterson had for some time been the victim of persistent physical abuse. Not the most serious, in terms of what many of us are used to dealing with, but a broken rib, bruising to the body, the kind of injuries that are often sustained within abusive relationships where the person perpetrating them has sufficient control over his or her temper not to strike out at the face or some part of the body where injuries would more easily be noticed."

Heads were turned in whispered comment and she waited for silence to return.

"I can't be sure how relevant this is to our primary investigation; but it can't be ignored. Which is why Detective Inspector Resnick, who most of you already know, is with us today."

Off to one side of the room, Resnick—clean shirt, second-best suit, clean tie—regarded the floor with interest.

"The inspector had met both Alex and Jane Peterson socially and had begun making inquiries into Jane's disappearance. So he has good prior knowledge here and it would be foolish to ignore it. And with the blessing of our respective lords and masters, he's going to be with us on this, concentrating on that particular aspect of the investigation. DS Kellogg and DC Khan will work with him, leaving the rest of us to concentrate on the wider picture.

"Right, questions?"

High-ceilinged, tall-windowed medical wards had once run more or less the length of both floors in the top half of the building. These had now been partitioned off to accommodate the squad's requirements: an open-plan office and large meeting room, Helen Siddons' own office leading off it, were on the upper floor; the computer room, communications room, and numerous smaller spaces, largely for the purpose of conducting interviews, were on the lower. Resnick and his small team had been allocated one of these, just large enough to hold three chairs, two desks arranged in an L, one computer screen, two telephones, a small cupboard containing empty files and a notional amount of stationery, and a metal waste-paper basket, color gray. The walls were a suspicious-looking shade of lime green; the suspicion being that it was a mistake. The window, open now by several inches at both top and bottom, afforded a generous view over the Roman Catholic cathedral and the restored Albert Hall and Institute down toward the various buildings of the city's second university and the bland ugliness of the flats that rose up without majesty above the Victoria Centre.

Helen Siddons had telephoned both Anil Khan and Lynn Kellogg earlier that morning to pass on the news; it had not been phrased as a request. Resnick himself had managed a brief word with Lynn, her response matter-of-fact, cool, everything would be fine.

"Okay," Resnick said, "two things we have to do. Confirm, if possible, Jane Peterson's injuries were caused by her husband. Find out what might have happened between them to drive him over the edge. So statements from friends, colleagues, relatives, will all need to be double-checked. We need to go through the records at Accident and Emergency, talk to her GP."

"And Prentiss," Lynn said, "the osteopath. If he was treating her, you'd've thought he must have seen something."

"He didn't say anything?" Khan asked.

"Nothing specific. Accused Peterson of bullying her, right enough, obviously didn't like him, didn't like him at all, but nothing more than that."

"Talk to him again," Resnick said. "Make it priority. And remember, there are seven days during which we've no idea where Jane Peterson was. And at some point in that time she met her killer. Could be accident, chance. Or it could be somebody she knew, had planned to see."

"It could be Peterson himself," Lynn said.

"Exactly. So the other thing we have to do is go back through that list of people at the day school. Busy building, middle of Saturday afternoon, somebody must have seen her leaving. She could even have been picked up outside. And let's double-check Peterson's movements that afternoon while we're about it."

"This whole disappearance business," Khan said, "he could have been faking it all along. Keeps her out of the way somewhere, secure, while he creates a fuss …"

"Right," Lynn said, warming to the idea, "plays the distraught husband just long enough, then kills her and dumps the body in the canal, so that we think she's been done by the same bloke as all the others."

"Which," Resnick said, "is exactly what we are doing. Most of us, anyway."

"Well," Lynn said, "if he did do it—Peterson—we're going to get him."

"Right," Resnick said. "And if he did do it, what interests me is why."

Thirty-three

"You know, dear," Hannah's mother had said, head half turned from where she was attending to the salad dressing, "I wonder if I shouldn't move after all."

Surprised, Hannah had looked up from the book section of the *Sunday Times*, her mother bending forward slightly, squinting above her glasses as she measured the required amount of raspberry vinegar into a spoon. "I thought you'd gone over all that, decided it was a bad idea. This house, the garden, you love it here."

"Yes, I know." Margaret's voice was flat and without conviction. Hannah laid the paper aside. "It's not the same, is it?"

"No."

They were both thinking of Hannah's father, out in France with Robyn, a girl when it had all started, a student, little more than a girl, younger than Hannah by far. Infatuation, intimations of mortality. One of those scarcely explicable affairs that flare up and just as suddenly burn down.

"Have you heard from him?" Hannah asked. "I mean, recently."

It was the wrong question. Anger fought back the tears in her mother's eyes. "He sent me … how could he have had the nerve? Why on earth he should ever think I was interested, I can't imagine. He sent me a cutting from the paper, or perhaps it was a magazine, something about this wretched book she's supposed to have written. Well, I don't know what he was thinking of. As though somehow that makes it all right, as if she isn't just some silly bit of skirt after all. As if I care what … what she is … the stupid, stupid …"

Hannah folded her arms around her, feeling the tension wound tight inside the brittle wiriness of her mother's body, the hardness of small bones, softness of white, lightly freckled skin.

"I'm not going to cry."

"No."

"She isn't worth it. They're neither of them worth it."

"That's right." Hannah was thinking of Andrew, her Irish poet lover, the way he had flung his final infidelity in her face like brackish water and expected her to be grateful for his openness, his honesty. How she had cried.

"He didn't think," Hannah said. "He wasn't thinking."

"Yes, he was. He was thinking of her. Not of me. Now, we could eat if you're ready. I'm afraid I forgot to buy any cheese. I hope that's all right. I ..."

"Mother," Hannah said, kissing the top of her head, "it's fine. Everything's fine." Tears bright in her eyes.

He had come back twice after that, Andrew. The first time had been midway through the evening, cold, a fire burning in the open grate. Hannah had been marking folders, grading papers, rereading the Lydgate and Dorothea chapters from *Middlemarch*. The first Mary Chapin Carpenter album had been playing quietly; she had had— what?—two glasses of wine or was it three? At the door, Andrew's breath had seesawed across the air; he had been wearing a thin coat, a scarf wrapped round his head as though he were suffering from toothache, gloves on his hands, a bottle of Bushmills clutched against his chest. Hannah had known from the first moment of seeing him that she should not let him in: known what would happen if she did.

She took his scarf and hung it in the hall, the coat he kept on, the gloves had somehow disappeared. "Have you glasses?" he said. And then, when they were sitting drinking, the smell of smoke faint from the fire, the shaded light dancing in his eyes, "So, Hannah, how've you been?"

He took her on the floor, the curtains only partly drawn across, touching her first with his tongue and then no time for niceties, Hannah's skirt pushed up and knickers pulled aside, Andrew having her there, wedged somehow between floor and chair, his long coat trailing round them as she moaned and he bit her breast and thrust deeper inside, stopping only to turn her round and push her down again face first onto the chair, hands clutching her, himself, not gentle, never that, the quick deep strokes and his fingers, damp, so far inside her mouth Hannah thought, if think she did, that she must surely choke.

He sat across the fire from her afterwards, uncovered, his lissome cock folding slowly back against his balls, savoring the whiskey, the cigarette he'd lit from the fire.

"I've missed you," he said.

Hannah hunched there, legs drawn up, arms raised across her chest, feeling him slowly dribble out of her, for those moments immune to tears.

There was another woman, of course; well, there were two, one in Belfast, one here. He wondered if he might not marry one of them this time, put an end to all this wandering, settle down. He'd written a poem about it, this yearning after hearth and home, but then he would.

When next he came round unannounced she bolted the door against him and immediately broke out laughing, unable to think of anything save the wonderfully melodramatic scene at the end of *The Heiress*, a film she remembered watching with her mother one long Saturday afternoon, Olivia de Havilland locking Montgomery Clift outside her door. Who said art didn't prepare you for life? She hoped Andrew could hear her laughter as he trudged away.

He had married, she heard, soon after; married and divorced and married again. His new book of poetry much acclaimed, he had given a reading at the university but she had not gone. She had glanced through the book once, displayed on the table in Waterstone's, smiling quietly at a poem she thought most probably about her. She missed the way he would read to her at night, his work and others—Heaney, Longley, Yeats—but Andrew being Andrew, mostly his own. She surprised herself by missing sometimes the way he would arrive unexpectedly home after a lecture that had gone spectacularly well or badly, and reach for her no matter what she was doing, taking her, hungry and fast, pinned up against the sink or stretched along the stairs.

Jim, the peripatetic music teacher who eventually took Andrew's place, had been far too sensitive and thoughtful to suggest anything so aggressive and uncaring. And Charlie … well, Charlie, bless him, was still a little hesitant and cautious at the best of times. A little lacking in that kind of fervor or imagination. Poets and policemen. Hannah smiled: at least she felt safe.

He was there when she finally arrived home, worn out after battling with the Sunday evening traffic on the motorway. A casserole of chicken and cured French sausage was in the oven, the kettle was simmering, ready to make coffee or tea. "You'd be So Nice to Come Home to." Billie Holiday was playing on the stereo in the front room.

"Why don't you let me run you a bath?" Resnick said. "Relax you. Then we can eat." Arms around her, he had no idea why she was crying.

"Charlie, why is it?"

"What?"

"You're forever trying to get me clean."

Less than fifteen minutes hater, he carried mugs of tea upstairs and sat on the edge of the bath, telling her about what was happening with the investigation, the fact that he was now fully involved.

"Poor Jane," Hannah said, "putting up with that for as long as she did. That bastard. That sanctimonious, know-it-all bastard. If he … if he …"

"If he did," Resnick said, "we'll catch him for it."

She rested her head sideways against his leg and he soaped her back, rinsing it with warm water and then, when she climbed out of the bath, helping to towel her dry. When he kissed her, she felt him starting to harden against her.

"Charlie," she said, "the casserole …"

"Isn't that the thing about casseroles? They just sit there and wait till you're ready."

Bubbles of water speckled the small of her back and the length of her thigh as she lay on the bed. "Is that all right?" he asked. "Is this?"

She curled beside him, her legs around his, feeling his heart beating through his ribs.

"Why are you so good to me, Charlie?" she asked.

Later still, they sat propped up by pillows, dipping bread into Portuguese blue bowls and soaking up the juice.

Thirty-four

Grabianski remembered the first time he had seen her, striding out between the traffic on Gregory Boulevard, her topcoat belted but unbuttoned, a tall, well-made woman of a certain age. Now, as he stood on the steps outside the National Gallery, scanning the crowds that moved without pattern across Trafalgar Square, he felt the anticipation of her like ice beneath his skin. All below where he was standing, students lounged and laughed and smoked across the steps, Italians, German, French. More of them sprawled on the grass that ran wide along the front of the gallery, sharing it with the homeless and their cardboard havens, cans of cider and ratty wet-nosed dogs tied up with string—as much a part of the tourist sights as the Horse Guards on parade.

Grabianski willed himself not to look at his watch again, and lost; in any case, there was the clock beyond the square telling him past doubt that she was close to an hour late. Of course, she wasn't coming, some emergency she had to deal with, one of the unfortunates she'd befriended had taken an overdose, thrown themself from a bridge; maybe one of the others, Sister Bonaventura or Sister Marguerite, had been taken ill. Or it could be simply the train, the train was late, seriously delayed, derailed, rerouted due to engineering works—wasn't that always happening on a Sunday, engineering works?—he believed it was.

No. She had decided against it, pure and simple: decided, on reflection, it was not a sound idea, not pure and simple at all. Meet at the National Gallery, Sunday, to see the Degas. Innocent enough. He would give it another five minutes and that was all. Go round on his own. Except that would be too depressing. No, a movie; he could go and see a film, dozens of them showing five minutes' stroll from where he stood. That slow jolt of pleasure, immersion in the dark.

The five minutes up and there he still was, fingers drumming the worn parapet of stone. Below him, buses crept past, red and green, some open at the top, Americans and Japanese craning their cameras toward the this and the that, guides blurred through their microphones; a bunch of dreadlocked, punked-up kids scrambling over one of the stone lions, pulling at each other's legs and feet; a small boy, no more than four or five, running between the pigeons, clapping his hands so that they rose on grimy wings and resettled on the far side of the square; the slow bass shaking down from the open windows of slick cars as young black men anointed the afternoon with soul. Almost before he had time to register her presence, there she was, Teresa, Sister Teresa, smiling as she stepped over the outstretched legs of youths from Perugia or Milan.

"I'm sorry I'm late, so sorry. One thing after another."

And Grabianski grinning fit to bust as, just to help her over the last hurdle, he takes her arm. "It doesn't matter. Really, it doesn't matter at all."

The exhibition was in the Sainsbury Wing and the clock alongside the ticket desk informed them their entry was timed for forty minutes hence. The slightly harassed young woman at the entrance to the brasserie found them a table toward the far corner, almost with a view of St. Martin-in-the-Fields.

"Cream tea?" said Grabianski, looking up from the menu.

"Just tea, thank you."

"You won't mind if I do?"

Teresa smiled her permission. Unlike some of her calling, it rarely occurred to her to deny others those pleasures she herself abjured.

Order placed, Grabianski was content to sit back and look. Teresa was wearing gray, a color she favored, but today in softer shades which accentuated rather than diminished the slight plumpness of her lower arms, the green that loitered in her eyes.

She was telling him of diversions via Milton Keynes, the thirty or so minutes they had spent, shunted onto a side line north of Willesden Junction due to signal failure; Grabianski half-listening, more than happy just to sit there, watching, watching the tilt of her head, the slow curling and uncurling of her fingers, the movement of her mouth—she knew he was watching her mouth—the stir of other conversations sealing them in.

The tea was served in china pots, Grabianski's scone a wholemeal disk studded with sultanas, harsh to cut and rich to taste, richer still once he had ladled it with jam and cream; the cream not of the clotted, Devon kind, but fluid enough to suggest it might easily slide off the blade of a knife, his half-moon of scone, his tongue.

"A good choice, then?" Teresa said, eyeing his plate.

"Oh, yes."

She smiled a private smile and added water to the pot.

"How are the other sisters?" Grabianski asked, wiping his face.

"Well. Sister Marguerite sends her love."

"Not Sister Bonaventura?"

"I'm afraid Sister Bonaventura regards this entire day as a foolhardy enterprise."

"Because of me?" Grabianski grinned.

"Oh, no. Because of Degas. What does she call him now? An over-the-hill representative of a dying bourgeois art form, eking out a talent for repetitive misogyny."

"She knows his work well, then. She's been down already."

Teresa laughed. "Not for Sister Bonaventura any of Thomas' existential doubts. She'd no more need to see a Degas in the flesh than press her hand against Christ's wounds before believing that he lived and breathed. Religion or politics, faith and dogma for her live side by side."

"She sounds hard work."

"Of course; it's the life we've chosen."

Grabianski finished his scone and washed it down with tea; summoning the waiter he paid the bill, careful to overtip generously.

"Shall we go?" he said, easing back his chair.

"Of course."

The first room seemed impossible and Grabianski's heart sank: what he had envisaged as an intimate afternoon, spent in close proximity and expressive silences, was instantly awash with earnest shufflers, shifting from painting to painting as slowly as breath would allow, parents with whimpering offspring dangling from backpack or sling, solitary listeners strapped into headphones listening to recorded commentary, girls from good homes sitting cross-legged, sketching.

Glancing around the walls, he glimpsed ballet dancers, bathers, hats, bouquets, a woman ironing, another standing, stern and staring out as if daring the artist to put a stroke wrong.

"Look," Teresa said, "the color. There. Isn't that wonderful?" At the center of a group of hats, the kind that for Grabianski existed only in the royal enclosure at Ascot, a scarf loosely knotted, hung down, lime green, so bright that it threatened to outshine all the other colors in the room.

When they moved on through the arch, the crowd already seemed to have dispersed a little, and they had an almost unimpeded view of five pictures hanging on the left-hand wall, five women drying themselves from the bath, or rather, the same woman in almost identical poses, the artist working on her again and again: ankle, leg, the deep cleft between the muscles of the back, broad swell of hips, arm raised to towel the now brown, now red hair, the curtains behind changing from orange fleck to fleshy pink, the wicker chair that is there and then not there. Working at it, Grabianski thought, until he got it right.

Except there was no right, he realized, each day a little different, the position, the light never the same: the way it would be if every day you were privileged to watch the same woman, unselfconscious, step, first one leg and then, steadying herself, the other, out from the bath and then bend forward to retrieve the towel that has slid to the floor, before drying herself slowly, then briskly, a snatch of song on her lips, a song she has surprised herself by knowing.

As Teresa turned in front of him, Grabianski followed her slowly into the next room toward the famous picture of a woman leaning back in a flame-red dress having the tangles brushed painfully from her flame-red hair.

"I never knew," Teresa said some minutes later, standing close. "What's that?"

"That she was pregnant, look. That's why she's so uncomfortable. That's why it hurts." And she smiled the secret smile that would forever keep Grabianski excluded, an outsider, more so even than herself, who had forfeited all right to so much that was womanly, to enter into the marriage she craved.

Turning sharply into the fourth room, Grabianski came face to face with the painting he would later believe he liked best; the body submerged in a near-abstract pattern of color and light, blue to the left and orange to the right. As he stood in front of this, Teresa, at his back, hurried past a canvas showing a woman bending forward unclothed, presenting her backside in a way that none of the others had, more frankly sexual, an invitation that lodged a thought in Teresa's mind and brought a rare blush to her throat.

When Grabianski looked closely at it later, it seemed to him the texture of the model's flesh was that of skin seen through wet shower glass, spied on, unannounced.

Teresa, meanwhile, had been relieved to escape from all that flesh into the last room, three gentle landscapes on the far wall threaded through with violet and mauve, so still that you could almost smell the woodsmoke on the evening air.

They hesitated before the exit: they had been there an eternity; they had been there almost no time at all.

Released into the afternoon, they walked without talking, down across the Mall and into St. James's Park: couples in deck chairs, a couple kissing on the bridge, couples holding hands.

"What did you think?" Grabianski asked.

"The exhibition?"

"Uh-huh."

"I liked it very much."

"But?"

"Is there a but?"

"I don't know. Yes, probably."

"I suppose I found it a little intimidating," Teresa said.

"The nakedness?"

"No, oh no, not that. Naked and unadorned. We are used to that. But, no, the warmth, the color, the beauty that he found there. Never tired of. This old man—old for those days—and going blind."

They sat on a bench near the lake, a group of shovelers and gray-winged teals arguing testily about some torn bread that had been tossed their way.

"I spoke to your friend, Charlie Resnick, not so long ago."

"Your friend, too."

"I think so," Teresa said.

"Did he know you were meeting me?"

"He knew it was a possibility."

"I see."

"He says you might be going to help him."

"I don't know."

When she moved, Teresa's arm brushed the back of Grabianski's hand, his wrist, certainly it was a mistake. "I think," she said slowly, "that if you could, you should."

He smiled, the skin wrinkling around the edges of his mouth, his eyes. "For the greater good?"

"For your good."

"Penance, is this? Atonement for my sins?"

"Perhaps. If you believe. But maybe something more practical, too. I'm not saying I wouldn't visit you in Lincoln, or whichever prison it might be, but that wouldn't be the same as in God's good air, would it now?" Briefly, she returned his smile. "No more exhibitions then."

"There's meant to be a good show in Cornwall," Grabianski said. "The Tate at St. Ives. Rothko. I don't know if you …"

"We'll see," Teresa said, already on her feet. "Maybe we'll see."

Thirty-five

"Someone to see you," Carl grinned.

Resnick looked up from the interview transcripts he was reading through and there was Mollie, skinny black trousers, a vivid Lycra top, clumpy sandals, two styrofoam cups balanced one on top of the other on the palm of one hand, a plastic bag clutched in the other. "This coffee might not be so hot," she said. "It's already been to Canning Circus. They told me you were here."

"Come on in," Resnick said.

Carl Vincent closed the door behind her and walked off in search of Lynn. Something she had wanted him to do.

"Black, gay, and a policeman," Mollie said with a backward nod of the head. "Things are looking up."

"How do you know?" Resnick asked. "He doesn't exactly advertize."

Mollie gave a small, enigmatic smile. "Oh, you can tell," she said. "You learn." She perched on a table corner, taking in the bare walls, the lightbulb that still lacked a shade. "Promotion, is it, then?"

"Not exactly."

"Smaller than the office I used to have and that's saying something." She jumped down and retrieved cups and bag. "We could have this outside. Better than being cooped up in here."

There was a bench, battered and heavily graffitied, but a bench nonetheless, by the top of the broad crumbling steps that led down to Park Valley. Mollie handed Resnick his cup and delved inside the plastic bag, lifting out a package wrapped in aluminum foil, which she placed between them cautiously.

"Is this getting to be a habit?" Resnick asked.

"Maybe."

Mollie carefully folded back the foil and there inside, squashed but not beyond recognition, lay two pieces of dark chocolate cake, a layer of what might be jam through the middle and coffee and vanilla icing across the top.

"It's my birthday," Mollie explained.

"Today?"

She shook her head. "Yesterday. But if I hadn't brought in some of the cake, the people at work would have killed me. And so I thought ... well, you brought something when you came to see me."

"Thanks," Resnick said. "And happy birthday."

He wondered which it was, thirty-four or thirty-five? Mollie prized the cake apart and set a slice, precariously, in his palm.

"I should have brought napkins."

"That's okay, don't worry." He took a bite and managed to catch the piece that fell away in his other hand. If he didn't drink some of the coffee soon, it would be colder still. "When I came to see you," he said, "there was a reason."

"Sheer delight at seeing me aside."

"Of course."

"Well," Mollie said, "I'm afraid it's true for me, too." Freeing herself to reach into her hip pocket, she pulled out a photocopy of the Broadway office telephone bill, two lines—number, date, time, and duration—highlighted in green. The numbers were prefixed 01223. "Here."

Resnick's hands full, she placed it on his knee.

He hooked at her inquiringly.

"The last quarter's telephone accounts just came through. As our esteemed finance director's wont to do, he pointed these out to me. You know, numbers he doesn't recognize. Exceptionally lengthy calls. The first was made on my mobile, oh, six weeks ago. That was short enough. A couple of minutes. But the second was from my office phone on the morning of the day school. Twenty-one minutes, forty-three seconds. You can bet he noticed that. And then, checking back, he spotted the first. The same number."

"And you don't know whose it is?"

Mollie shook her head.

"You didn't make the calls?"

"No."

Resnick's stomach tensed, waiting for what she was going to say next.

"I hadn't remembered, didn't think anything of it at the time, but as we were coming out of one of the early planning meetings, Jane asked if she could use my mobile, just a quick call. I said, sure. I presumed she was making arrangements, meeting someone, somebody picking her up. As I say, I didn't give it another thought."

"But this second call, the longer one, you didn't know anything about that?"

"Uh-uh." Mollie was getting in her share of the cake now, licking her fingers.

"Could Jane have had access to your office while the day school was going on?"

"The downstairs door should have been locked, but with people popping in and out all day, yes, it could have been left on the catch. She could have used it without anyone knowing."

"Isn't it possible she could have asked someone else if she could use your phone?"

"It's possible, yes, but as far as I know it's not what happened. I asked around. The staff who were there." Mollie sat forward. "You really think this might be important?" she asked. "You think it might help?"

"It might. At least it's something. We've precious little as it is." Resnick smiled and when he did Mollie couldn't help but notice the smudge of coffee icing just above the corner of his mouth. "Thanks," he said, "for letting me know so promptly. And," smile broadening, "for the birthday cake."

Mollie's face darkened. "I just hope it helps. Poor Jane. No more birthdays for her."

Resnick put a trace on the Cambridge number as soon as he got back to the office. It belonged to a pub on the outskirts of the city, the Dray Horse out on the old Newmarket road; a pay phone in the corridor outside the lounge bar.

193

Alan Prentiss smiled as he opened his front door to Lynn Kellogg, a smile which tapered off when he saw Carl Vincent standing behind her. Lynn introduced Carl and thanked Prentiss for agreeing to see them at short notice.

"I had a cancellation," he said, stepping aside to let them in.

Carl nodded, taking the man's measure as they walked through. With Khan busy, Lynn had wanted a second opinion, hadn't wanted to talk to Prentiss alone.

"You said you had one or two more questions about Jane Peterson," Prentiss said, when they were all sitting down. "It's terrible, of course, what happened to her. Such a waste."

"When you were treating her," Lynn asked, "I wonder whether you noticed any marks on her body?"

Prentiss blinked. "Marks?"

"Bruises," Carl said.

Prentiss shifted uncomfortably in his seat.

"Did you ever see any bruises on Jane's body, Mr. Prentiss?" Lynn asked.

Another little fidget, something irritating along his thigh. "I might have once … There were, there was bruising once, yes. Around the hip and along this, this side."

"Severe?"

"No, no, I wouldn't necessarily say severe."

"And you asked her about it?"

"Yes. She said she'd been in a fall. Coming down the stairs from the living room. Carrying a tray. Cups and so on. She fell. I don't know, as many as a dozen steps. Halfway."

"Had she been to her doctor?"

"I don't think so."

"And the hospital? Accident and Emergency?"

"It's possible. I don't know."

"Would you say," Carl asked, leaning forward, "the bruises on Jane Peterson's body could have come from a fall such as she described?"

Prentiss' mouth was dry. "They could have, yes."

"It never occurred to you that they might have been caused in any other way?"

Prentiss shook his head. "Not … not really, no."

194

"Not," Lynn said, "after what you told me about her husband? You said he was a bully, you remember that?"

"Yes, but I didn't mean ... That wasn't what I meant."

"What did you mean, then?"

"Verbally. Mentally. The way he got on at her. Not the sort of thing you're talking about now."

"Really?" Lynn said. "It never occurred to you that Alex Peterson might have been behind those injuries? You never for one moment thought he might have been hitting his wife?"

Prentiss sat on his hands. He didn't say anything for some little time. It was quiet in the room, quiet outside. "All right, if I'm honest, it did go through my mind. Just the possibility. But Jane, she'd been so clear about what had happened, so detailed. To have questioned her would have been like calling her a liar. So I said nothing. She ... we never mentioned it again."

"A shame," Carl said, "in the circumstances."

"The circum ... what? You don't think, you're not suggesting ...?"

"This friend of yours you spoke about," Lynn said, "Patricia, she used to teach with Jane?"

"Yes. Yes, that's right."

"You wouldn't have an address for her, I suppose? Just in case we need to get in touch."

"Yes," said Prentiss distractedly. "Yes, I must have it somewhere. If you'll just give me a few minutes to look ..."

"Wanker," Carl said dismissively when they were back on the pavement.

"As long as that's all," Lynn said.

"You're serious?"

Lynn unlocked the car door. "Maybe. As far as we know he's unattached, doesn't seem to mix much with other people, works from home. There's a lot of things on our offender profile that he fits."

Carl slotted his belt buckle into place. "Checking him out some more won't hurt."

"Right. And this Patricia, where did he say she was?"

"Peterborough."

195

"Close enough to be worth a call." Lynn checked the rearview mirror and pulled away.

"You know what's getting to Prentiss, don't you?" Carl said. "Thinking if he'd done something to stop this happening back when he had the chance, Jane Peterson might still be alive now. Maybe that's what's making him twitchy. Bad conscience, nothing more."

"Probably," Lynn said. "We'll see."

Thirty-six

"Thirty thousand the pair?"

"That's the going price."

"Bullshit!" Grabianski said, his voice louder than intended.

"Take it or leave it." Eddie Snow shrugged as if he didn't care.

They were sitting in a pub in Camden, one of those places that had been fashionably stripped back to bare boards, tat and clutter peeled away, a large room lit by candles and a few tastefully concealed ceiling lights, guest beers, a menu that included samphire and lemon grass, scallops and black pudding served on mashed potato.

The rest of the place was more or less empty at that time of day: a couple of thirtyish men in bad suits dragging out their last beer over the remains of a business lunch; an upmarket mum sitting outside with her two kids, waiting for them to sit back down and finish their fruit sorbet.

Grabianski was drinking a large tomato juice with Worcester sauce, Tabasco, ice, and lemon. He needed a clear head.

"I thought you wanted to get rid?" Snow said.

"So I do."

"And fast?"

"Fast doesn't mean throwing them away."

One of the children outside was crying; the men in suits were preparing to haggle over their bill. Round the corner on Arlington Road, a car alarm sounded and then was still, sounded and was still.

"Clearly," Grabianski said, "someone's heard of him in Dubai."

"Bahrain, actually, but who's counting?"

"I am."

Fast enough to take Grabianski by surprise, Snow covered one of his hands with his own and squeezed. "Jerry, don't be such a hardass all the time, know what I mean?" When he let go his grip, save for several bright red marks, Grabianski's knuckles were white.

"What's your cut on this?" Grabianski asked. "What do you call it, finder's fee?"

Snow leaned back and crossed his legs, signaled to the barman for a fresh glass of wine. "Forty percent and cheap at the price."

"Okay. All I'm saying," Grabianski said, conciliatory, "if you can push a little, without putting the whole thing at risk, get a few thousand more, where's the harm?"

The barman lifted Snow's glass away and set another in its place.

"When we first started talking about this," Snow said, "you were coming on like you was Linford in the Olympic Games. Couldn't wait to get on the move. Now all of a sudden, 'Yeah, Eddie, no rush, take your time, let's get the best deal we can.'" Snow was looking at him, direct. "What happened?"

Grabianski shrugged impressive shoulders.

"Only," Snow said, "if I thought you was back in touch with that cunt Thackray, playing us off, one against the other, I'd see you lived long enough to regret it."

Thackray had left his car where Grabianski had suggested, not in the car park directly behind Kenwood House, but the one farther along toward Jack Straw's Castle, left it there and walked back down to where Grabianski was waiting, seated near the faded rhododendron bushes either side of Doctor Johnson's summer house. It was early in the evening and the breeze carried with it a certain chill now the sun had dipped behind some wavering cloud. Wearing a sheepskin car coat, Thackray looked like a man expecting winter.

"We've hit," he announced, "something of a problem." As yet, he had barely stopped walking. "My buyer in Japan, he only wants the one piece. The *Departing Day* study, of course. The other," Thackray sighed, "he claims it's not worth the price of air freight. Never mind the insurance."

"How much," Grabianski asked, "is he prepared to pay?"

"Twenty-five thousand sterling, dollar equivalent, of course."

Grabianski moved along the bench and Thackray, tugging at his trousers so they didn't bag unnecessarily at the knees, sat down. Grabianski caught himself wondering if there was anyone born after 1955, any male, for whom that was still an automatic gesture.

"You know," Thackray said, "I don't think I'm going to be able to push him any harder on this."

"That's fine," Grabianski said. "If that's the best deal there is …"

"Excellent." Thackray sealed the bargain with a sheepskin-warm handshake. "Now, if you'd care to join me, I thought a quick look round Kenwood House here before closing. There's a lovely little Vermeer."

Grabianski made a show of glancing at his watch. "Better not."

"Suit yourself. I'll be in touch." And Grabianski stood watching Vernon Thackray walk along the narrow, jinking path and across a small diagonal of lawn. Whatever risk there was of being seen with Thackray, best, especially now, to keep it to a minimum.

There was a steady roll of traffic coming off Spaniards Road at Whitestone Pond and turning down toward the Heath. Grabianski pushed his phone card into the slot and waited for the little illuminated message telling him it was okay to dial.

"Faron," he said, recognizing her flat, nasal tone, "Jerry Grabianski. I'd like to talk to Eddie."

She told him to wait and he heard the receiver being set down with a soft chunk. There was music in the background, none of the three or four things Grabianski might have recognized: music never his strong point.

Whatever it was, it rose in volume as Faron came back on the line. "He says is it important?"

"Probably. Tell him it's to do with what we were discussing earlier today." Grabianski could hear other voices now, something of a party, warming up, he guessed, for the night ahead.

"What?" Snow's voice was unnecessarily loud, pitched against the noise.

"The deal you mentioned. I've been thinking about it and what you were saying makes sense. If this is the best deal we're going to get, let's take it now."

199

"You're sure?"

"Sure."

"You know we're not talking the day after tomorrow, right? Prob'ly not even next week. There's always money to be moved around, transportation, na-de-na-de-nah."

"That's okay. I know you're not going to hang about. I'll leave all that up to you."

"Great. Oh, and Jerry ..."

"Yes?"

"Not right now, but there's something else I wanted to talk to you about, okay? Piece of business I might be able to put your way. Your line, know what I mean?"

Oh, yes, Grabianski thought, maybe he did; in the small square of mirrored glass, he watched his face brighten into a smile.

Table lamp shining, chilled glass of Stolichnaya close at hand, Grabianski shuffled through the cards he had bought at the exhibition, deciding which to choose. It had to be *The Millinery Shop*, the vividness of that lime green scarf not so striking in reproduction, but she would remember all the same. He uncapped his fountain pen, a silver-inlaid Waterman's with gold nib he had come across in a seventeenth-century-style writing desk which had proved disappointingly fake. He wanted to be careful what he wrote.

Thirty-seven

Thinking about Jill, the way she had looked when he had left that morning, Khan overshot his exit from the motorway and had to drive south another seventeen miles before he could make a turn. The Dray Horse was a sprawling three-story building whose white stucco frontage had long since turned a carbon monoxide shade of gray. There were two car parks, one to either side, pot-holed and in need of resurfacing. Even the horse itself had seen better days, plodding along in front of a bulging brewery wagon, shoulders straining, head bowed, paint flecked and faded on a sign which swayed creakily in the burgeoning east wind.

Khan left his car facing the road and rattled the handle on the front door. The sign written in white paint above his head read *Lawrence Gerald Fitzpatrick, licensed to sell wines and spirits.* Khan was about to try the bell when he saw someone approaching through the mottled glass.

"If it's a drink you want, you're too early; if it's something you're selling, we're not buying."

He was a bearded man who wore his belly the way a camel wears its hump, except at the front. The whiskers around his mouth were stained reddish-brown with nicotine.

"Mr. Fitzpatrick?"

"Depends who's asking."

Khan identified himself and the man shook his head. "Them lights you saw on, round midnight was it? That was just the bar staff clearing up. And if it's the music, well, the renewal license is in the post."

"It's not that I've come about, it's the phone."

"Bloody hell! Sending the likes of you out here for that now, are they? I stuck a check in first class mail, Sat'day."

Patient, Khan explained why he was there. The telephone matching the number Mollie had passed on to Resnick was, indeed, out in the hall, directly across from the ladies toilet. The gents, smelling richly now of disinfectant, was farther along. The harness that kept the phone attached to the wall had worked itself loose by a couple of screws, and the mouthpiece, originally cream, was now virtually black with the residue of phlegm and so much bad breath. A calendar listing the dates of the principal Newmarket race meetings hung from the wall at a convenient height for doodling and several neat pornographic conceits shared its margins with a myriad of numbers and barely decipherable messages.

"I'll have to borrow this," Khan said, indicating the calendar. "You'll get it back all in good time."

"Aye, when it's good and out of date, I'll wager."

Khan took out his notebook and began to copy down the irregular curve of telephone numbers that had been written directly onto the wall. By the time he had done a quick check in the local directory, he'd ascertained two-thirds of them belonged to taxi companies, and one of the most frequent of the others seemed to connect with a sauna and massage parlor in Saffron Walden.

"I wanted to ask you," Khan said, "about a call that came through here just after eleven thirty the Saturday before last."

"Morning or night?" Fitzgerald asked.

"Morning. Ring any bells?"

Fitzgerald thought back; from the pained expression on his face it wasn't something he bothered with too often. "No," he said finally, "can't say as it does. You could ask Len, though. He's in later. He might have picked up on something."

Len Bassett was a soft-spoken man in his late fifties who walked slightly on a slant as the result of a replacement hip. He came up with three possibilities more or less straight off: a market gardener from Burwell who sometimes used the pub to take orders, a commercial traveler in fancy goods who provided all and sundry to corner shops and sub-post offices from Lowestoft to Northampton, and that bald feller, tall, you know the one I mean, Lawrence, always carrying one of them black briefcases wherever he goes, never lets it out of his sight. What's his name now? Small whisky and ginger ale, that's what he has. Grants, Bells, Teachers, doesn't care. Once you've smothered it with ginger ale, tastes the same anyway.

"You can't remember his name?" Khan asked.

Neither man could.

Khan set two of his cards on the bar counter. "If either of you do remember anything more, I'd appreciate it if you got in touch."

The men looked at one another. "Right," they both said.

Khan stopped off on the A45 near Fen Ditton and bought some cut flowers; if he made good time getting back, he might take a chance and nip to the flat before reporting back to the station. It was Jill's day for the late shift at Central and with any luck she might still be around.

Alex Peterson's dental surgery was on the raised first floor of one of those large, bay-fronted buildings on College Street, leading down the Hill to Wellington Circus. The receptionist viewed Resnick with suspicion, a man trying to muscle in on the appointments list by dint of waving his warrant card around. But after some discussion on the intercom, Peterson's dental nurse, a young Muslim woman with her head and lower face covered above her white uniform, came through and informed Resnick in a soft voice that if he could wait for just five minutes, Mr. Peterson would be able to see him.

Five minutes, as they do in dentists' waiting rooms, became fifteen. Peterson emerged in conversation with a middle-aged woman holding a handkerchief to one side of her face and doing her best to look brave despite the pain.

"Inspector ..."

"If there's somewhere we could talk privately?"

Peterson led him back into the surgery, from which the nurse had now disappeared. "You've found something? About what happened?" His voice was anxious, the dark hollows scooped below his eyes suggested tears, lack of sleep. The lingering smell in the room—metallic, medicinal—brought Resnick suddenly back to his childhood, be brave, this is going to hurt just a little bit.

"Really, it's a question," Resnick said. "It may be nothing."

"Go on."

"Your wife, as far as you know, did she have friends in the Cambridge area? Newmarket, possibly. Somewhere around there. There was no one on the list you gave us."

Peterson blinked. "No, I don't think so. Why?"

"It might not be important …"

Peterson's hand was on Resnick's arm; his breath, mint-flavored, on his face. "Tell me, please."

"A phone call she may have made, that's all. We can't even be certain it was her."

"But you think she made a call to Cambridge, that's what you're saying? I don't understand. When was this? Is that where you think she might have gone?"

"As yet we just don't know."

"But it must be important, otherwise why would you be here?"

Resnick sighed. "I'm here because we're checking everything, every little thing that might give us a lead to what happened." He looked at Peterson for a moment. "Believe me, as soon there's anything definite, I'll let you know."

"Really? I'd like to believe that was true."

"Your wife was killed," Resnick said. "I've no way of knowing how that must feel. But I do know how important it is to understand what happened. And why. You have my word. If this leads any-where, I will keep you informed."

Slowly, Peterson nodded. "Thank you. And I'm sorry if …"

"There's nothing to be sorry for."

Back at the Ropewalk there were two messages waiting: one from Lynn to say that she had tracked down Prentiss' ex-girlfriend Patricia Falk in Peterborough and arranged to meet her; the other was from Hannah—monkfish with grilled aubergine, how did that sound? Resnick thought it sounded good.

Thirty-eight

On either side of the road as Lynn drove, neatly hedged fields spun away to small horizons. At dinner last night with Sharon Garnett— a curry washed down with bottles of Kingfisher, and the usual bad coffee made palatable by After Eights—she had tried to talk through how she felt about working again with Resnick, so soon after thinking she had made the break. And the truth was, it didn't feel too bad.

Well, as she had sought to explain, it was different, being part of a far larger team, not cooped up in that substation at Canning Circus with just a handful of others and Resnick looming over everything. She was a sergeant now, more status, expected to use her initiative, take responsibility. And the case they were working on, a murder, possibly five murders all down to the same person— how much more serious could Serious Crimes get?

"So you see what I mean?" Lynn said, lifting a piece of lamb with her fork. "It's not the same at all."

Grinning, Sharon tore off a piece of naan bread and scooped it through what was left of her coriander and green chili sauce. "You know what I think?"

"No. Go on."

"I think you should marry him and have done with it."

"Very funny!"

"Maybe."

Watching Lynn reach for the water jug to refill her glass, Sharon laughed. "Hot is it, that lamb passanda of yours?"

She had only been to Peterborough a few times, and only once by car. The outskirts of the town seemed dominated by low-level industrial estates, which the development council optimistically called parks, and units of neat brick housing only now beginning to show serious need of repair. The signs for the town center were frequent and clear and the green neon outside the multi-story told her there were spaces available. She could walk from there directly into the newish shopping center, which was where she'd arranged to meet Patricia Falk.

As those places went, Lynn thought, it was pleasanter than most. At least there seemed to be plenty of natural light—or was that an illusion?—and the walkways were wide enough for people to stroll without feeling they were running a gauntlet between Our Price and Etam, Saxone and WH Smith.

Patricia Falk was precisely where she had said she would be, on a stool at the right-hand side of the Costa Coffee Boutique, wearing, as she had promised, a brightly colored cardigan with a parrot that looked as though it came from Guatemala. She was nibbling at a hazelnut wafer and reading the G2 section of the *Guardian*.

Lynn introduced herself before ordering a cappuccino and dragging over an empty stool.

Patricia Falk was in, she guessed, her early forties but could have passed for less. Her eyes were alert and bright behind simple round spectacles with gold rims; her dark hair had been cut short, but stylishly, and azure blue birds hung down from her ears. When Lynn had asked her on the telephone what she did, she had said, somewhat dismissively, "Oh, I work with voluntary groups," as if that were explanation enough.

A few minutes' chat about the journey and the day and then she plunged in. "This is about Jane," Patricia said. "Jane's murder."

"Yes."

"I couldn't believe it when I read it. It was just ... You never think, when you hear about these things, it's going to be anybody you know. I mean, burglaries, yes, someone losing a bike, their car stereo, but this ..." She drank some coffee and shifted her position on the stool. "You know, I only worked with her for a year. Less. I left halfway through the summer term."

"Had something happened?"

Patricia smiled. "I'd seen the way things were going. National curriculum. Testing. The days when you could expect to be creative as a teacher were at an end. And if the teachers aren't allowed to be creative, what chance is there for the kids?"

Lynn nodded, uncertain; the only kids she regularly came in touch with didn't seem to have a problem with creativity: they could be relied upon to find new ways to cheat and steal and the stories they told to cover up for what they did would have made Hans Christian Andersen seem like a candidate for Special Needs.

"Would you say, though, you knew her well?"

"Pretty well, yes. Considering the amount of time we spent together."

"You went out with her a few times, I think. Her and her husband. A foursome."

Patricia, whose head had begun to tilt inquiringly to one side, let out a knowing laugh. "Oh, you've been talking to Prentiss. I thought someone had been doing a diligent trawl through old staff records at the school. But, no, now I see. Well, that's a name from the past I hadn't expected to hear again."

"You haven't kept in touch, then?"

"In touch and Alan aren't terms that go together. Which is strange, considering his chosen profession. I told him, he should have been a priest instead of an osteopath. No need for physical contact other than a religious laying on of hands."

"He wasn't what you'd call," Lynn asked, "a particularly passion-ate man?"

"In his head, maybe." Seeing Lynn's raised eyebrow, she gave a rueful smile. "Sorry, I sound bitter, don't I?"

"Yes. Yes, you do."

"Are you married?"

Lynn shook her head.

"A man?"

"No."

"A woman, then?"

"No."

"Maybe you're lucky."

And maybe I'm not, Lynn thought.

"God help me," Patricia said, "what I did with Prentiss was, made

207

this image of him. It was as if I'd taken bits of him, all the different bits, and put them together in some totally different way. And that was what I saw, that was what I wanted, but, of course, he wasn't there, he wasn't like that, only inside my head. And it took me— what?—five months of miserable, disappointed evenings before I finally realized. Five months of going out with this ... this phantom." Patricia laughed. "Can you believe that?"

Even Lynn was smiling. How long had she shared her life with the cyclist, shared her flat with him? Cog wheels on the carpet and time charts taped to the kitchen wall. Whatever had she thought he was going to turn out to be? "Yes," she said, "I'm afraid I can."

"Whereas Jane, poor Jane. She knew what she wanted and she got it in spades."

"Which was what?"

"Someone strong, intelligent, absolutely committed to her. Someone who, no matter what else, needed her."

"He was in love with her, then? Alex?"

"If that's a definition of love, yes."

"You don't think it is?"

"Oh, I think it might be missing a few things, don't you? Tolerance. Space. Freedom. Room to develop, change. Just room to breathe."

"And she didn't have those?"

"Did you ever meet Jane? Did you ever see her and Alex together?"

Lynn shook her head; she didn't want to say the only time she'd seen Jane Peterson was when she was dead.

"When she was on her own, working, for instance, with the kids, she ... well, she had a mind, she was lively, fun to be with, she became involved—a little too much so at times, she could be over-intense about things. In Alex's company she was this ..." Patricia finished the last of her coffee. "She was like his little dog, you know, a pet dog. Alex would be all for showing her off, bragging about how attractive she was and all of that, and then it was as if he'd encourage her to say stuff, you know, get excited, do tricks, and when she was really into it, he'd slap her down."

"Slap?"

"Not literally. Slap." Patricia's hand steadied in the middle of putting down her empty cup. Never taking her eyes off Lynn, she asked, "He didn't hit her, did he? Alex? He didn't ..."

Lynn was looking back at her, not answering, but Patricia could read it in her face.

"The bastard. That cruel bastard."

"You didn't know?" Lynn asked quietly.

Lips tight together, Patricia shook her head.

"And Jane, she never said anything?"

"Not one word."

"But you're not surprised?"

"When I look back on it, it makes perfect sense. I mean, I knew that in a way she was frightened of him. That when he said jump, if you like, she jumped." Patricia looked around toward the counter. "Look, I don't know about you, but I could do with another coffee."

"Maybe in a minute," Lynn said. "I just wanted to ask, if all this was going on, why you think she put up with it?"

Patricia folded the paper that had held her wafer in half, then half, then half again. "I think in a way it's what she wanted, that kind of almost domination. And I think, in any case, she would have been frightened to have done anything about it."

"Anything. Such as?"

"Oh, the whole range, from suggesting family therapy to leaving him. Having an affair."

"And you don't think she did that?"

"An affair? Jane? She'd have had to be a combination of Houdini and Mata Hari if she had."

Lynn nodded, stood away from the stool to get more coffee.

"Although she might have thought about it," Patricia said quietly.

For a moment, Lynn held her breath. "What makes you say that?"

Patricia half-smiled, remembering. "We were nattering one day in the loo. Girls' stuff. One of the games staff was having this big thing with someone from another school. Everyone knew about it and they didn't seem to care; everyone except for their respective partners, I imagine. I remember Jane saying it's amazing what you can get away with if you've got the guts. I think she said balls. Anyway, I told her it was okay for her to talk, she wasn't the type to have an affair even in her wildest dreams. And I remember she gave me this little smile and said, 'If only you knew.'"

"That was all?"

"That was all."

"But you thought ...?"

"I suppose I thought, well, she's been thinking about it, at least."

"Cappuccino or espresso?" Lynn asked.

"Straight, please. Straight black."

"All right," Resnick said, "correct me if I'm wrong." They were in their room on the Ropewalk, Resnick, Khan, and Lynn, the window open several inches top and bottom, the air heavy and promising rain. To the northwest, the sky was darkening like an overripe plum. "What we're supposing is this. One, despite any previous evidence to the contrary, Jane Peterson was carrying on an affair. How far this had got or how long it had been going on, we've no way as yet of knowing, but some kind of affair.

"Two, both of the calls she made from Broadway, were made to the other person involved, which places him in the Cambridgeshire–Newmarket area, if not permanently, then at those times.

"And three, after the second of those calls, somewhere, somehow, Jane ran out on her husband and joined her lover. We don't know what happened then, where they went, anything. All we do know is that a week later she was dead." He looked from Lynn to Khan and back again. "Now why, as a story, do I not find that convincing?"

"There are too many gaps," Khan said. "Too much conjecture. We don't *know* she was having an affair at all."

"We know she phoned someone before she disappeared."

"Okay, but if she's on the point of meeting him, why talk for almost half an hour?"

"Maybe there were a lot of arrangements to be made."

"Or," Resnick said, "maybe one or other of them was getting cold feet."

"Probably Jane," Lynn said.

"We don't know that," said Khan.

"She was the one who'd stayed in an abusive relationship for years," Lynn said. "If she was all that keen to run off, surely she'd have done it sooner. No, it makes perfect sense to me she'd have doubts."

"Right at the last minute?"

"Especially then."

"Okay," Resnick said, "here's what we do. Lynn, we should check back through all of Jane's known friends and relations; if she let that one remark slip to Patricia Falk, she just may have said something to somebody else. Something that until we jog their memory they might have honestly forgotten. And push the Cambridgeshire connection, see if you can get them to come up with anyone Jane knew there."

Lynn nodded.

"Anil, I want you back out at that pub, asking around. If this bloke we're looking for calls in regular, daytimes, it might mean it's on his route from here to there. But equally well, it might be his local. How close is the nearest village? Couple of miles? Happen he's got good reasons for not wanting to take calls at home. Some calls. Okay?"

"Yes, sir."

"Right." As Resnick pushed up to his feet, the first rumblings of thunder were heard, rolling across the middle distance. By the time he was down at the main entrance, spots of rain the size of ten pence pieces were darkening the street.

Thirty-nine

Standing in the kitchen, Resnick seated at the table in front of her, Hannah vigorously toweled his hair dry. "Why is it," she asked, "I feel like I'm in a short story by D. H. Lawrence? Seeing to my man after a hard day at the pit face. All it needs is the coal in the bath to be perfect."

"Or me in the bath," Resnick suggested.

Hannah dipped her head to kiss the back of his neck. "We'll get to that later."

After dinner, they sat in the front room with the lights out and watched a video of Woody Allen's *September*. Brittle, rich people with money enough to indulge their own small hurts. And in its midst a writer whom half the women seem unfathomably to be in love with. He was, Resnick thought, as manipulative and self-obsessed as he supposed writers might be.

"Switch it off, Charlie, for heaven's sake!" Hannah exclaimed as, yet again, Resnick let out a groan at the behavior of one or other character on the screen. "Or else stop complaining."

But there was one thing that kept him watching—or listening: the album Art Tatum once made with Ben Webster was forever on the record player. People danced to it, listened in the dark to it, kissed and quarreled to it, exclaimed how wonderful it was.

Which was true. Almost the only truth Resnick could divine from the whole charade.

"You know what it reminded me of?" Hannah said, once the end titles had come up, switching the remote to rewind. "You remember the first time we went to Broadway, that film we saw based on the Chekhov play?"

Resnick could recall the occasion very well; about the film he

212

was less certain. He reached up to switch on the light. It was still not eleven o'clock. "The thing that got me," he said, pausing on his way to the kitchen, "wanting us to believe that twerp of a writer with the morals of an alley cat would have the nous to choose Tatum and Webster as his favorite record."

Hannah looked at him, smiling. "Morality, Charlie, is that what it's about?"

And Resnick looked right back at her, as if not believing what she had just said.

Candlelight flickering across walls and ceiling, and only a light rain now falling, they lay and stared up through the skylight at the midnight sky.

"After things went wrong between you and Jim," Resnick said suddenly, "how long did it take you to come to terms? Yourself, I mean. You know, feel okay again."

Hannah turned lightly onto her side, facing him. "What made you ask that?"

"Do you mind?"

"No. It's just that you've never asked before. About that or anything much else." She was stroking her fingers down along the inside of his arm.

"I suppose I always figured it's your life."

"Not wanting to interrogate me, eh, Charlie?"

"Something like that."

"And now?" She raised one knee so that he could slide his leg between hers.

"It was watching the film, I suppose. Mia what's-her-name, taking two years off in the country to get over some bloke who's dumped her."

"She could afford to, that's all."

"And you?"

"All I could afford was a week in France, visiting my dad and his doxy."

"Doxy?"

"You know what I mean."

"Do I?"

Her breasts were pressed against his chest and when she moved only slightly along his thigh, he could feel that she was already wet.

"So how long did it take?" Resnick asked, his mouth close to her ear.

"Getting over Jim?"

"Uh-huh." Difficult to speak when she was kissing him.

"About two years," Hannah said some moments later. "If, that is, you ever really do."

She slid herself over him and, though he wasn't quite ready, deftly took him inside her. Leaning forward, she teased his nipples with her tongue and then, knees fast against his side, arched back, arms wide, and hung there, her voice arousing, enthusing, attacking, and imploring.

Resnick raised a hand toward her face and, broadly smiling, she took his fingers in her mouth and languorously started licking them, but that was not what he had meant. He moved his hand again till it was behind her neck and gently brought her down and round until once again she lay facing him.

"I'm sorry," he breathed. "I don't know …"

"Charlie, Charlie, shush. It doesn't matter. The earth doesn't have to move every time." And then she threw back her head and laughed. "Sleep with an English teacher, Charlie, and that's what you get. Literary references the whole evening." And continued to laugh, rocking on her hip until she spilled him out.

Forty

As soon as the car crested the hill across the moor and he saw the rose window of the abbey outlined against the stubborn blue of the sea, Resnick remembered when he had been here before. Whitby. The summer of '76. Himself and Elaine young enough and still in love enough not to care if the cups they drank tea from in the café on the West Cliff were cracked, if the wind laced chip papers around their feet each time they crossed the harbor bridge, or if the seagulls woke them at dawn in the B&B where they stayed. Especially that.

Why was it, Resnick wondered, dropping down a gear to make a show winding descent into Sleights, that those were the times he rarely thought of? Elaine working as a secretary for that firm of solicitors on Bridlesmith Gate, typing heaven knows how many letters and invoices by day and going off to evening classes when she was done, business management and administrative skills; Resnick a young copper new to CID but eager already to mug up for his sergeant's exam. Nights when he and Elaine would sit up in bed, blankets wrapped round them to keep back the cold, testing one another on what they had read. Elaine with the glasses slipping off the end of her nose as she fidgeted for the biro that had got lost in the sheets.

Some people, he knew, invented rose-tinted versions of their past; lives spent together in barely screened dislike and studied acrimony became, with the benefit of time and absence, near idyllic passages of mutual bliss. What he remembered were the petty rows, the jealousies, arguments about the bill that she forgot to pay, the meal he missed; what he saw in her face were want and pain, when the wanting was no longer for him and the pain was his to share.

He could still remember the carelessness of Elaine's infidelity, like a child who can't say no to sweets.

A vague geography of the town coming back to him, he turned left in front of the small municipal park, right again at the top of the street, and parked. Walking down past still impressive Georgian houses set well back from the road, he cut through onto Back St. Hilda's Terrace, then down again into one of the narrow yards, snug there, almost hidden above the outer harbor.

The house he was looking for had flowers spilling from hung baskets and window boxes, the already small windows cloistered behind pink and white petals.

He wasn't sure what he had expected of Diane Harker from their sparse conversations on the phone, but possibly not this trim woman in cut-off blue jeans, a lemon top knotted above the waist, and violently bleached blonde hair that sprang wildly from around her head. If there was a resemblance to her elder sister, Resnick could not see it yet.

A small child—a boy he thought, though he was less than certain—sat on Diane's right hip, supported by her arm, and a second child, a girl of three or four, clung to her other hand.

"You found it all right, then?" she said, glancing at his warrant card.

"Yes."

"People get lost."

"I can imagine."

"You'd best come inside. But mind your head."

Resnick negotiated the first beam but not the second, the hard edge grazing away a good square inch of skin. He had the grace not to cry out or complain. The room was small yet somehow bright, every surface above four-year-old height crammed with ornaments and photographs, postcards rearranged into surreal collages, pieces of weathered driftwood in the shapes of fish or birds. A one-eared cat, the color of pale marmalade, sat, sphinx-like, on the arm of the one easy chair. The elder of the two children sat on the bottom tread of the curving stairs, jiggling a faceless doll in her lap.

Diane pushed a mug of herbal tea into Resnick's hands. The

younger child was nuzzling her breast. "We'll go out," she said. "In a minute. It'll be easier to talk."

They walked toward the West Pier, slow progress between the fish dock and the tat and glitter of amusement arcades and shops selling Whitby rock or doughnuts, six for a pound. Outside the Magpie Café, where he and Elaine had eaten gargantuan plaice and chips, followed by hazelnut meringue, Resnick bent low to retie the little girl's shoe, for all the world, in his loose dark suit and flowered tie, like a flustered uncle come to visit.

Diane stood jiggling the small boy—it was a boy—on her hip and talking to him in a low voice: seagull, fisherman, boat.

At the lifeboat station, they crossed the street and walked past the wooden bandstand, out onto the pier, Resnick asking Diane about her family and hearing a familiar tale of jealousies and jumbled expectations. The oldest child, the brother, who did well at school and university, leaving three sisters uncertain in his wake. While James was successfully pursuing wife and career, the oldest daughter was poised to bury herself beneath the hard work and constant grind of being a farmer's wife, and the next, Jane, had a secure job and was respectably married, even if she had failed to provide the necessary grandchildren by the expected time.

"And you?" Resnick asked.

"I was the one who bunked off from school, started going out with boys when I was thirteen, got drunk on Southern Comfort and cider, smoked, sniffed glue. It's a wonder, as my dear mother never tired of telling me, I didn't get into more serious trouble than I did." She glanced across at him. "I didn't even get pregnant till I was seventeen."

"But ..." Resnick was looking at the four-year-old, skipping up ahead.

"Oh, I had an abortion. More than one. Funny, really, Mum being a midwife and all. A miscarriage at twenty-one." She laughed, the sound silvering away, brittle, on the wind. "I was beginning to think I'd be like Jane, never have kids at all. That was before I met their father. He painted some Pentecostal sign on my belly and played Jimi Hendrix at full volume. Oh, of course, he had to stick it in as well. Worked first time, just about."

"He's not still around?" Resnick asked.

"I think he heard voices telling him to move on. The last we heard he was living in a bothy on the Isle of Mull and practicing white magic. Presumably on the sheep."

"And you stayed here."

"I like it. Besides, I was pregnant again at the time. Making up for Jane." She stopped and there were tears in her eyes. "God, poor Jane!" She shifted the child across to her other hip, tugging a tissue from the pocket of her jeans. "If anything awful was going to happen to anyone, you'd have thought it was going to be me. All the stupid things I used to get up to, the risks I took. And Jane, I doubt she took a serious risk in her life—you can't even include Alex, he wasn't a risk, he was just a bloody mistake. So how, how does she end up the way she did? How does she end up bloody dead?"

Distressed by her mother's tears, the girl clung to her leg while the younger one pressed his face against her chest. Resnick hovered on the verge of putting an arm around her, putting an arm around them all, but then Diane was wiping her face and smiling and promising ice cream on the way home and the moment had passed.

They stopped again near the end of the pier and leaned against the rail, the ruins of the abbey and the weather-beaten church high behind them on the East Cliff, below them the tide dragging the sea back along the Upgang Shore. Dogs and children ran and chased balls and a few intrepid souls swam in the nearer edges of the water. With a stick in the sand, someone had scratched the words *I think* and nothing more, having thought, presumably, better of it.

"Were you close, you and Jane?" Resnick asked.

Diane didn't answer right away. "Not really close, no. When we were growing up, it was she and Margaret who were friends, did stuff together. I was ... I was just the little one getting under everyone's feet and getting in the way. Real runt of the litter. But there was a while, it must have been when Margaret had gone off to university and Jane was in the sixth form, I suppose, we became sort of close then."

"And more recently? Since you've been here?"

"Oh, Jane would occasionally persuade Alex to drive up for the day. I mean, he hated it, just hated it. You could see it in everything about him from the minute they arrived—that supercilious manner of his, just the way he stood. It was all I could do to get him to sit down in the house. I think he was always afraid there'd be something organic and squashy beneath the cushions. And, of course, he didn't know what to do with the kids, didn't have a clue. Creatures from another planet, as far as he was concerned." She gave a mock shudder. "No wonder children are afraid of dentists."

"How about Jane," Resnick said. "How was she with the kids? Did they get on okay? Did she like them?"

"She loved them. And they loved her. I remember once, it couldn't have been so long after this one was born, Alex must have been off at some conference or something, anyway, Jane got to come over on her own for the whole day. It was wonderful. We just fooled around on the beach in the morning; made up a picnic and drove up onto the moors." For a moment, Diane's voice was breaking up. It must have been the last time she saw her sister; Resnick didn't need to ask, and she didn't need to say.

"It wasn't her decision then, as far as you know, not to have children?"

Diane squeezed her hands around the metal of the rail. "Decision? In that relationship, there wasn't much question of Jane making decisions. Oh, I dare say mustard or cranberry sauce with the turkey, two pints of milk or three, but that was about as far as it went."

"Why did she put up with it?"

Diane shrugged, turned around, and leaned the small of her back against the railing. Her daughter was tugging at the uneven hem of her cut-offs, eager for ice cream. "Why does anyone put up with anything? Because we're too lazy to do anything different? Too frightened."

"You think she was frightened of Alex?"

Diane looked at him. "Probably. But that wasn't what I meant. Frightened of the alternatives, that's what I meant, all that great unknown." She cuddled the smaller child to her, and nuzzled her chin down into his hair. "Frightened of being alone."

"You don't think," Resnick said—they were walking now, back along the way they had come—"you don't think she could have been having an affair?"

"God!" Diane said. "I wish she had. I wish she'd had the gumption, never mind anything else."

"But you don't think she was?"

Emphatically, Diane shook her head.

"Would she have said?"

"To me, you mean? I'm not certain. Once I might have said, yes. And maybe that day she was here, if anything had been going on ..." A smile brightened Diane's face. "The only time I can remember her going on about something like that, you know, boys, men, love, she was home from university and we went off into town, shopping for clothes. There was this lad she'd met and she just couldn't stop talking about him. On and on and on. 'I'll never want anyone else,' she said, 'not as long as I live.'" They stopped at the curb and waited for a car to ease past. "Well, you say things like that, don't you? Young and in love. It doesn't mean anything."

Back in the house, radio playing, children stalking the cat, Diane blew the top layer of dust away from a cardboard box she had pulled out from under the bed. Inside were photographs, old Christmas cards, torn concert tickets, letters, badges. Diane shuffled and sorted while Resnick watched.

"Here," she said, finally, separating one small colored photograph from a batch of a dozen or so others. "Jane and Peter. Love's young dream."

Resnick looked down at two nineteen-year-olds, arms wound about each other on a white bridge, smiling not at the camera but at each other.

"Where's this taken?" Resnick asked.

"Cambridge. It's where they went to university."

Resnick looked at the young man with a wide face and a shock of dark hair, unable to see anything other than the young woman beside him. Even in that small, slightly battered photograph, it was impossible not to respond to the adoration he was feeling, not to see her beauty through his eyes.

"You've no idea where he might be now?" Resnick asked.

"Peter?" She shook her head. "I haven't a clue."

"And Jane never mentioned him? More recently, I mean."

"Never, no."

Careful to avoid cat and child, Resnick got to his feet. "If I could just borrow this, a few days? I'll make sure it gets back to you in one piece."

"I suppose so," Diane said, a little surprised. "Can't do any harm."

Forty-one

"Peter Spurgeon," Resnick said, holding out the blow-up reproduction of the photograph. "I don't have to tell you it was taken a while ago."

"Childhood sweethearts," said Lynn, not quite able to keep the dismissiveness out of her tone.

"College, anyway," said Khan.

"And we're assuming they've kept in touch?" Lynn asked.

Resnick lowered the photograph onto the desk. "We're assuming nothing. What we're doing is checking as thoroughly as we can. Let's see if we can track him down through vehicle registration; otherwise, it's voting registers, directories, you know the kind of thing. And let's check his college while we're about it; there's bound to be some kind of organization for former students and he just might belong."

When the phone went some little while later, Khan identified himself, listened for a moment, then passed the receiver across to Resnick. "For you, sir. Something about a nun."

Sister Teresa was waiting for Resnick outside the main doors, a dark gray shawl draped over a light gray dress, gray tights, and black laced ankle boots.

"You're busy," she said, reading some concern in Resnick's face.

"No more than usual. Time for a cup of coffee, at least."

"Ah, I'd best not. There's two people to call on still, and then another of those meetings Sister Bonaventura's forever hauling me off to. *Christian Interface and the Diocese*, something along those lines."

Still smiling, she drew an envelope from her bag and from that lifted out a postcard. "It arrived yesterday. I thought you might want to see."

Resnick glanced quickly at a picture of a young woman sitting among a lot of hats, before turning it over to read the reverse:

> *Your favorite, I think. Almost mine too. Entrance to exit it was a perfect afternoon. Thank you.*
> *I thought you'd like to know, after your lecture, I've decided to be active in the cause of righteousness.*
> *Till St. Ives,*
> *Jerzy*

"St. Ives?" Resnick said.

"Oh, that's nothing. Just some foolishness." She was, Resnick thought, perilously close to blushing.

"The rest of it, then ..."

"I did as you asked, tried to show him that in helping you, he could only be helping himself." She waited until she had Resnick's eye. "That is right, isn't it?"

"Oh, yes," Resnick said. "I think so."

Teresa reached her hand toward the card. "You'll not be needing this?" As he relinquished his grip of it, she replaced the card inside the envelope, the envelope safely inside her bag.

"Thanks for making the time," Resnick said.

She slipped her hand for a moment into his and smiled.

Helen Siddons was shouting instructions down the corridor, a plethora of younger officers stumbling in her wake. Midway down the stairs, she paused to light another cigarette and that was when she spotted Resnick, on his way back into the building. "Charlie, how's it going?"

As they walked, he filled her in on the progress of his end of the inquiry, letting her know just enough to see they hadn't been wasting their time.

"Well," Siddons had stopped outside the main computer room, hand to the door, "not that I want to knock you off your stride, but it looks like we've got a live one just crawled out of the woodwork.

223

Went down for attempted rape six months after the Irene Wilson murder; released three weeks before that girl turned up in the Beeston Canal. Oh, and Charlie, we may have got a line on her, too. Dental records. Should have confirmation in a day or two."

And with a wave of cigarette smoke she disappeared.

Carl Vincent finally got through to the Arts and Antiques Unit at the Yard after a solid fifteen minutes of trying. Tracking down Jackie Ferris took five minutes more.

On the line she sounded brisk and businesslike, prepared to give him exactly as much of her time as importance warranted, but no more.

"My DI," Vincent said, "in a roundabout sort of way, he's had a message from Grabianski. Seems as if he's ready to push ahead. Could be soon."

"Right. Maybe you should get yourself down here sharpish. Any problem with that?"

"None that I can think of."

"Fine. Ring me as soon as you arrive." Jackie Ferris hung up.

Holly had told Grabianski he should buy root ginger and lemons and make ginger tea; it would help to clear away a lot of the toxins that were troubling him. He was almost back from a trip to the fruit and vegetable stall, purchases in a small plastic bag, when he noticed someone sitting on the steps outside his building. It was Faron.

She was wearing a shiny silver dress and there were new gold highlights in her hair. Between the bottom of the dress and the expected clumpy shoes, her legs, thin in spangled tights, seemed to go on forever.

"Hi-ya!" She dropped her magazine as Grabianski came through the gate and, quickly to her feet, caught hold of his arm and kissed him on the cheek.

"Don't tell me, Faron," he said, "you were out for a walk on the Heath, and before you knew it here you were outside my house. You thought you'd stay for tea."

She peered along her sharp little nose. "You're sending me up, aren't you?"

"Maybe. Just a little."

"That's all right. Eddie does it all the time. And worse. Downright rude, sometimes. Know what I mean? No respect."

Grabianski unlocked the front door and led her through what it always delighted him to remember were called "the common parts." Several flights of stairs and they were standing in the combined living room-kitchen, an elevated skylight drawing in the light from above their heads.

"Have a seat," Grabianski said, pointing toward the low settee. "I'll put the kettle on."

"I don't suppose you've got any white wine? I should've brought some myself, but I didn't think. Well, sometimes you don't, do you? Not till it's too late."

Out of the mouths of babes and five-thousand-a-show models, thought Grabianski. He took a bottle of Sancerre from the fridge and uncorked it. Faron was back on her feet again, prowling the room.

"It's nice here. Cozy."

"Thanks." He gave her a glass of wine and she gulped the first mouthful as if it were pop. "Only one thing, though, I thought there'd be paintings, you know, all round the walls, like at Eddie's."

What Grabianski had were landscape photographs; a few enlarged shots of birds that he'd taken himself. On the glass-topped coffee table in front of the settee, there was a black statuette of a falcon in flight. A few shelves of books, mostly reference, and that was all.

"Where's your tele, then? In the bedroom, I suppose. Eddie keeps his in there, too. Still, at least you've got a few CDs."

It was difficult not to think Faron would be disappointed with his selection: *Bird Calls of Africa and the Near East; Tropical Storms*; a recording of Prokofiev and Janáãek violin sonatas he'd bought because he liked the look of Viktoria Mullova on the cover; Steven Halpern's *Spectrum Suite*, recommended by Holly for the way it resonated within specific areas of the body. After the African bird calls, it was the one Grabianski played most.

"You know," Faron said, turning, "what Eddie don't trust about you? He thinks you don't know how to have fun. Too serious, right?"

225

"Is that why you're here?" Grabianski said. "To help me have fun? Ask a few questions. See if I don't talk in my sleep."

She batted Oxfam eyes at him from across the room. "I don't like the way that sounds."

"No. Nor should you." Just for a moment, he touched the back of his hand to her cheek.

Faron sipped at her wine and then, from the tiny leather rucksack she'd had on her back, shook out a smart red notebook and matching pen. "I was going to nip to the loo and scribble it all down before I forgot."

"And now?"

Faron shrugged.

Grabianski reached out for the notebook and tore it in two, letting the halves drop to the floor. When he touched her face again she didn't pull away and he was surprised, despite the makeup she so expertly wore, at the softness of her skin.

"I wonder," he said, "if you'd consider doing something for me?"

"Oh, yeah," she grinned. "And what's that?"

"That man Sloane. The artist. I'd like to meet him."

It was twenty past five that evening, when Lynn and Khan came into the office and caught Resnick just on the point of leaving.

"Peter Paul Spurgeon," Lynn said, "thirty-seven years of age. Married with three children, Matthew, nine, Julia, eight, and Luke, five. Wife's name's Louise."

"Currently resident," Khan said, "27 Front Street, Bottisham. That's just …"

But Resnick knew where it was. "It's a village, northeast of Cambridge."

"Yes, sir. Seems he left the area for a while after getting his degree; came back six or seven years ago."

"After university, he worked in publishing," Lynn said. "London and Edinburgh. Set up some kind of firm of his own, apparently, but it didn't take. Sounds as if he might still be keeping it going in a small way, but what he does to pay the bills, he's a sales rep for a number of other publishers, mostly academic ones, all over the eastern counties."

"His wife works, too," Khan said. "A librarian at one of the colleges."

"Well," Resnick said, looking almost as pleased as they were themselves. "Good work. Very. Now what d'you say we break the habit of a lifetime, hike up the road, and beat everyone else to the bar in the Borlace Warren?"

Forty-two

Number 27 was sideways on to the road and deceptively small. The spiraling hedge separating it from the narrow pavement was in need of cutting back, causing passersby to step around it or raise an arm to brush it aside. The green wooden gate could have used a coat of paint. A ten-year-old Ford Fiesta, dingy cream, sat by the curb.

"Doubt he does his repping in that," Khan remarked.

"Let's hope not," Resnick replied.

"According to records, he owns a Vauxhall estate, L reg."

"Left early," Resnick suggested.

"Maybe never got home last night."

The two of them had stayed in the vehicle, sixty yards back down the road, while Lynn took a slow wander past the house.

"Someone's home anyway," she said, returning. "Caught a glimpse. A woman, I think. Back door's open and there's a radio playing."

"Houses like this," Khan said, "how d'you tell which is the front and which is the back?"

"It's like one of those tests they give you," Lynn grinned. "You know, intelligence."

"Likely the front door then, after all."

"If it is the wife," Resnick said, "no call getting her alarmed without reason. Lynn, why don't you go and have a word? Anil and I'll hang on here."

Before she was halfway there, a maroon estate came slowly around the far curve and signaled that it was going to stop. The driver eased across and parked close behind the Fiesta. By now, Lynn had stopped in her tracks and Resnick and Khan were out of the car and beginning to walk toward her.

The man who emerged from the Vauxhall was tall enough to have the slightly stooped posture of someone who habitually dips his head in conversation. He wore heavy-framed glasses and though his dark hair was still quite full, the crown of his head was bald.

"Spurgeon?" Lynn said quietly, once he'd clicked through the gate.

"Unless he's got a brother."

They moved on toward the house.

"Louise!" Spurgeon called, pausing at the open door. "Louise?"

But by then Resnick had pushed the gate back open and was walking toward him along the path, the two other officers close behind.

"Mr. Spurgeon?"

"Yes, I ..."

"Peter Spurgeon?"

"Yes."

"Peter, what is it?" Louise Spurgeon was short to medium height, a couple of inches shorter than Lynn. She was wearing a smart suit skirt, but with an apron still fastened over the front of her white blouse.

"I don't know, I ..."

"We're police," Resnick said. "Detective Inspector Resnick." He held out his card. "This is Detective Sergeant Kellogg, Detective Constable Khan."

"Whatever's the matter?" Louise Spurgeon said. "Is it one of the children? Peter, Peter, it can't be the children, you've only just taken them to school."

"We believe you know a Jane Peterson," Resnick said.

Spurgeon blinked. "No, I don't think ..." He half-turned toward his wife.

"Peterson," said Louise. "No. Unless it's someone, Peter, from work. A buyer, perhaps? Someone from the University Press?"

Spurgeon removed his glasses and rubbed them against his trouser leg.

"Sir?" Resnick asked again. "You're sure?"

"Yes."

"She used to be called Harker. Jane Harker."

"Oh. Oh, yes." Spurgeon took a step back, fumbling his glasses back onto his face. "Louise, it's Jane, you remember ..."

"Yes, I know who she is." Louise turned abruptly and went back into the house.

"Louise, please ..." Shaking his head, Spurgeon gave an apologetic smile. "I'm sorry."

"You did know her, then, Mr. Spurgeon?" Resnick persevered. "Jane Harker? Peterson as she became."

"Yes. Yes, of course. But a long time ago."

"And you haven't kept in touch?"

"No. No, not at all."

"In which case," Resnick said, "likely you wouldn't have heard?"

"Heard what?"

"I'm afraid she died, sir."

"Jane ... Oh, my God, how ..."

"She was murdered."

A shiver ran through Spurgeon's body; his face was the color of fine ash.

"I'm sorry to have to be the one to break the news," Resnick said.

Spurgeon removed his glasses, put them back into place. "Tell me what happened. Please."

Levelly, evenly, not goading him, Resnick told him the facts. Tears fidgeted in the corners of Spurgeon's eyes, his hands knotted and pressed against his thighs. Then, silently at first, he began to cry. After several moments, Resnick touched Spurgeon gently on the arm and led him inside the house.

His wife was sitting at a plain kitchen table, still crowded with breakfast things, cold anger the only expression on her face.

"She's dead," Spurgeon said, voice cracking. "Jane's dead."

Louise tilted up her head. "Good," she said. "Not before time."

Some minutes later, Louise Spurgeon reappeared in the kitchen with her suit jacket and makeup in place. Switching on the ready-loaded washing machine as she passed, she lifted her car keys down from the hook alongside the door and stepped briskly out without uttering another word.

Her husband leaned against the table, then sat, head pitched forward into his hands, alternately sobbing and reaching for breath. Khan fetched a length of kitchen roll and placed it near at hand, where it stayed unused. Resnick waited until the edgy sound of the Fiesta's engine had faded before touching Peter Spurgeon lightly on the shoulder. "Perhaps there's another room where we can sit quietly, have a chat?"

Unsteadily, Spurgeon got to his feet, wiping his face with his sleeve. "We can go through here."

Following him, Resnick turned his head. "Tea?" he said to Lynn.

"Tea, Anil," Lynn said, once they were alone. "I'm going to take the chance for a quick look round."

The room Spurgeon led Resnick into overlooked a muddled garden in which swings and a climbing frame rose above some rather desultory rose bushes, a lawn that was threadbare in patches, over-grown in others, and cabbages that had gone to seed. A fruit tree, pear, Resnick thought, though he could never be sure, straggled up alongside the far wall. A pair of child's trainers sat in the center of the room, stray items of clothing vied for space with comics and magazines. A small computer was set up on a table near the window, the cursor rhythmically blinking its green eye.

"I'm sorry," Spurgeon said, "about the mess."

Resnick negotiated space on an old Parker Knoll armchair, bought secondhand or someone's hand-me-down. How seriously had they suffered financially when Spurgeon's publishing venture had gone bust, he wondered, and were they still suffering from that? Financially and perhaps in other ways. Was this simply the house of two busy people with three children, never time to keep up? Or was this what it was like when things had unraveled beyond the point of care?

Spurgeon pushed a pile of publishers' catalogs to one side and slumped onto a sagging two-seater settee. Resnick waited until he had looked at him and looked away, looked at him and then away.

Resnick wondered if Spurgeon could hear as well as he could those footsteps he assumed were Khan's or Lynn's upon the upstairs boards? No, Resnick almost allowed himself a smile, they would be Lynn's; she would have been sure to have told Khan to make the tea.

And, yes, when the tea arrived, along with milk and sugar on an improvised tray, it was Khan who handed it round and, catching Resnick's eye to see if he should go or stay, carried his own mug to the side of the room and sat on a straight-backed chair near the door.

"I ... I don't know," Spurgeon said at last, "what it is you want me to say."

"The truth," Resnick replied.

"But about what?"

"Everything."

Spurgeon tasted his tea, stirred in more sugar, left it alone.

"Mr. Spurgeon ..."

"I've told you the truth."

"About Jane? You didn't know what had happened to her?"

"Of course not."

"And you haven't seen her in a long time?"

Spurgeon shook his head.

"How long? Fifteen years? Ten?"

"Ten, something like that. Ten. I can't remember exactly."

"What happened," Resnick asked, "for you to stop seeing her?"

"I suppose we just drifted apart, you know how it is. And then, of course, I married Louise."

"Your wife knew her, then?"

"No. They never met."

"Strange then," Resnick said mildly, "that she should react the way she did."

For an instant, Spurgeon closed his eyes. "Louise used to say I talked about Jane all the time. She said I made comparisons, between the two of them. It preyed on her mind. I suppose that's why, when she heard what had happened ..."

Leaning forward, Resnick set his mug of tea aside. "There was no other reason for your wife to be jealous in this way?"

"I told you, I haven't seen Jane ..."

"In ten years."

"That's right."

"Nor spoken to her."

"No."

"Mr. Spurgeon," Resnick raised his voice a touch, shifting his weight back in the chair, "don't you think it's time we stopped all this?"

When Spurgeon spoke again, his voice was so quiet that both Resnick and Khan had to strain to hear. "When I first met Louise, I was still getting over Jane. I don't think I even realized it at the time, but it was true. First love, I suppose that's what you'd say. But I hadn't kept in touch with her at all, didn't know where she was, I never expected to as much as hear from her again. And then a couple of months after the wedding a card came. From Jane. I don't know how she'd found out, but she had, and she sent this card, wishing me good luck. Congratulations. Of course, I should have shown it to Louise straight away, but I didn't. Perhaps there was some kind of guilt, embarrassment, whatever." Spurgeon was twisting his wedding ring round and round on his hand. "It's so easy to get caught up in a lie." He looked Resnick in the eye. "Louise found the card, almost a year later; I hadn't thrown it away. She … the way she behaved was out of all proportion. And she hasn't forgotten. Not even now."

"Tell me," Resnick said, "what was written on the card."

Spurgeon looked away. "Congratulations and good luck, with all my fondest love, Jane." He hesitated. "Then underneath she'd written, I wish it was me."

"You didn't reply?" Resnick asked.

Spurgeon shook his head. "I'd made my bed. And besides, there was no return address."

"Until later."

"I'm sorry?"

"Jane's address, you found out later what it was."

"What are you saying?"

"What I'm saying, Mr. Spurgeon, is that if you hadn't got back in contact with Jane Peterson in some way, she would never have phoned you at the Dray Horse on the Newmarket Road, just ten minutes' drive from here, on the day that she disappeared. Exactly one week before she was found dead."

233

Forty-three

Faron had scarcely spoken on the way over. Stripped of its makeup, the face that looked out through the mini-cab window seemed even younger than its nineteen years. Hoxton, Haggerston, Hackney, Bethnal Green, London Fields: all of her ambition was in moving away from this, not driving back.

For Grabianski it was alien. The moment he passed—where?—Highbury Corner? Stamford Hill?—the minute he crossed that indefinable boundary between North and East, he felt himself slipping into a world he didn't know and if not feared, was at least wary of. Discounted shoes and rebuilt cycles, fashion watches and made-to-measure suits, Lycra in forty-five styles a snip at £14.95 a meter, chopped herring, cheap curries, salt-beef bagels, dry salted fish, pigs' trotters, pigs' tails in a bag for 99p. There ought to be a wall, Grabianski thought; probably there was.

The driver turned and spoke over his shoulder and Faron answered him. Not far now.

Grabianski had read somewhere, probably around the time of the Whitechapel Open, there were more artists living in this part of London than in the rest of the city stacked together. Studios in houses, old bakeries, breweries that had folded too soon for the boom; studios in arches underneath the railway lines that still criss-crossed from Stratford and Bromley-by-Bow to Willesden Junction and Kensal Green. Sloane had been here before most of these, not his natural home either, south of the river that, but here was where he had produced his first serious paintings after art school, here was where, if the years in the States were forgotten—as largely they were—he had stayed.

The cab pulled up outside a row of tall, flat-fronted buildings with broad stone steps worn smooth at the center with use and age.

Grabianski told the driver to wait and followed Faron out onto the wide pavement. A collarless dog that had been sniffing at the dustbins stacked inside the low wall came and sniffed at them instead. Absently, Faron petted its head.

"Which one?" Grabianski asked.

She pointed. "The end."

There were steps down to the basement, steps going up. Bins aside, the space at the front sported the plastic and paper debris of casual passersby, an old chimney stack someone had filled with earth but in which nothing apparent grew, some bottles and a can or two.

Reaching up, Faron rang the bell. After a while they heard music and then footsteps, fast and heavy, on the stairs. Sloane shot back the bolt and threw open the door, staring out. He was wearing the same dungarees Grabianski had seen him in before, the same interrogation in those strong blue eyes.

"What the fuck d'you bring him for?" Sloane asked.

Carefully, Faron unfurled her eyes. "He asked me," she said.

Sloane sniffed and wiped a hand across his face. To Grabianski he said, "Now you're here, I guess you better come inside."

The last sound Grabianski heard before Sloane slammed the door shut was the clunk of Faron's heels along the pavement, the closing of the cab door.

At some stage, the entire top floor had been laid bare, stripped back to plaster and board, beyond plaster to the rough brick. Paint was speckled and smeared across the floor and the farthest wall. Metal shelves held a massed assemblage of brushes, palette-knives, and paints, sheaves of paper spilling from brown, loose-tied folders, books illustrating other artists' work, catalogs, a collection of LPs with covers that were bent and torn. Raised off the floor by bricks at either end of the room, two four-foot speakers splayed out a raucous, arrhythmic sound that Grabianski thought might be some kind of abstract jazz, but like nothing he had heard before.

Canvases in various sizes leaned against one another haphazardly around the walls; propped on an easel near the far window, half-finished, was an oil Grabianski recognized as being in the style of William Stott of Oldham. Grabianski had stolen one once, a small seascape, from a private collector in Leeds.

Towering over all this, constantly claiming Grabianski's eye, was a single huge canvas, wider and taller than the span of two men's arms, which had been stretched and tied within a free-standing wooden frame. Fervid and loud, the paint lay thick in sheets of color, vermilion and magenta overlaid with crystal blue. Closer to, you could see where earlier attempts had been scraped back and covered over, scraped and covered, punched and gouged and pummeled closer to the painter's vision.

"What?" Sloane yelled across the noise.

Grabianski didn't take his eyes from the canvas. "It's yours."

"Course it's fuckin' mine!"

"I mean it's not a copy."

"I know what you mean."

"It's amazing."

"It's crap."

Like the surface of water breaking, music stopped. Sloane moved closer to his canvas, then away.

"What's wrong with it?" Grabianski asked.

"What's wrong," Sloane said, "is it's no longer nineteen-fucking-fifty-nine. Now why don't you tell me what you're here for, so's I can get on?"

When Grabianski had told him, Sloane ambled to the window and gazed out. "Why," he said, moving to the record deck, "should I want to get so far up Eddie Snow's nose?"

Grabianski shrugged. "The fun of it? The challenge?"

Sloane looked at him. "The money?"

"That, too."

Sloane lowered the pickup arm and the cacophonous sound of the Art Ensemble of Chicago refilled the room.

Forty-four

"You won't have any objection, sir, to our taking a quick photograph?"

Resnick had informed Colin Presley, the senior local CID officer, of his impending visit, and now a second call to Cambridge HQ secured an interview room with tape facilities, car parking, use of the canteen. Lynn's brief stroll around the premises on Front Street had yielded nothing aside from the fact that the Spurgeons' life would be easier—and tidier—with the services of a good house-keeper or au pair. Even kids who picked up after themselves would help. Now Khan had been sent off to the Dray Horse with a Polaroid of Peter Spurgeon, seeking confirmation that this was the man who consistently called there and from time to time made use of their telephone.

Resnick and Lynn sat in the interview room, high at the rear of the building, watching Spurgeon wipe the lenses of his spectacles over and over with a yellow cloth. After all the backtracking and deception, Resnick believed a change of scene to somewhere more institutional might more quickly loosen Peter Spurgeon's tongue.

"Your earlier denials," Resnick said, "of having any continuing relationship with Jane Peterson ..."

"We didn't have a relationship ..."

"Or of knowing about her death ..."

Spurgeon wrapped his head in his hands.

Oh, God, Lynn thought, he's going to lose it totally.

"I'm willing to accept," Resnick said, "all that was due to the immediate stress of the situation. But now I want us to be clear. This is a murder investigation. Any further attempts to throw us off the track, impede that investigation in any way, will be treated very seriously indeed."

No response other than a vague fluttering of hands.

"Mr. Spurgeon, is that clear?"

"Yes." Weakly. "Yes, yes, of course."

"Then tell us in your own time everything you can about yourself and Jane."

Spurgeon fidgeted his glasses back onto his face, half-removed them again, pushed them back into place; Resnick reached across the desk and lifted them away, the last prop Spurgeon had left.

"It ... it was true," Spurgeon finally began, "what I told you about the card. Coming the way it did, out of the blue."

Resnick nodded encouragingly, even smiled. "When Jane and I first met, it was the first day of college, the first evening. We just started talking. The next thing we were going out together, going steady. It just seemed, I don't know, natural, the natural thing to do."

"And this carried on all the time you were here," Resnick asked, "at the university?"

Spurgeon nodded. "Yes."

"No little mishaps," Lynn said. "No falling-out?"

"Not really, no."

"The perfect couple."

"That was what everyone said."

"So what happened?" Resnick asked.

Spurgeon coughed, fidgeted, cleared his throat. "At the end of the ... after graduation, Jane went down to Exeter to do her PGCE year, her teaching certificate, and I stayed on here and started working on some research. At first we saw one another every other weekend, until the Christmas vac. That was when Jane said wouldn't it be a good idea if we stepped back a little, that was the expression she used, gave ourselves room to think about what was going on."

"What was going on?" Resnick asked.

"I don't know. As far as I was concerned, nothing, I still felt the same."

"She'd met somebody else," Lynn said.

"No. I mean, yes, maybe. I don't know."

"She didn't say?"

Spurgeon didn't answer straight away. "She said we should be mature enough to respect one another's privacy."

"She'd met somebody else," Lynn said again.

"Do you think," Spurgeon said, "I could have a drink? My mouth feels really dry."

Resnick nodded at Lynn, who slid out of her chair and left the room.

Without his glasses, Spurgeon's eyes were restless and pale. "After Easter, she stopped writing. Didn't phone. I went down to Exeter on the train and she refused to see me. I couldn't understand it, she just wouldn't listen to reason. As soon as I got back 1 wrote, letter after letter. If I phoned, she wouldn't take my calls."

"And she didn't give you any explanation?"

Spurgeon shook his head again. "She refused. Point blank. I didn't know what to do."

"What did you do?"

"I packed in my research, moved away, found a job in publishing. I was lucky. I did well, got on. Fine, I thought, I'll forget her, I'll do this."

"And did you? Forget her?"

"Of course not."

There was a slight clink from outside, which Resnick registered and maybe Spurgeon did not; Lynn had arrived back and would have listened at the door, hearing enough of a flow in the conversation to know she should stay where she was.

"I borrowed some money and started up in business on my own. A small press, you know, specialist titles. All the forecasts showed there was every chance I could break even after a couple of years, pay back the debt, start forging ahead after that. That wasn't the way it worked out." Spurgeon wiped his hand across his mouth. "Some of the money I'd borrowed from Louise, well, from her family, I suppose. We were together by then, engaged, and it only seemed the natural thing. I remember after the wedding, her father making this speech, how his daughter was going to be sitting at the right hand of the next Lord Weidenfeld, the next Alan Lane. A little over four years later I was broke, virtually bankrupt. Louise's family would scarcely speak to her, except to malign me, tell her what a fool she'd been, throwing herself away on a bigger fool like me."

He paused and Lynn slipped back into the room with glasses and a jug of cloudy water.

Spurgeon waited until she had sat down. "It was around then that Jane got back in touch with me. She'd seen something in one of the papers about the firm going under, just a paragraph, but it had been enough to help her find me. She phoned one afternoon, a Sunday, it was only luck that I picked up the phone. "Hello," she said, "this is Jane Peterson," and for a moment I didn't know who that was. I hadn't even recognized her voice."

He poured himself water from the jug and drank.

"We arranged to meet in Cambridge, Heffers bookshop in the middle of the town. If anyone saw me, saw us, said anything to Louise for any reason, well, I would have had a good reason for being there. There's this sort of balcony that runs round three sides of the shop and that's where I was standing, I wanted to be sure of spotting her when she came in. I suppose I was afraid of not recognizing her, but, of course, as soon as she stepped through the door, I knew who she was.

"We drove out to Grantchester and sat in this outdoor, well, tea place, café, right away from everyone else, shaded by the trees. We sat there for ages, drinking tea, apple juice, Jane telling me about her life. About Alex, how paranoid he was, possessive. And—she didn't tell me this straight away—how he'd been hitting her. Where nobody would see. I could have ... If I could have laid my hands on him, I swear I would have killed him."

Spurgeon rocked back sharply in his chair, eyes closed. Resnick and Lynn exchanged a quick glance.

"I'm wondering what it must have been like," Resnick said, not wanting the distraction of more tears, "seeing somebody you loved again after all that time."

Spurgeon opened his eyes. "It was wonderful," he said simply. "It was as if we'd never been apart; as if she'd never been away."

"But you were," Lynn said. "She was married. You were both married."

"I know. I told her to leave him. After what he'd done …"

"And your wife?" Lynn asked. "Louise?"

"That was over."

"And the children?"

Spurgeon pushed his fingers through his hair. "I would have left them in a moment, all of them. The kids would hardly notice, Louise would be glad. As for her parents, they'd be delighted, thrilled."

"What did she say to all this?" Resnick asked. "Jane?"

"She'd been hoping, when she came to see me, hoping that I'd ask her, I could see that. That's what she wanted to know, if I still felt the same."

"And did she," Lynn asked, "feel the same about you?"

"Yes, yes, I'm sure she did. But she was frightened. Terrified of Alex. Just terrified of what he would do if he found out we'd as much as seen one another, talked, never mind anything else."

"So how did you leave it?" Resnick said. "After that first occasion? Would you say there was—what would you say?—an under-standing?"

"She was going to think, very seriously, about what we'd said. Of course, nothing was going to be easy, we realized that. She had all these problems with Alex and I had to work hard to pay off all my debts. We agreed we'd keep in touch as best we could, make plans."

"And you did?"

"It was difficult. Sometimes there wouldn't be a chance to speak for months on end. He seemed to monitor every minute of her time. And because of all the resentment Louise had built up about Jane, I didn't dare risk her calling me at home."

"Which was when you started using the Dray Horse for calls?" Lynn said.

"Yes. I'd try and be there at certain times, sometimes she would call and sometimes not."

"And this went on," Resnick said, "not just for months, but years?"

"Yes."

"And all this time you were waiting for Jane to leave her husband and live with you?"

"Yes."

"It never occurred to you," Lynn said, "that she might have been stringing you along?"

"Of course not. She was in love with me, we were in love. It was the same as before."

It was Resnick's turn to pour and drink a little water. "Tell us about this last few months," he said.

"Jane was almost at breaking point with Alex. There was no way she could carry on like that forever, something had to happen. And I think helping to organize this day school helped, gave her an impetus. But she was still scared of telling him to his face. So what we arranged was she would write to him, post it that day, and just go. I'd drive up and collect her in the middle of the day school and we'd simply leave. Stay in a hotel. Anywhere. As far as Louise was concerned, I was off on business, East Anglia, Hull, it's a trip I make every few months. She wasn't expecting me back till the end of the week." He folded his hands, one over the other. "That would be that."

"Except," Resnick said, "that it wasn't."

Spurgeon sighed. "She hadn't written the letter. That was what we argued about that day. She promised she'd do it once we were away, but every letter she wrote, she'd tear up. She even dialed his number, but then didn't go through with the call. By Wednesday, she was saying she had to go back and face him. She thought she could do that now, after being with me. I tried to talk her out of it, but she'd made up her mind. She would go and see him, tell him she was leaving him and why, and then come back to me."

"This was Wednesday, you say?"

"Wednesday morning, yes."

"And she went back that day?"

"Yes."

"You drove her?"

"Only as far as Grantham. She wanted to make the rest of the journey on the train. She said it would be best, give her a chance to think over exactly what she was going to say, clear her mind."

"You didn't think you should be with her?" Lynn asked. "That maybe you should face him together?"

"Well, of course. But it wasn't what Jane wanted. She wouldn't hear of it. She wanted me to stay in Grantham and wait for her there. I booked a room in a hotel; she was going to catch the train back that evening. She never came."

"So what did you do?" Lynn asked.

"What could I do? I waited and waited. Went to the station and met every train the next day."

"What did you think had happened?" Resnick asked.

"At first, I thought Alex must be keeping her there by force, against her will. But then, when I still didn't hear, I thought, one way or another, he's persuaded her to change her mind. So I went home. I couldn't think what else to do. Then when I switched on the TV and it was all over the news, I didn't know ... there was no one I could talk to, I didn't even have any way of knowing whether anyone—whether you, the police, would ever connect her back to me. And then when I saw you coming down the path ..."

Resnick nodded, paused. "What do you think happened?" he asked. "What do you think happened to Jane?"

Spurgeon didn't hesitate. "He killed her, didn't he? Alex. Killed her and threw ... threw her into the canal."

No way to stop the tears returning now and neither did they try.

A uniformed officer was keeping an eye on the interview room while Resnick and Lynn bustled off to the canteen.

"After the best part of an hour with him," Lynn said, "I can understand the attractions of a bloke like Peterson. Something about him, at least."

"Even if it means taking yourself off to Accident and Emergency once in a while?"

She shook her head vigorously. "No, not that. But Spurgeon ... It's all too easy, telling yourself you're in love with some fantasy. Especially one you almost never see. A sight simpler than knuckling down to what you've got, a difficult wife and a bunch of mardy kids in need of a good sorting. No, he's nothing. A failure, through and through."

"You don't fancy him for it, then?"

"'Less I saw it, I'd not fancy him for tying his own shoe."

Resnick was still laughing as Khan came hurrying toward them, photograph of Spurgeon in his hand. "Him, sir, without a doubt."

Resnick nodded. "He's not denying that part of it, at least. But there's a sight more to do, so don't waste the effort sitting down. There's a hotel reservation to check in Grantham, we need to know how many days Jane Peterson was there with Spurgeon. Anything else you can dig up. Lynn and I'll drop Spurgeon off to his wife's tender mercies, nothing we can really hold him on and I doubt he'll do a runner anyway. Then we'll get back and see what Peterson's got to say for himself."

"Right, sir." Khan was already wondering when he'd next get the chance to phone Jill, get a bite to eat; thinking also that for all the talk there'd been about Lynn applying for a transfer because she was up to here working with Resnick, he couldn't say these past days it had showed.

Forty-five

Eddie Snow unfolded his paper napkin, wiped his fingers, folded the napkin again, and picked up what remained of his quarter pounder, medium rare with bacon and Swiss cheese. They were in Ed's Diner, not the one in Hampstead, which Grabianski often walked past and sometimes walked into, but this one on Old Compton Street in Soho, maybe the original, Grabianski didn't know. The style was fifties—early sixties retro, school of *American Graffiti*, red and chrome, padded stools, rock 'n' roll on the jukebox, apple pie.

"Exporting rare works of art to the Middle East," Snow said, "any-one'd think you were trying to sell arms to Saddam in the middle of the Gulf fucking War."

Grabianski drew on the straw of his banana milkshake; it was a great shake, creamy and thick, but required considerable suction to get it up the straw. "There's some kind of trouble, Eddie, that's what you're saying?"

"This kind of line, there's always trouble. Otherwise, you think everyone else wouldn't be doing it?"

Grabianski nodded. "I suppose so."

"It's like having sex with the same woman after too many years: no matter how keen you might be, how much you want her, a little more difficult every time."

Grabianski pushed the milkshake aside. "Bottom line," he said.

"Bottom line? Applications for transit of goods, pro forma invoices, import-export licenses, cargo shipment, customs and excise. Four more weeks. Possibly six."

"Six?"

"Outside, eight."

Grabianski shook his head and stared at his abandoned hot dog.

"What?" Snow said. "You've got a problem with storage? I thought you'd solved all that?"

"I have, I have, it's just ..."

"A long time since the original job was done."

"That's right."

"A long time before you see any cash recompense for your labor."

"Precisely."

Snow put down an uneaten section of bun, leaned forward toward the white-uniformed server standing the other side of the counter and ordered a Diet Coke.

"Jerry?"

"No, thanks. No, I'm fine."

"Good, good." And when the Coke arrived and he'd swallowed enough to make him belch, he said, "That very problem, cash flow, yours, it's been exercising my mind."

Grabianski waited. The box was playing Ricky Nelson. "Poor Little Fool." Who's to say, Grabianski thought, him or me?

Snow lowered his voice but only a little. "This talent you've got for getting in and out of places unannounced. There's a few things I could do with being deposited, safe and secure, where nobody would ever think of looking for them until they were told."

"What kind of things?" asked Grabianski.

"Bona fides. Documents. Nothing difficult."

"And these places you'd be wanting me to gain access to ..."

"Museum offices, archives. For the most part, low security."

Grabianski slid the menu out from between the ketchup and the mustard.

"What d'you say?" Eddie Snow asked.

"You mean aside from how much?" Grabianski thought he might order the pie after all. Why not à la mode?

Resnick found Helen Siddons in the first-floor bar of the Forte Crest, sitting in a gray lounge chair across a low table from Jack Skelton, who was looking chastened even before Resnick appeared, and when he did, assumed the aspect of someone who's been caught pissing down his own leg.

Resnick raised a hand in greeting and moved on toward the long bar, shifting a stool down to the far end and, when the barman noticed him, ordering a large vodka with lots of ice. He thought he might be in for quite a fight.

Siddons was leaning toward Skelton now, voice low, before suddenly throwing herself backward in the chair and pointing at him with the red-tipped cigarette in her right hand. "Fuck d'you think you are, Jack?" Resnick heard, and "miserable bitch of a wife." Not so long after, and without a wave or a word in Resnick's direction, Skelton got up and left.

Resnick wondered whether he should go over to where Helen Siddons was sitting, or if she would come to him; he was still considering when she stubbed out her cigarette and, grim-faced, headed his way.

She lit up again as soon as she sat down. "Scotch," she said, not bothering to look at the barman. "Large. No water, no ice."

"So, Charlie," she said, "how's it all going?" And before he could answer, "What is it, Charlie? What is it with just about every man in the fucking world? The minute you lose interest is the minute they become convinced you've got a cunt of gold."

She drank the first half of the scotch fast, the rest at even speed, and called for another. Resnick wondered how long she had been there, whether this particular session had started at lunchtime and simply flowed.

"This woman of yours, Charlie, what's she called?"

"Hannah."

"Hmm, well, promise me this; promise me this about you and darling Hannah …"

Resnick waited while she dragged deep on her cigarette.

"Promise me if ever she wants to leave, if ever the day comes when she wants to walk away and call it quits, promise you'll let her go. God's blessings, Charlie. Godspeed and goodbye. None of this sniveling and whining, you're-the-most-important-thing-in-my-life crap. Right?"

"Right."

"I'm serious, Charlie."

"I know."

Her hand was on his knee. "You and me, Charlie, you never fancied that?"

"No."

She threw back her head and laughed. "Christ, Charlie! The last honest man."

Resnick wondered what it was about her that made that sound almost like an insult. "I was going to ask you ..." he began.

"What I'm doing here half-pissed? Triumph or adversity?" She ducked her head forward till he couldn't avoid the nicotine and whisky on her breath. "That little sniveling little shortshanks the computer spewed up for us, David Winston Aloysius James, five years for attempted rape, except of course he's out after serving not much more than three, not only has he got two other priors for assault, one more charge of indecent exposure which got thrown out of court, guess what he had tucked snug underneath the mattress of his bed, along with more porn than the average newsagent's top shelf and a score of semen-stinking handkerchiefs?"

Resnick couldn't guess.

"Miranda Conway's Euro Railcard, complete with photograph attached."

"You've brought him in?"

"What do you think?"

"Charged?"

"Not yet."

"What does he say about the card?"

"Says he found it, what do you think?"

"Is there anything else linking him with the girl?"

"Come on, Charlie, what do you want? Love letters? A length of rope?"

Resnick shrugged. "Someone who saw them together earlier that evening. She'd not been in Worksop that long, but she hadn't exactly kept her head down. There's folk knew who she was."

Siddons lit a fresh cigarette from the butt of the last, tipped back her head, and released smoke into the air. "Charlie, he fits the profile, he's got the photo ID, and we can put him here in the city four nights before that one you claimed who was fished out of the canal."

Instead of responding directly, Resnick told her what they had

248

discovered about Jane Peterson and Peter Spurgeon. She listened with interest, went thoughtful, and asked for a large coffee, black, two sugars.

"Fronted him with it yet? The husband?"

Resnick shook his head. "Up to now, he's always denied seeing her or hearing from her after that Saturday she disappeared. I'd like something else to hit him with aside from Spurgeon's accusation, which as things stand we've no way of proving. We've only his word for it, she went to see Peterson from Grantham."

"She went somewhere."

"Agreed. We'd already canvassed the neighbors, in case they'd seen anything of her during the week, but came up short. Now, though, we've got a good idea, if she did come here, which train it would have been. I'd like everyone on duty at the station that after-noon and evening talked to, shown photographs, taxi-drivers the same. Regular passengers, too."

"That's a major operation, Charlie."

"I thought this was a major case."

"And we've got someone a few hours from being charged."

"All right," Resnick conceded, "but even if he's responsible for the others, all or some, he doesn't have to have done this."

Helen Siddons gave him a look pitched somewhere between contempt and disgust. "I didn't think this was you, pedaling your own corner no matter what."

"What evidence is there says Jane Peterson was killed by the same person as the others?"

"Aside from an identical MO?"

"Naked, not molested, dumped in water, what else?"

"What else?" Incredulous.

"Helen, that's all circumstantial, flimsy at best. Unless there's something you haven't told me, you've got nothing links Jane Peterson directly to your suspect, no physical evidence, no DNA."

"Oh, and what have you got, Charlie, aside from a selection of lovers' lies?"

"Then lend me some bodies, authorize the overtime."

"I can't."

"Helen ..."

Her mobile phone jumped to life and she fumbled it from her bag. "Right," she said, after listening. "Right, I'll be there." She had a grin that would have challenged a Cheshire Cat. "He's owned up to talking to her, Miranda, buying her a drink, taking her for a walk along the canal. We've got him, Charlie. He'll have his hands up for it this side of supper-time."

Resnick followed her across the room. "If you're right, you'll have officers, time on their hands. Twenty-four hours, that's all I'm asking."

She stopped at the head of the stairs. "Talk with Support Department. If they can spare a few bodies, fair enough. But like you said, twenty-four hours and that's your lot."

Resnick was on his way back to where his drink sat unfinished on the bar when he changed his mind.

Jackie Ferris was wearing an unbuttoned denim shirt with a snug white T-shirt underneath, blue jeans; in the comparative heat of the car, she had kicked off her shoes. Carl Vincent, beside her, was smart and cool in a fashionable stone-colored suit and a collarless white shirt.

"You always dress this way?" she asked. "It doesn't bring you any grief?"

"How d'you mean?"

"Get you noticed? Draw the wrong kind of attention?"

"Aside from being black and queer?"

Jackie Ferris leaned back along the seat. "Down here in the sophisticated South, we call it gay."

"Uh-huh, that's what I'd heard."

She hesitated only a moment before asking, "Are you out?"

"Yes."

"Long?"

Carl shook his head. "Year, more or less."

"How's it been?"

He looked out through the car window at the slow stream of people taking the exit from the underground station, automatically checking every face. "You know, like a lot of stuff, worse before it gets better."

Jackie nodded and wondered again about a cigarette.

"How about you?" Carl said, keeping it light, not quite looking at her direct. She was a detective inspector, whatever else.

She took out and lit the cigarette, winding the window low. "There was this woman I was living with, well, more or less. She was a singer, one of those little indie bands. Did session work once in a while. But that was the kind of life she led."

"She must have been young."

"She was. She said she couldn't keep seeing me if I was living this secret life. That's what she called it, this secret life. So the next time I went for a drink with the lads from the squad, I took her along."

"How did they react?"

"You mean, aside from the ones that wanted to fuck her? Oh, they were fine. People confuse you sometimes, straight people, by being a lot less prejudiced than you expect. Mostly they were fine. Six weeks later, she dumped me anyway. I think she came home early and caught me listening to Doris Day."

"I'm sorry."

Jackie Ferris shrugged. "What did Oscar Wilde say, never give your heart to a child or a fairy? I'd done both."

But Carl was no longer really listening. He was watching Grabianski approaching along the opposite side of the street, starting to cross toward them now. Jackie pushed her feet back into her shoes and turned the key in the ignition.

As soon as Grabianski was in the rear seat, she pulled away, careful through the traffic turning west into Victoria Street.

"How did we do?" she asked over her shoulder.

"As long as you don't mind a little indigestion, and rather too much of Ricky Nelson, I think it went fine." And, taking the cassette from his pocket, he passed it forward into Carl Vincent's waiting hand.

Resnick had thrown four or five stones up at Divine's flat, before the window was pushed awkwardly open and Divine's head leaned out. He was about to give whoever it was a piece of his mind but then grinned when he realized who it was.

251

"Hey up, boss! What's up?"

"Come to see you."

"Hang about, I'll be down."

"You sober?"

"Yes, I was just having a kip."

"Eaten?"

"Not so's you'd notice."

"Good. I'll treat you to a curry. There's a bit of work, unofficial, I might be able to put your way."

Divine beamed like someone had brought back the sun.

Forty-six

Six thirty a.m. Breakfast in the café near the Dunkirk roundabout. Resnick, Lynn Kellogg, and Anil Khan, three members of the Support Group, Steve Neale, Vicki Talbot, and Ben Parchman, along with a weary-looking Kevin Naylor, prevailed upon to set aside a day off in a good cause. Mark Divine, cautious on the edge of the rest, cautious especially with Lynn, but pleased to be there nonetheless, sat tucking into his egg and bacon sandwich with gusto, unable to disguise the grin that kept sliding around his face.

Resnick knew enough to let them finish their meal, order another tea or coffee, light up; his briefing was clear and to the point.

"One thing, boss," Ben Parchman said. "Are we doing this so Peterson can't turn round and say his wife was never here that Wednesday, he never saw her? Or because we don't necessarily believe the boyfriend's story about her coming here at all?"

"Both," Resnick said. "It's both."

The two most likely trains for Jane Peterson to have arrived on were the five forty-seven and the six fifty-two. When Steve Neale spoke to the guard on the latter, the man thought it a possibility Jane had been on his train, but no way was he certain enough to make a positive identification. The wall-eyed official who had been collecting tickets on the forty-seven took a quick look at the photograph and shook his head. "No, duck, alus remember't pretty ones." He tapped his middle finger against his temple. "Keep 'em filed away, like, somethin' to set against cold nights."

Lynn, Anil, and Vicki had positioned themselves inside the sliding doors at the back of the busy booking hall, close to the stairs heading down to the Grantham platform. A good number of

253

passengers would be regulars, out in the morning, back on one of those two trains after work. The three officers spoke to people as they passed, handed out hastily printed leaflets, detaining anyone who admitted making the relevant journey and asking them to look at Jane Peterson's photograph. After the best part of an hour, they had logged three maybes and one fairly definite for the earlier train, a couple of possibles for the latter. But these were commuters whose schedules were cut to a fine line and more hurried past, eyes averted, than stopped.

With the first morning rush more or less over, Khan and Vicki Talbot took the eastbound train themselves; they would question the staff at Grantham station, drop off more leaflets for distribution there.

Kevin Naylor and Ben Parchman had divided the black cabs between them, leaving Divine to have a crack at the freebooters, drivers for mini-cab firms who were not authorized to ply for hire within the station concourse. It was a fact, however, that if one of them drove in to drop off a passenger and there was a fare waiting but no black cabs, well, business was business. They were also known to hang around at busy times outside the station, hoping to catch the eye of any potential customers for whom the regular queue was too slow and too long.

By mid-morning, between them, Naylor and Parchman had spoken to some fifty drivers and come up blank each time.

The first time Resnick spoke to Gill Manners, who ran the flower stall in the station concourse with her husband, Jane's picture didn't mean a thing, but later, when Resnick was walking past after talking to the station manager, she called him over and asked to look again.

"I've seen her, I know I have, I just can't fit it in with what you said. Times and that."

"Her picture would have been in the *Post*. On TV. You don't think you're remembering it from there?"

She shook her head. "You, now, Mr. Resnick, I've seen you on the local news a time or two. But this one, no, I've seen her I know, but where or when? It's wedged in this poor head of mine some-where, but I can't shake it down."

254

Resnick gave her one of his cards. "You'll let me know, if you do remember? It could be important."

"'Course. I'll have a word with my Harry when he gets here, see if he can't come up with something. Hanging's too good for him, Mr. Resnick, whoever done this."

Nodding noncommittally, he hurried across to WH Smith. It wasn't inconceivable that Jane would have stopped in to buy a newspaper, tissues, something of the kind, or that one of the assistants might have noticed her walking by.

It was past noon before anything definite broke. Kevin Naylor had just wandered across the street from the cab rank south of Slab Square and called Debbie from outside the Bell, Debbie sounding remarkably cheerful and reminding him there was a little errand he had to run for her at the chemist's on his way home.

Naylor fancied something from the barrow close alongside and treated himself to a couple of bananas, one for now, one for later. It gave the drivers a laugh anyway, everything from, "Okay, punk, make my day," to the inevitable, "Is that a banana in your pocket, officer, or are you just here to arrest me?"

He dropped his peel in the nearest ornately decorated, black-painted bin and, photograph in hand, continued working down the line. Second was a young Asian who scarcely seemed old enough to be in charge of a cab without a minder. Naylor had even half a mind to check his license, but the thought went away the moment the driver tapped his finger twice against Jane Peterson's face and said, in a strong local accent, "Yes, I had her in my cab not so long back. Remember her, right. Picked her up, yeah, at the station, and took her to an address in the Park. Those newish places up near Derby Road. Flats, are they? Houses? I don't know. But you know where I mean, right?"

"You're sure it was her?" Naylor asked.

"Yeah, she was—I don't know—she was all worked up about something, right? Dead nervous. Dropped her money all over the inside of the cab when she was fixing to pay me. I jumped round and helped her, like, pick it up." He looked at Naylor, open faced.

Feeling the adrenaline starting to kick in, but keeping it all nice

255

and simple, nonetheless, Naylor noted the driver's name and address, then asked him, not putting too much into it, the other things he needed to know. Yes. The date and time checked and so did the address.

"Here," the driver said, "this is important, yeah? All this stuff you're asking. I bet there's got to be some reward, right? Or else maybe I'll get to be in one of them programs on tele, yeah? True crime."

But Naylor was no longer listening.

Just Resnick, Lynn, and Naylor in the office on the Ropewalk: close to old times.

"You think he's got his details right, Kevin?" Resnick said.

"Didn't seem to be in any doubt, sir."

"Which means," said Lynn, "she caught the later train, the six fifty-two. And according to the guard Steve spoke to, it was in on time. Two or three minutes at most to get to the cab rank; allowing for traffic, what, another ten minutes to the Park? Fifteen tops. She'd have been home by quarter past seven."

"Quick bath, change, mash tea, and settle down to *EastEnders*," Naylor grinned.

"Likely, Kevin," Resnick said, "she had more pressing things on her mind."

The receptionist in Alex Peterson's surgery was half out of her seat in protest when she recognized Resnick and held her tongue. Lynn was standing close behind him, Naylor at the door.

"This patient," Resnick said, "how much longer will he be?" Flustered, she looked from her desk to the clock behind Resnick's head, then back to her desk again. The telephone sounded and she let it ring. "I don't know, it should have been over, let me see, at quarter past. But his next appointment's waiting and there's somebody else Mr. Peterson's promised to try and fit in. I'm sorry but I really don't think he'll have time to talk to you till the very end of the afternoon."

Resnick leaned toward her, close across the desk. "Explain to these people there's an emergency. Apologize. Don't make a fuss."

"Well, I don't know, I don't really see how I can."

"Do it. And don't bother telling Mr. Peterson, we'll do that for ourselves."

"Oh, but you can't ..."

The Muslim nurse was holding out a metal cup at the end of a tube for the patient to spit into; Peterson was making notes in small, precise writing on the man's chart. When Resnick appeared in the doorway, the dentist hesitated a little before finishing what he had begun.

Since his wife's death, he had used his work more than ever as a way of exerting control; not only over those around him, those he came into regular contact with, but over himself, his emotions. He had accepted condolences from colleagues politely and they had not sought to intrude; the letters from Jane's family he had acknowledged with a cold, formal hand. Mourning was something to be held at bay for as long as possible, allowed only privately and then in small doses, like a glass of strong Scotch sampled alone and late, just himself and the moon. Grief frightened him: it threatened to undo him.

"If you'll give this in at reception, Mr. Perry," Peterson said. "Make another appointment for, oh, two weeks' time. We'll see how that's settling down."

Lynn stepped aside in the doorway to allow him past.

"Govinda," Peterson said, "let us have a minute, will you?"

With a slight uncertainty, the nurse left the room. There was a smell of mint and analgesic; a distinct but faint background hum.

"Inspector ..." Peterson began, offering his hand. When Resnick made no move to accept it, he took a step back, one hand resting on the head of the chair. "Somehow I don't get the impression you've come simply to give me news."

"There has been a development," Resnick said.

"You've made an arrest?"

"Not yet," Resnick said. The pause before he spoke alerted Peterson to his meaning.

"We'd like you to come with us and answer some questions," Resnick said.

"Now?"

"Now."

Methodically, Peterson fastened the cap on his pen and clipped it inside the breast pocket of his jacket. "Is that merely a request or am I the one about to find myself under arrest?"

"Whichever you want," Resnick said flatly. "Whichever it needs."

Peterson stared at him, then slowly shook his head; taking off his jacket, he slipped on a navy blazer in its place. Outside on the pavement, just before getting into the back of the waiting car, Peterson turned to Resnick and said quietly, "What is it, sheer spite? Or have you simply run out of other ideas?"

They sat him in the same room as before and made him wait. In search of Helen Siddons, Resnick found her in the squad office, tearing a strip off a group of officers whose background checking she'd found to be less than diligent. The details of Aloysius James's story were beginning to look particularly frayed, and, emboldened by his solicitor, James was proving a less tractable suspect than they had imagined.

Resnick waited till the air had cleared a little, then filled her in quickly on the day's discoveries. "You've got him in now?" Siddons asked, frowning.

Resnick nodded.

"Fancy him for it, don't you? Have all along. Topping his wife. That anger getting out of control."

"It's possible."

"If you're right …" She shook her head. "Christ, Charlie, they don't call you Golden Bollocks for nothing."

Almost before Resnick had closed the door, Alex Peterson was out of his seat. If leaving him there dangling had been intended to make him nervous, break down his resistance, it hadn't worked; what it had done was steady his mind, steady his nerve.

"I thought this was urgent; I thought this was something that couldn't wait. You drag me down here in the middle of the afternoon, prevent me from treating my patients, and for what? So I can sit here for half an hour with a cup of stewed tea and, presumably, somebody outside the door to make sure I don't run off."

"You're at liberty," Resnick said, "to leave whenever you wish." Pulling out a chair, he sat down, Lynn to his left. "You've been kind enough to agree to answer our questions, assist with our inquiries. You are not under arrest."

From the look in Peterson's eyes, it was clear he was deliberating what to do: make to go and see what happened, force the issue and become embroiled in a farrago of blundering officialese, solicitors, even handcuffs for all he knew; or stay and see it through, debate, defend. As much as anything, it was the latter which appealed. He sat back down and even smiled. "How can I help?" he said.

They took him through everything from the moment Jane walked out through the door on that Saturday morning, excited, apprehensive, setting off for Broadway, to the night, a week later, when her body was lifted from the canal. Step by slow step. At no point had Jane been in touch with him, not by letter, not by phone; they had not met, she had not called. The last thing he had said to her, a remark called over his shoulder from the breakfast table where he sat reading the international section of *The Times*, "Bye. Hope it goes well."

"You are certain?" Resnick said.

"Oh, God. Of what? Can't we be done with this?" Peterson was bored. This wasn't a debate, this was a boring litany of the obvious, square pegs into square holes.

"That you didn't see your wife at any time between that Saturday and when she died?"

"Yes. How many more times?" He stared at them and they stared back. "Right, I'm sorry ..." Peterson on his feet now, fingers automatically buttoning his blazer, "but this is patently absurd."

"How about Wednesday?" Lynn said, speaking for the first time.

"Wednesday?" He stopped, head angled round, almost at the door.

"Wednesday evening at around quarter past seven?"

"What about it?"

"That was when she came to see you, remember? Your wife. That was when the taxi dropped her off at your door."

Peterson laughed, or at least he started to.

"She caught the six fifty-two from Grantham, then a cab from the station."

"Grantham? Whatever would she have been doing in Grantham?"

"She was there with a man called Peter Spurgeon," Resnick said. "The man she was leaving you to go and live with."

Slowly, mind churning, Peterson moved across and sat back down.

"You know him?" Resnick asked. There was a fly, fat and lazy, hazing around the upper half of the window, and he tried to clear it from his mind.

"No, I don't *know* him."

"You know who he is?"

"Jane went out with him at Cambridge. That was more than ten years ago. Fifteen."

"You didn't know she'd seen him since?"

"That's preposterous."

"Is it?"

Peterson started to say something and then stopped. Resnick asked him again.

"No. No, I didn't know."

"Did she ever talk about him?"

"No, not really. I mean, a few times, possibly, in passing. Maybe once or twice, late at night, you know, those slightly drunken conversations when people start reminiscing. What it was like back then, idyllic summers punting down the Cam."

"Idyllic?"

Peterson shrugged. "She obviously thought so at the time."

"She was in love with him."

"Apparently. Though heaven knows why. Even when she was trying to paint this heroic portrait of him, learned and romantic, he came over as rather pathetic. Not the kind of person who was ever really going to do anything with his life."

"Does that matter?" Lynn asked.

"Not to me."

"But what did you think of him?"

"I didn't. Why should I? He was of no possible relevance to me."

260

"So if your wife, if Jane, had wanted to contact him, I don't know, phone once in a while, see how he was getting on, you wouldn't have minded?"

"No," Peterson practically scoffed. "Why should I?"

"I wonder why, then," Lynn said, "when she did get back in touch with him, after his business failed, she didn't let you know? Unless she was frightened of how you would react."

"Jane was never frightened of me. She had no reason."

"Not even when you were angry?"

"No."

"Those times you hit her, then," Lynn said, "you were just hitting her for fun?"

Peterson clenched his fist and then, aware of what he was doing, allowed his fingers slowly to relax.

"If you had known Jane was carrying on some kind of relationship with Peter Spurgeon," Resnick said, "it's fair enough to say you wouldn't exactly have approved?"

"Approved? Of course not, Spurgeon or anyone. She was my wife, you can understand that."

"Yes," Resnick said, leaning a little toward him, lowering his voice. "Absolutely. Of course I can. Just as I can understand when she finally got around to telling you, not simply that she'd been seeing him all this time, but that she was going away with him, well, it would be enough to test anyone's temper. Any man's. I can see that."

Peterson laughed and shook his head. "Is that how you do it?" he asked. "Charlie Resnick, Detective Inspector, catcher of thieves and murderers, is that how it works? Push me around enough and then when you've got my back up sufficiently, uncork the compassion. Oh, yes, yes, of course I understand. And they sit here, poor innocent bastards, feeding out of your hand. Well, I'm sorry, because even if I wanted to help out, confess, unburden my sins, I'm afraid I can't. If Jane was running off with her childhood sweetheart or whatever she thought of him, I knew absolutely nothing about it until a few moments ago when you told me. And if she came to the house that Wednesday, if that's what really happened, well I can assure you she didn't knock on the door, didn't ring the bell, didn't use her key. I was in all evening from a little before six, just as I was every evening that week, sick with worry about what had happened to her, where she might be.

"And if you seriously think, had she come to me and told me this fairy story about herself and Peter Spurgeon, that my response would have been so uncontrolled that I would have taken her life in a fit of jealousy, then, Inspector, you are about as far from understanding me as you will ever be."

Resnick and Lynn were silent, waiting.

"If you intend to charge me with my wife's murder, then go ahead, but let me warn you I will pursue you with the biggest wrongful arrest suit this constabulary has ever faced. And whichever course of action you intend, I believe I am within my rights to telephone my solicitor and that is what I wish to do now."

Peterson gripped the table hard and sat back down; as soon as he reasonably could, he slid his hands from sight, hoping no one would see how they were beginning to shake.

Forty-seven

One simple question and answer, repeated, with slight variations, again and again.

Naylor: After you'd dropped her off, did you actually see her go inside the house?

Driver: I saw her go up to the door, yeah, there's these steps, you know, leading up. And like I say, she'd been in a bit of a state. But then, when I saw her on the step, I thought, like, she's gonna be fine and I drove away. I never actually, what you'd say, saw her go inside, no. No way.

Peterson's solicitor, Maxwell Clifford of Clifford, Taylor, and Brown, didn't even bother talking to Resnick direct; his first call was to the chief constable designate, who referred him to Malachy, who took great delight in chewing out his DCI, getting in a passing shot to the effect that she wasn't having much luck with her other suspect either and maybe she should consider tossing everything up in the air and starting again. His tone made it clear that tea lady was the kind of thing he had in mind.

Alex Peterson stepped back out onto the pavement of the Ropewalk less than three hours after he had been marched in, turning down the polite offer of a ride home in a police vehicle in favor of a brisk stroll along Park Terrace and Newcastle Drive and then home.

"Now then," Helen Siddons smiled maliciously, cupping a hand in the direction of Resnick's balls. "Not so golden after all."

Resnick was pleasant with Hannah when she called, and although he felt himself sounding cold, pleasant was the best he could do. He felt as flat as water trapped in a rusted sink, flat and stale.

Jealous husband, violent man, love spurned: it had been so simple. Perhaps it still was.

When he arrived home, there was no Dizzy to greet him, preening himself on the side wall. Inside the house, there was the unmistakable reek of cat piss; someone was telling him something and he'd better listen quick. Coffee he ground fine and made strong, the first thing he did after feeding Pepper and Bud, pausing to give the smaller one a touch of the cosseting he seemed to need. Of Miles and Dizzy, so far, there was nothing to be seen.

In the living room with his coffee, having found only a few sad slices of salami at the back of an almost empty fridge, he pulled down his old album of Monk playing solo piano—fractured, dissonant, ends refusing to be tied. "Monk's Mood." It suited him perfectly.

Slumped in the armchair, he almost failed to register the phone when it rang.

It was Lynn, plain and matter of fact. "There's a woman, says she spoke to you this morning? At the railway station." Gill Manners, Resnick thought. "Anyway, she says she's remembered."

"What exactly?"

"She didn't say."

"Okay, where is she now?"

"Still at the station. Till half past eight, she said."

"Right, I'll get along."

"Is this likely to be important?" Lynn asked.

Resnick hesitated. "I don't know."

The moment he set the phone back down, hand still on the receiver, it rang again.

"I forgot," Lynn said, "Mark called. He may have something but he's not sure. He said he'd be in the Market Arms; till closing I shouldn't wonder."

"All right," Resnick said. "Pick him up, bring him to the station. I'll meet you there. Soon as you can."

He went out leaving his coffee unfinished, the record still playing.

Gill Manners' husband was a bristling, fit-looking man with strong wrists and small, almost delicate hands. Gill looked womanly beside him, motherly, a bright yellow apron sailing across capacious breasts.

"Harry reminded me, Mr. Resnick, when he got back after lunch. Where I saw that woman you was asking about. Jane, is it? Yes, Jane. Anyway, it wasn't here at the station. No, not at all. The market, that's where it was. The wholesale market, you know. Well, we're down there every morning come five, Harry and me."

Just when Resnick was expecting more, she stopped. "And that's where you saw her?" he asked.

"Like I said. The morning after you was asking about, the Thursday."

"And this was close on five?"

"I was just parking up. So, yes, ten minutes either way. She was standing by this car, estate, dark blue, black. Wasn't no farther off than, oh, here to them doors."

Twenty yards, Resnick thought, no more than twenty-five. When he looked across, there was Lynn heading their way, Divine hanging back by the entrance. "She was on her own?" Resnick asked.

"No. With this bloke. Bald. Tall. 'Course I don't know what'd been going on, not exactly, but they'd been having some kind of row, you could tell. Tears an' all, the pair of them. Got themselves worked up into a right state. Soon as they saw me get out the van, he said something to her and they got back in the car. Looked at me though, she did, before she done so. Dreadful, she looked. Dead miserable. But it was her, the one in the picture, I'd swear."

"And the man?"

"Forty, forty-five."

Lynn took a copy of the Polaroid from her bag.

"Yes," Gill exclaimed. "That's him. That's the bloke there."

"And the car was a Vauxhall estate?" Resnick asked.

"Estate, yes. As for Vauxhall, Harry'll tell you I don't know one make from another. Shapes I can do, it's names I'm bad at."

"What they used to say about me," Harry said, "before you got your hands on me."

His wife laughed and aimed a mock blow at his head, Harry bobbing and weaving out of the way like the bantamweight he once was.

Resnick thanked them both and hurried across with Lynn to where Divine was waiting.

"What Mark's got," she said, "it could fit in."

Divine gave Resnick a nervous half-smile. "Mini-cab drivers, I carried on asking questions, even after Kev'd found that bloke as picked her up at the station. No real reason, just felt good, I suppose. Like I was back doin' the job again. Doing something. Anyhow, this guy I spoke to, Castle Cars, he reckons he saw a woman, could have been her, Peterson, right by where them gates are, top of North Road, you know, entrance to the Park off Derby Road. Staggering, he says, almost out into the road. Thought she might've been coming right out in front of him so he slammed on his brakes. That was how he saw her face."

"And she was staggering how? Like she was drunk? As if she'd been hurt? Hit?"

"Crying. Upset. When she heard his brakes, she pulled herself up, you know, gave herself a bit of shake. Driver called out, was she all right? And she said, yes, she was fine, and hurried off."

"Which way? Back into the Park?"

Divine shook his head. "On up Derby Road, toward town."

"Do we know what time this was?" Lynn asked.

"Yes," Divine said. "He reckons he looked at his watch and the clock on the dash both. Seven thirty on the dot. He got a call right after, pick up somebody at Queens. Turned round and went right back down. It's in his log. I checked."

Resnick's mind was racing. "All right, here's Jane. She leaves Spurgeon in Grantham and catches the train, fully intending to have it out with Alex, come clean about the whole business, the whole affair. In the cab from the station, she's worked up, excited, most likely frightened, there's a history of violence between them remember, he's hit her before. But when she gets to the door ..."

"She can't go through with it," Lynn said. "She can't face him."

"Right. But are we sure why? Is it because she's scared of Alex, or because she's changing her mind?"

"We don't know," Lynn said. "And, anyway, does it matter? Now. To us, I mean."

"Likely it determines what she does next."

266

"How 'bout she phones him," Divine suggested.

"The husband?" said Lynn.

"No, this bloke in Grantham. No matter what she says, he can tell she's in a right state. Wait there, he says, I'll come over and get you."

"And there they are," Resnick said, "arguing it over, back and forth, back and forth."

"It's not just that she's frightened of her husband," Lynn said, "it's more than that. It's worse. She's realized she's making a mistake. That's what all those tears are about, she's telling Spurgeon, after keeping him dangling all that time, she's not about to go through with it after all. She doesn't love him. She doesn't love him enough. And he spends all night trying to convince her that she's wrong; that she still does. And it doesn't do any good."

Jealous husband, Resnick was thinking, violent man, love spurned: he hadn't been listening. Had heard only what he expected to hear.

"Let's go," he said, anxious at the slowness of the automatic doors. "We'll phone Cambridge on the way."

Divine stood beside the car as Lynn slipped behind the wheel. "I don't suppose, boss," he said, "there's any way I could come along?"

"Sorry, Mark," Resnick said, climbing in. "'Fraid not." He raised a hand and as he closed the door, Lynn pulled away.

It was dark enough for the blue lights of the emergency vehicles to be seen from some distance, spiraling out across the flat English countryside. A uniformed officer stopped them at the edge of the village and checked their credentials; another waved them over only a little way into Front Street and advised them to park. Colin Presley was standing in the roadway level with the gate of number twenty-seven; the house itself an incongruous blaze of light. When the DS turned toward them, Resnick recognized only too well the look on his face.

"The children ..." he began.

But mercifully, Presley shook his head. "With a neighbor. Safe."

"And the wife?"

Louise was sitting at the center of the kitchen table, almost the last place Resnick had seen her; what stray color she had once managed had now disappeared.

267

"Are you all right?" Resnick asked, as much from the use of saying it as anything else.

Slowly her head tilted up until she had fixed him with her eyes. "I'm only surprised he had the guts to do it."

There was a card torn to small pieces beside her elbow and partly burned, the writing mostly beyond recognition, although Resnick believed he knew who had written it, what it said.

"Sir," Lynn said softly. She was standing in the far doorway and he followed her through into the living room and stood a moment beside her, looking down the garden in the direction of the lights.

They walked out there together, down past the cabbages and the rusted swing and the ambulance men and uniformed officers and finally the police surgeon, who was anxious to have the body lowered carefully to the ground, which it would be once Scene of Crime had finished with their video equipment, their photographs.

Peter Spurgeon was hanging from the uppermost of the branches, a length of narrow rope knotted close to the trunk and then again around his neck. His legs were splayed out at odd angles, like a man who has been desperately trying to climb something and has failed.

Forty-eight

Three weeks later, a family out picnicking on the edge of Laughton Forest found a bundle of women's clothing and a blanket, thickly matted with blood, buried beneath the undergrowth where their labrador had been digging. The last days of Peter Spurgeon's life were beginning to fall into place.

Late on the Thursday afternoon, he had booked into a Little Chef motel on the A1, south of Bawtry. The receptionist and the maid confirmed that he had been alone. Jane, presumably, was already dead. Her body had lain in the boot of the estate car, or possibly in the back, covered by its blanket and surrounded by boxes of books thick with learned footnotes and appendices. Analysis of the interior of the Vauxhall yielded samples of Jane's hair and of her blood. What Spurgeon had done during that day, killing Jane aside, was never clearly established. Resnick imagined them driving somewhere secluded and quiet to continue their argument, he heard the voices winding louder and louder, Jane's words the more wounding, more final; saw the despair on Spurgeon's face, the first frantic blow—but with what? Tire jack, iron railing, spade? A weapon had yet to be found.

On the Friday, incredibly, Spurgeon drove north to Hull and called in on some of his clients, the university bookshop and others, securing a small number of orders. What did he think? That if he behaved as normal, all the rest would go away? That night, he stayed at the same hotel he regularly used and on the Saturday began a long and meandering journey south that would take him through Brigg and Caistor, down through the Lincolnshire Wolds and finally east again—Sleaford, Newark-on-Trent. Jane always behind him, always filling his head, cold, naked, dead.

Was the decision to lower her body into the still water of the canal a conscious attempt to link her murder with that of others, shift the blame? Or had it finally seemed the only perfect place? Did he think that she would drown and disappear or merely float? How much did he think at all? Resnick saw the legs, stiff, breaking the surface of the water, the torso, trunk and arms; the splash as Spurgeon finally let go.

"God," Hannah said, holding Resnick close. "How could he?"

"I don't know," Resnick said.

But, of course, he did; they both did, deep inside.

A month to the day after he was first arrested, Aloysius James was released from custody without further charge. He is currently suing for compensation and despite the best efforts of the Serious Crime Squad no further suspect has been identified.

Faron came round to see Grabianski as a messenger one more time. Eddie Snow wanted to meet him at that new place, you know, Ladbroke Grove, Italian, used to be a pub.

Didn't they all, Grabianski thought? "Something to celebrate?" he asked.

Faron shrugged. "One of Eddie's deals."

"You going to be there?"

"Maybe." She looked at him and did that thing with her eyes.

Grabianski touched his hand to her cheek. "Don't," he said. "Find an excuse, anything. Just don't go."

Eddie Snow wore a red silk shirt, black leather waistcoat, tight white trousers, hand-stitched boots. Downstairs in the bar he ordered champagne and slipped an envelope into Grabianski's pocket, his profit from the sale of two pieces of English Impressionism to Bahrain. Up in the restaurant, surrounded by dazzling apricot walls, they had stone crab with celery, lamb cutlets with a *timbale* of aubergine. Snow was in an expansive mood, stories of his record company past and Chablis première cru. While they were waiting for the espresso, he leaned across the table and gave Grabianski a second envelope, sealed.

"What," Grabianski said, articulating carefully, "do you expect me to do with that?"

Eddie grinned back. "How 'bout slipping it into the archives at the Sir John Soane, somewhere dusty where it'd conveniently be turned up next time they're doing a search."

Without the service, the bill must have set Snow back well in excess of a hundred quid. Maybe more. Jackie Ferris and Carl Vincent were waiting in an unmarked car across the street.

"I'm off this way," Grabianski said, "31 bus, right?"

"You and your buses," Snow laughed. "Bit of a bloody affectation, don't you think?" He waved goodbye and walked a block before turning his head at what he thought was the sound of a cab. Why walk when you can ride? Except it wasn't a cab.

Resnick read in the paper about a British art dealer named Thackray who had been arrested on a warrant from Interpol for attempting to smuggle a painting by the little-known English artist, Herbert Dalzeil, into Japan. More importantly, the Arts and Antiques Squad raided premises in Notting Hill, Hampstead, and Hackney in connection with a worldwide racket in the false authentication and sale of forged paintings. Eddie Snow was among those helping Scotland Yard with their inquiries. A few days later, Resnick also had a message from Sister Teresa to meet him in the city, after she had finished her weekly stint on local radio.

"Any interesting calls?" Resnick asked. They were sitting in the Food Court, drinking coffee out of paper cups.

"A seventy-two-year-old woman looking after her ninety-three-year-old mother, wondering isn't she entitled to a little help? Another pensioner, wanting me to pray for his cat, that it might have a merciful release. Two women, neither of them more than twenty by the sound of them, both of them in relationships with men that beat them. He loves me, sister, what should I do?"

Only two, Resnick thought?

Teresa opened her bag and gave him a postcard and a package. The card was from Lisbon, white buildings leading down toward a true blue sea. *So these are the paths of righteousness*, Grabianski had written. *I always thought they went to St. Ives.*

"The package," Teresa said, "it's for you."

It was a CD of the Duke Ellington Orchestra, recorded in 1968 and containing "The Degas Suite."

"Possibly," Teresa said, "I could come and listen to it some time. I'm afraid the order doesn't see the need for our having anything more than a little Roberts radio."

"It would be a pleasure," Resnick said. And it was.

It didn't seem that Grabianski stayed in Lisbon long. One morning, making her way a trifle gingerly into the drawing room, Miriam Johnson stopped in her slow tracks and stared: the two Dalzeils which had been stolen were back in place on the wall.

It would only be after her death, thankfully some little time into the future, that the question of whether these were forgeries came to be discussed. Meanwhile, once the delighted Miriam Johnson had informed Resnick of their miraculous return and Resnick had passed on the news to Sister Teresa, Teresa was left thinking, not for the first time, that the Lord did indeed move in mysterious ways.

Resnick and Hannah talked about the cats. As a result, he began to stay over at her place rather less in the week, rather more at weekends and when he did, paid the thirteen-year-old son of a near neighbor to go in and administer to the animals' needs. "Pick them up," Resnick told him. "Stroke them, make a bit of a fuss. Not the big black one, though. He'll have your fingers if you don't watch out."

Over Hannah's half term, they took the Eurostar train to Paris and Resnick realized, from looking at a poster outside Gare du Nord, he'd missed Milt Jackson by two days. They went to see the singer Dee Dee Bridgwater instead, joyously swinging through her versions of Horace Silver tunes.

More than six months now; if they weren't careful, it would be a year. Hannah occasionally thought of her former Irish lover, mused from time to time about other lovers she had never had, but most of the time seemed content.

And Resnick ...?

One night, more than a little drunk after dinner with some friends, aroused, he and Hannah started making love upon the stairs, continued on the sanded floor and then half on, half off the bed. Hannah with her head thrown back, eyes wide, fingers clutching tight into his back, breaking skin. "Hold me, Charlie! Hold me down!"

He didn't hear, at least not the final word; not till, his face sweating next to hers, she screamed it in his ear.

He was sitting down below, shirt unbuttoned, boxer shorts, feet bare. Hannah came and sat opposite him, feet pulled up beneath her on the chair.

"Charlie ..."

"Every day," he said, "most days, so much of what I have to deal with, it comes from that."

"That?"

"People having power over one another, using them. Submission. Hurt." He looked at her, the beauty in her eyes. "It's not a game."

She moved across to him, sat on the floor with her arms around his legs, resting her head against his thigh. "Charlie," she said after a while, "the fact that I can say that to you, that I can ask you ... That fantasy—that's all it is, a fantasy—I could never show that, expose myself in that way if I didn't trust you. Absolutely. It shows how safe I feel with you, how close we are, don't you see?"

Resnick reached down and stroked her hair and touched his fingers to the fine line of her back, but still, no, he didn't see.

"I'm going back up," Hannah said, getting to her feet. "You'll be up in a little while, yes?"

Resnick nodded but he didn't move; he didn't move until much later, when, stiff-legged, he went to the window to pull back the curtains and by then the first light of day was stretching out across the park.

REFERENCES

Herbert Dalzeil
(1853–1941)
Dalzeil was born in London and studied in Paris.
A member of the New English Art Club, he was primarily
an orthodox painter of landscapes and rural scenes.
While in his fifties, something changed radically
in his stylistic approach and he produced
a number of impressionistic oils which owed
much to the later Turner and to Whistler's nocturnes.
Departing Day is the best known of these.

*

In the Cut
Susanna Moore
Picador, 1996

*

The End of Alice
A. M. Homes
Scribner's, 1996

*

The Degas Suite
Duke Ellington
Duke Ellington: The Private Collection
KAZ CD 5O7

*

Broadway Media Centre
is an independent cinema
showing a wide range of films
and organizing related media events.
14 Broad Street, Nottingham NG1 3AL

*

To find out more about
JOHN HARVEY and CHARLIE RESNICK
visit the Mellotone website at www.mellotone.co.uk

The CHARLIE RESNICK series is published in the
United States by Bloody Brits Press.
For more information visit
www.bloodybritspress.com

John Harvey

John Harvey was born in London in 1938. After studying at Goldsmiths' College, University of London, and at Hatfield Polytechnic, he took his Masters Degree in American Studies at the University of Nottingham.

Initially a teacher of English and Drama, Harvey began writing in 1975 and now has over 90 published books to his credit. After what he calls his apprentice years, writing paperback fiction both for adults and teenagers, he is now principally known as a writer of crime fiction, with the first of the Charlie Resnick novels, *Lonely Hearts*, being named by *The Times* [London] as one of the 100 most notable crime novels of the last century.

Flesh and Blood, the first of three novels featuring Frank Elder, was awarded both the British Crime Writers' Association Silver Dagger and the U.S. Barry Award in 2004. His books have won two major prizes in France, the Grand Prix du Roman Noir Étranger for *Cold Light* in 2000 and, in 2007, the Prix du Polar Européen for *Ash & Bone*. Also in 2007, he was the recipient of the CWA Cartier Diamond Dagger for Sustained Excellence in Crime Writing.

After a gap of ten years, Harvey has returned to the character of Charlie Resnick in his most recent novel, *Cold in Hand*.

Having lived in Nottingham for a good number of years, Harvey has recently returned to London, where he lives with his partner and their young daughter.

www.mellotone.co.uk

Bloody Brits Press

LAST RITES
A Charlie Resnick Mystery

John Harvey

"*A fitting final brick in the wall to what has been one of British crime fiction's most impressive series of the last decade*" —Time Out (London)

"*Harvey has set a benchmark which the genre must now measure up to*" —Literary Review (London)

Lorraine Preston's brother, Michael, was sent down for life for the murder of their father—and now he's being allowed out for their mother's funeral. A hardened criminal, Michael Preston is the last person Resnick wants back on his patch, even if it's only for a matter of hours.

Heartsore and world weary, Resnick is struggling to contain an explosive situation on the streets, where the spread of guns has led to a frightening escalation in drug-related crime. The local force, meanwhile, is riven by internal rivalries and rumors of corruption. And now, with his previously stable relationship with Hannah Campbell wavering, Resnick is forced back on his self-belief, his understanding of people. Why they—himself included—do the things they do.

Last Rites is the tenth Charlie Resnick Mystery

ISBN 978-1-932859-61-4 $14.95

Available at your local bookstore
or call toll-free 866-390-7426
or order online at www.bloodybritspress.com

Bloody Brits Press

ROUGH TREATMENT
A Charlie Resnick Mystery

John Harvey

"Rough Treatment *combines a gripping and well-handled plot with subtly-drawn characters and believably witty dialogue*" —British Book News

A kilo of cocaine. Hardly what two small-time crooks were expecting to find when they broke into TV director Harold Roy's shabby mansion. But nor was Harold's frustrated wife expecting to fall in love with one of the intruders. Now she's willing to make a deal with him—for both her husband and the drugs.

But the precious white powder belongs to someone else, who wants it back. And if he feels he's been double-crossed, there's no telling what might happen.

Detective Inspector Resnick has a hunch that there's more to a series of burglaries than meets the eye. And as his investigations lead him down the mean streets of an inner city drugs ring and into the backstabbing world of the TV industry, it's obvious that more than one person has something to hide …

Rough Treatment is the second Charlie Resnick Mystery

ISBN 978-1-932859-45-4 $13.95

Available at your local bookstore
or call toll-free 866-390-7426
or order online at www.bloodybritspress.com

Bloody Brits Press

CUTTING EDGE
A Charlie Resnick Mystery

John Harvey

"*Harvey's police procedurals are in a class by themselves—near Dickensian in their portrayal of human frailty, cinematic in their quick changes of scene and character, totally convincing in their plotting and motivation*"
—Kirkus Reviews

"*The characters in John Harvey's urban crime novels are so defiantly alive and unruly that they put these British police procedurals on a shelf by themselves*"
—Marilyn Stasio, The New York Times Book Review

A savage assault with a scalpel leaves Dr. Tim Fletcher's body badly slashed in a deserted walkway. The first victim in a series of brutal assaults on hospital staff.

As panic grips the city, it's up to Detective Inspector Charlie Resnick to find the killer. Faced with a mass of clues that lead nowhere and a past he cannot forget, Resnick is soon pushed close to breaking point …

Cutting Edge is the third Charlie Resnick Mystery

ISBN 978-1-932859-46-1 $13.95

Available at your local bookstore
or call toll-free 866-390-7426
or order online at www.bloodybritspress.com

Bloody Brits Press

OFF MINOR
A Charlie Resnick Mystery

John Harvey

"*Suspects, cops, grieving relatives, alarmed teachers, creepy kids from the neighborhood—no one escapes the glare of the author's insights or the warmth of his compassion for the pathetic frailties of human nature*"
—The New York Times Book Review

"*This Nottingham vibrates with crooked and tender tensions, the dialogue snaps with wit and Harvey has surprises for the most jaded reader*" —The Times (London)

Little Gloria Summers' body has been found hidden inside two plastic bin bags in a disused warehouse. Somewhere in the city, a child killer is on the loose, free to strike again.

Then Emily Morrison vanishes on a Sunday afternoon. A week later, there are still no clues. Inspector Charlie Resnick is as appalled as the media. But years of patient police work have taught him a thing or two—including his conviction that those who jump to easy conclusions are often the last ones to solve a crime.

Off Minor is the fourth Charlie Resnick Mystery

ISBN 978-1-932859-47-8 $13.95

Bloody Brits Press

WASTED YEARS
A Charlie Resnick Mystery

John Harvey

"*From Resnick's bruised marriage to his flamboyant sand-wiches, from the precisely drawn characters to the surpris-ing (yet strangely inevitable) climax, from the wonderfully telling details ... to the desolation of a decaying city,* Wasted Years *is a novel without one false note*"
—The San Francisco Chronicle

A series of brutal robberies takes Detective Inspector Charlie Resnick back ten years. To a time when a rash of very sim-ilar incidents left him face to face with a frenzied sociopath who nearly brought his life to a premature end—and to a time when his wife ran off with her lover, putting paid to their marriage and leaving him with an emotional wound that still hasn't healed. Now with the lookalike robberies escalating in violence, Resnick fights to track the men down before they kill, just as he fights to stem the poignant mem-ories that threaten to overwhelm him.

Wasted Years is the fifth Charlie Resnick Mystery

ISBN 978-1-932859-55-3 $14.95